RAFE

HEROES AT HEART

MARYANN JORDAN

ISBN ebook: 978-1-947214-10-1

ISBN print: 978-1-947214-11-8

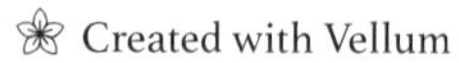

AUTHOR INFORMATION

I am an avid reader of romance novels, often joking that I cut my teeth on the historical romances. I have been reading and reviewing for years. In 2013, I finally gave into the characters in my head, screaming for their story to be told. From these musings, my first novel, Emma's Home, The Fairfield Series was born.

I was a high school counselor having worked in education for thirty years. I live in Virginia, having also lived in four states and two foreign countries. I have been married to a wonderfully patient man for thirty-seven years. When writing, my dog or one of my three cats can generally be found in the same room if not on my lap.

Please take the time to leave a review of this book.

Feel free to contact me, especially if you enjoyed my book. I love to hear from readers!

Facebook

Email

Website

Author's Note

I have lived in numerous states as well as overseas, but for the last twenty years have called Virginia my home. All my stories take place in this wonderful commonwealth, but I choose to use fictional city names with some geographical accuracies.

These fictionally named cities allow me to use my creativity and not feel constricted by attempting to accurately portray the areas.

It is my hope that my readers will allow me this creative license and understand my fictional world.

I also do quite a bit of research on my books and try to write on subjects with accuracy. There will always be points where creative license will be used to create scenes or plots.

As an adolescent counselor for over twenty-five years, I had the opportunity to work with many young people. One young man, upset over a poor choice he had made, came to me. As I listened to his story and his confession, I told him that the true measure of a man was not in the mistakes he made, but in how he handled those mistakes. I remember the look on his face when I told him I was sure he was going to be a good man. So, this book is dedicated to all the students over the years who allowed me to be a part of their lives.

1

Rafe wiped his bloody nose, smearing his dirty face streaked with tears. Shuffling home from school he kept his head down, eyes on the sidewalk. Normally, he enjoyed looking at the yards on either side of the street, but not today.

He liked the way the homeowners tended their yards in the neighborhood. Some with flowerbeds lining front walks, others with evergreen shrubs hugging the fronts of the porches. He knew the houses were old, but that's why the oak trees were so large, their acorns dropping in great number every year. To him, the trees definitely made up for the age of the houses. The maple trees with their red, early-spring leaves, stood as sentinels in front of many of the homes.

Azalea bushes, their pink flowers mixed in with the box hedges, created pockets of floral color amidst the lush green. Crepe Myrtle trees, late to leaf, would burst forth in colors of pink, fuchsia, and white in mid-summer, lining the sidewalks with their beauty, along with the stately Magnolias.

The house at the end of the street, its yard just as pristine and carefully tended, loomed ahead and his pace slowed as he swiped a hand across his face once more. Sucking in a shuddering breath, he heard running footsteps coming down the sidewalk from behind. Cael and Asher pulled along either side of him, both with faces full of concern.

"Don't cry, Rafe. Zander's taking care of him," Cael said.

The news did not make him feel any better. After all, Zander should not be fighting his battles. Before he had a chance to respond, he heard more running footsteps coming from behind. This time, the twins, Jaxon and Jayden, caught up, Jaxon grinning from ear to ear.

"Zander's busted his nose and given him a black eye!" Jaxon called out in glee, hopping from one foot to the other, his fists out jabbing the air.

Jayden, his voice softer, said, "Come on, Rafe. Let's get you inside so Miss Ethel can take a look at you."

Rounding on his friends, he glared, "No. I don't want her to know."

The boys stopped in the middle of the sidewalk, all staring up at Rafe as he made another swipe at his eyes. He pulled up the hem of his shirt, beginning to wipe the dirt, tears, and blood, but his hand was stopped by Jayden. Bending down to open his backpack, Jayden pulled out an old shirt from his PE class.

"Here, use this. Then Miss Ethel won't see the blood and wonder what's going on."

Tossing a grateful nod his way, Rafe took the t-shirt and carefully cleaned his face. Looking down at it, he asked, "How you gonna explain this?"

"I'll just tell her I got bloodied in a basketball game in PE. She'll get it all washed up and won't be the wiser."

Nodding, he handed the shirt back, then heard more pounding footsteps coming from behind. Zander, the oldest, his face split with a huge grin, came flying around the corner, skidding to a stop at their gathering. "I got him good. Dickie was pissing his pants by the time I got through with him."

Wide-eyed, Asher asked, "You gonna get in trouble?"

"Nah," Zander bragged. "When I said he was pissing his pants, I meant, he was really pissing. I threatened that if he told anyone, then I'd tell them all about his wet pants."

The others broke into grins, and even Rafe had to admit, it made him happy to know that his nemesis had been so easily taken care of. Zander was older by a year, and already thirteen. At twelve, Rafe had Zander's height, but the gawkiness that plagued most pre-teen boys was in full force with him. His hands and feet appeared too large, while his arms and legs seemed too skinny. Awkward and ugly...that's what Dickie had called him. A beast. Shrek. An ogre.

Miss Ethel told him that he would be a big man, like his father, but he wanted to be big now. *Waiting is too hard.* That thought sobered him. *His father.* He wished he knew what his father would have thought of him now. *Would he be proud or embarrassed of me?* The unknown answer to that question haunted him, especially when he lay in bed at night, listening to Zander and Cael sleeping. It was getting harder and harder to remember his dad's face...or his mom's. Miss Ethel made sure he had pictures, but it was not the same.

Startled out of his morose musings by laughter from

the others, he tried to smile as Zander threw his arm around his shoulders, tugging him along the sidewalk, saying, "Come on, Rafe. It'll be fine."

"That's easy for you to say," Rafe grumbled. "You manage to scare all the bullies...I just manage to attract them."

Zander looked him up and down before shaking his head. "You're already almost as tall as I am. You remember what Miss Ethel said about that puppy we rescued? She took one look at his paws and told us he was gonna be a big dog. Said he'd grow into those huge paws and, sure enough, he did."

Rafe bumped Zander's shoulder, hiding his grin with a scowl, "You callin' me a dog?"

The others laughed as they turned into the front gate of Miss Ethel's house, their footsteps slowing.

"Uh oh," the twins said in unison. The whole gang looked up toward the front porch, spying Miss Ethel standing on the top step. Her grey hair was neatly pulled back in her old-fashioned bun at the back of her head. A light blue striped shirt-dress, belted at the waist, emphasized her tall, thin frame. Sharp blue eyes peered at them from behind wire-frame glasses. Her face, with its usual smile in place, still made the boys scuffle along.

"Don't say anything," Zander warned. "No way she coulda heard about it."

"Are you kidding," Cael whispered. "She knows everything. I don't know how...maybe she's got magical powers."

Rafe glanced around at his five brothers as each attempted an innocent expression, but he knew there was no way Miss Ethel was going to be fooled.

Zander urged him on, saying, "I got this. It's all on me."

Once again, Zander was stepping up to fight his battles. Squaring his shoulders, Rafe pulled himself up to his full height. As they met Miss Ethel at the top of the stairs, she greeted each of them, her smile sincere. Hugs all around and offers of homemade cookies on the kitchen table had them scurrying inside. The last one to enter, he stopped as her hand landed on his shoulder. Looking up, his heart pounding, he met her smile as she peered deeply into his eyes.

"Are you okay, son?" she asked, her voice as calm and warm as always.

"Yes, ma'am," he lied, his palms now sweating.

"Your day go okay at school?"

"Yes, ma'am," he lied again.

Her thin hand patted his shoulder and she nodded, her smile still in place. "Well, you go on in and get some cookies for yourself before the others take them all. I made chocolate chip oatmeal...your favorite."

With that, he hurried inside, glad he had gotten away with the deception and determined to not miss out on her treats.

That evening, after supper had been served on the large, old, scarred dining room table, they all settled around, some spilling into the living room, their homework spread out before them. Rafe, finished with his math problems, closed the book, looking out into the living room.

Miss Ethel was ensconced in her wing-back chair with her knitting bag at her feet, her hands busy with the needles as she kept an eye on the twins sitting on the worn, braided rug on the floor nearby. Occasionally, they would ask a question, and then she began quizzing them on their spelling words. Cael and Asher sat on the couch, working on a writing assignment, a dictionary on the coffee table in front of them. Zander, at the table with Rafe, had finished his homework and, per usual, had a large, fiction book open in front of him, lost in the words. Rafe had no doubt that Zander would be reading to them before they went to bed.

He smiled at the thought. It did not seem to matter how old they got, Zander's stories at night seemed to chase away the worst memories...for all of them. With a sigh, he thought of how they all came to be with Miss Ethel. He knew he was lucky, he had had wonderful parents. But traveling on a wintry highway ended with a deadly crash and, with no other relatives, he ended up in the foster system.

His eyes sought out Miss Ethel again, a small smile slipping over his face. He knew he was lucky—he had heard some stories, from the other boys who had passed through her home, of foster families that were not so good. But Miss Ethel? Even the social workers claimed she was the best. His gaze drifting over the room again, he took in the five boys that had stayed with her the longest, all like brothers to him now. They had vowed their friendship and sealed it with an oath.

As though hearing his thoughts, Miss Ethel looked over, her smile landing on him. He could swear she had untold wisdom in her eyes. Sucking in a quick breath, he gave a nod before opening another book.

Later that night, after she tucked Asher, Jaxon, and Jayden into their beds in their room, she crossed the hall to the room he shared with Zander and Cael. Both rooms contained a bunk bed set and twin bed, allowing three boys a place to sleep. A shared bathroom was at the end of the hall. There was one other small bedroom with a single bed and connecting bathroom upstairs but Miss Ethel kept that ready for an emergency child, one who might be overwhelmed with the others. She had said the oldest could have it for their room, but Zander preferred sharing with the others. Miss Ethel's room was downstairs, across from the kitchen.

The furniture in each bedroom was old, but clean. For some of them, it was the nicest place they had ever known. For him, Rafe remembered a similar room in his parents' house.

Pajamas on, teeth brushed, backpacks ready for the next day, the three of them were piled in their beds ready for Zander to read another story from his large edition of abridged classics. They especially loved the fairy tales and were not ashamed to admit it. Perhaps, they all felt the need to believe in happy endings after their unpleasant beginnings in life.

Zander looked up as Miss Ethel entered and sat on the foot of his bed. She sat primly, her back straight and her hands folded in her lap.

The serene expression on her face did not change, as she asked, "Now boys, I think there are some things you need to talk to me about." The room was quiet, so she continued, "I would like to think that you trusted me enough to talk to me."

Zander opened his mouth, "It was me, Miss Ethel—"

"No, ma'am, it wasn't," Rafe blurted, his heart rate speeding. Not knowing how she knew about the fight, he watched as she swung her warm gaze on him and he continued. "Dickie Malten was teasing me again today. Calling me Shrek and ogre and beast, and...other things.

He says I'm too ugly to live." Swallowing back the shame, he admitted, "So I took a swing at him. I missed...but then he hit me in the nose. I jumped on top of him, still swinging. Don't expect I did much to him other than just make him mad."

"Rafe was just defending himself, Miss Ethel. I was the one who jumped in and started punching," Zander confessed. "Honest, Dickie deserved it."

Nodding as she listened, Miss Ethel said, "No doubt."

That response drew surprise from all of them, including Jaxon, Jayden, and Asher, who had snuck out of bed, their curiosity getting the better of them.

"You know, sometimes I have wondered about raising so many boys all alone, knowing that you are missing a man's hand in your upbringing."

Zander immediately protested. Rafe knew his best friend had never had a good man in his life so he didn't know what he could be missing. But he was right, Miss Ethel was amazing all on her own.

Before the rest of them could chime in, she raised her hand. "Thank you for that vote of confidence, Alexander, but I am not perfect. And while I love each of you, I do know my limitations." She grew quiet for a moment, then said, "My George was a peace-loving man, but I remember one time, long ago, when we were dating. A man made a rude comment about me and George punched him in the nose."

A chuckle slipped from her lips and her face eased into laugh lines that Rafe thought were beautiful, as she recalled, "I was mortified, but also knew that a good man won't allow someone to bully others. So, Alexander, while I do not condone violence, I do appreciate you defending one of your friends."

Turning her gaze to Rafe, she said, "But, son, I think that perhaps tomorrow morning, you and I should spend some time in the garden."

He loved to work in the yard, so he said, "But that's hardly punishment, Miss Ethel."

"I didn't say anything about punishment, dear boy. I just think you and I need some time to tend the plants."

With that, she stood and kissed them goodnight before turning out the light. Scooting the younger ones back to bed, Rafe heard her soft footsteps descend the stairs. Lying in bed, he could not help but replay Dickie's words over in his mind, fighting against their power. *I'm not a beast. I'm not ugly.* As he drifted off to sleep, he dreamed of the beast in the castle, visited by beauty.

The sun beamed down on Rafe and Miss Ethel as they bent over their gardening tasks. The front flower beds had been weeded, bushes trimmed, and now they were in the backyard, checking on her small vegetable garden.

He loved the outdoor chores, one of the few activities that brought memories of his father back to the forefront of his mind. His father had owned a lawn care business and often took Rafe along on his many jobs. He used to watch his father blowing leaves, riding the mower, trimming low-hanging tree branches, weeding, and planting. His favorite was seeing the rose bushes in full bloom, which a few of his clients requested and that they had in their own garden as well.

"Are you thinking about your father?" Miss Ethel asked as though reading his mind—again.

Maybe Cael is right and she does have magical powers!

Grinning as he nodded, he replied, "Yes, ma'am. He didn't plant any vegetables, but he loved to plant rose bushes. I remember he would plant them for my mom every year."

"Your father was a wise man," she said. "Many men just buy store-bought roses for a woman, when it is convenient for them. But the blooms soon die and the gesture can be forgotten. But your father planted the beautiful plants so your mother could enjoy the bounty all season, knowing they would come back again."

He wiped his hands on his jeans as he listened to her.

"Of course, you know rose bushes are terrible when they are first planted. Do you remember?"

"Yeah," he agreed. "They were just sticks...ugly sticks with thorns."

"Exactly! Just looking at the rose bush when it's been pruned and recently planted, you would never know what beauty it will become."

He knelt in the dirt, still listening as he helped her tie the tomato plants to the stakes. Finishing, he stood, facing her as she placed her hand on his shoulder.

"You do know, son, that we humans are just like that pruned rose bush."

His brow creased in confusion, looking from the plants to her face. "Huh? I mean, how Miss Ethel?"

She met his polite correction with an indulgent smile. "We all look like pruned bushes at times. You've gained height, and your hands and feet have grown, but the rest of you still needs time to grow and catch up."

He dropped his chin to his chest, heaving a great sigh.

"Look at me, son," she said. When he sent his gaze back to her, she continued, "But remember, real beauty lies within...it comes from the care given to the thorny, pruned rose bush. You remember your father and mother. I've looked at their pictures and they were such a handsome couple." Placing her hands on his shoulders, she peered deeply into his face. "And you, my dear Rafe, will become a handsome man. But that beauty on the outside, will mean nothing if you don't have beauty on the inside as well. And thank goodness, you're as good as they come."

Smiling, she said, "I'll go get us some lemonade and check on the other boys. You can come in when you're ready."

Nodding, he watched her walk up the back steps, leading into the kitchen. He turned, taking the twine and tools into the shed near the back gate. As he closed up, he detoured toward the front, going straight to the rose bushes. They were still sticks with thorns, but the buds were already starting to show. Grinning, he thought of the beautiful flowers that would burst forth soon. *That'll be me, someday.* His heart lighter, he went inside to join the others.

2

"Arms down."

He dropped his arms.

"Head up."

He lifted his chin.

"Tilt your head to the left."

He did that too.

Standing in the California heat, a swimsuit hanging low on his hips, his chiseled abs, muscular chest and arms on display, he flexed his legs, showcasing his massive thigh muscles. Adopting the carefree grin that had graced calendars, magazines, and billboards, he looked to the world as a man enjoying his time in the sun.

A woman, from off to the side, jumped in front of him as soon as the photographer lowered his camera, dabbing the sweat from his brow before spritzing his face and body with water from a spray bottle to simulate sweat. *Fuckin' hell, this is stupid.* Gritting his teeth, Rafe Walker kept from biting her head off, knowing the assistant was simply following directions.

At six feet, four inches and close to two hundred

pounds of solid muscle, he knew what he brought to the business. *A body...that's all...just a body.*

The photo shoot continued for another three hours, moving from the sandy beach, to under palm trees, to the surf, first by himself, and then with two female models in bikinis that barely covered their stick-thin bodies. With zero percent body fat, the size and lift of their breasts in comparison pointed to augmentation. Preferring a more natural look on a woman, he inwardly grimaced at how cutthroat this industry was and wondered if the women were happy this way. Looking down into their faces as they pressed in tightly, too tightly to be honest, he knew they had nothing more on their minds other than how they looked in the shot, just the way he used to be.

As they draped themselves over him, taking direction from the photographer, he began praying for the last shot. His mind wandered to the phone conversation he had that morning. Getting up early, he had called Zander, hoping to get him before he went in to his job.

"I was afraid I was calling at a bad time," he confessed, hearing a female voice in the background.

"Nope," Zander replied. "Rosalie's got a teaching job now, so she gets up early. I don't have to climb outta bed at this hour, but I like being up when she's up."

A teasing comment danced on Rafe's tongue, but he swallowed it, because Zander sounded happy...*really happy.* Not one to hide his thoughts, he said, "I'm glad for you, man. She's a wonderful woman."

"She makes me complete, that's for sure," Zander admitted, no hesitation in his voice. "So any particular reason you're calling this morning?"

"I'm thinking about taking a break—"

"Thank God!"

"Seriously, Zan, why don't you tell me how you really feel?" he laughed, knowing his friend would always tell him the truth.

"Look, Rafe, you've said over and over that modeling isn't your forever career. It's just a stopgap between the Army and whatever else is coming. But I don't think you're gonna find your forever out there in California, so far from your roots."

"Yeah, I know. I really called to say that I'm gonna make a trip home."

"You've got your room here whenever you want it," Zander reminded.

"Hell, you've got a home with Rosalie now. I'm not gonna crash that. I figure I'll stay with Miss Ethel."

"She'd love to have you. Any of us would. You just come home and don't worry about where you'll stay."

"Rafe! Fucking focus!" the photographer shouted.

Jolted from his thoughts, he battled the desire to flip the pompous ass off, but just nodded instead. Following the directions, he was unable to keep his thoughts away from Zander and Rosalie. *Zan is lucky...but then so is Rosalie.* Envying their new relationship, he wondered if there was someone for him. Someone away from the spotlight. Someone who just wanted him for himself...*and not Mr. July.*

Another assistant rushed over, a makeup airbrush in her hand, and began drawing lines on his already-washboard abs, creating more definition. About to bark at her, he was startled when someone else, from behind, began mussing his hair, giving it a windblown look when the breeze was doing just that naturally. As long as he had been modeling, he never could get comfortable with someone's hands constantly on him. Taking deep breaths, as Miss Ethel had taught as a way to manage frustration, he managed to not lash out at the assistants just doing their jobs. *How the hell did this use to be a cool way to make a living?*

After another hour, the shoot finally concluded. As the female models sauntered off, Rafe snatched the towel being handed to him by the assistant and wiped down, smearing the makeup off onto the towel.

Walking into the tent set up for them, he almost stumbled over a male model, whose pants were at his ankles, a woman's head bobbing between his legs.

"Jesus, get the fuck out," he roared, and watched as the overeager fan jumped up, her naked breasts bouncing as she grabbed her shirt and hurried from the tent. Shooting the model a glare, his phone vibrated before he had a chance to say any more. As the model jerked his pants up and hurried after the girl, Rafe looked down at the sender. *Fuckin' hell. Cherelle.* He growled as he checked the message.

Hi baby. Miss you...Marty is working on something for us. Call me.

Sighing, he deleted the message. Cherelle Parkinson. A casual hookup that turned into a few hookups. Until she became possessive, clingy, and downright neurotic. It was six months ago, but at least once a month, she texted, trying to hook up again. *Nope, not happening.*

Pulling on his loose track pants, he heard his name called and, looking up, saw two other male models walking into the tent.

"You looked good today," Todd said, a smile on his face that did not reach his eyes.

Grunting, his mind was already on the shower and dinner he was planning...alone in the efficiency, garage apartment he rented. He had made a few friends in California, but nothing like the ones back home. And Todd and Tommy did not fall into the friend category…more like suck-ups.

"You up for some partying?" Tommy asked, his wide, white-toothed grin shooting toward the females on the periphery of the shoot, eliciting giggles and shouts of phone numbers. "Looks like the pickings are good today."

"Rafe! We love you!" screamed a few of the girls at the fence.

"Nah," he replied, ignoring the women still calling his name, and snagged his keys from a small, padlocked locker. "I'm heading home."

"Shit, man," Tommy exclaimed. "If you go, the women will follow."

"Too good for us?" Todd asked, his brow lowered.

Glaring, he stood to his full height, hands on his hip, and faced the two. "Seriously? What are we? Fifteen years old?" Seeing the blush rise on Tommy's cheeks, Rafe said, "What the fuck do you care what I do?"

"Rafe!" Hearing the voice of his agent…*former agent*… he dropped his chin to his chest.

As Marty Robbins stepped into the tent, he threw a narrowed-eye look at the others. "Out."

The models scurried out and Rafe could hear them approaching the young women hanging by the fence. He knew they would soon be taking a group back to one of their houses, drinks flowing and orgies in every room. *God, had that been me?* He knew the answer to his own question…*well, not the orgies. Never got into public sex.* But the girls had been easy when he first came to California. So had the parties. Before he had time to travel down that morose road into past thoughts, Marty stepped into his space.

Marty's time in the salon showed, with his hair dyed a sandy-blond to cover the grey and his nails buffed to a sheen. His thin frame was covered in a silk suit and Rafe could not figure out how the man never seemed to sweat. A sharp agent, Rafe was, at one time, convinced he had his best interests at heart. It took a while, amidst the glitter of the business, to realize that he only had one interest—and that was himself.

Marty ingratiated himself to whoever was necessary to get a client, a contract, a negotiation, all with the intent of making more money. Pretending to be Rafe's best friend only so far and, once his eyes were open, he realized how slick—or maybe slimy—Marty really was. Eyeing him cautiously, he waited to see what Marty was going to say, considering his contract with him ended today.

"That was a great shoot. I saw some of the preliminaries, Rafe. Looks good." He snapped his fingers to the young assistant at his side, who began immediately tapping on a tablet. Marty looked down at it and began rattling off upcoming events. "I've lined up the next swimwear shoot, a tuxedo shoot is coming up, the ski equipment company wants to shoot next month in the mountains, and I've just landed you—"

"Told you I was taking some time off after today," Rafe interrupted, pulling a t-shirt over his head, settling the soft material across his thick chest muscles.

Marty smiled benevolently, "Of course, of course. A few days off is good for anyone—"

"The summer," Rafe interrupted again, bending to grab his worn backpack before standing again, facing the red-faced agent. "The whole summer."

"But Rafe, I've just scored a shoot with you and Cherelle Parkinson...she made number forty-nine in People Magazine's 50 Most Beautiful Woman of the Year, and she's been interested in shooting with you."

Rafe winced, realizing this was what she was texting him about. He met the model-turned-actress last year at one of the many parties he attended. *Beautiful, for sure, but manipulative.* Shaking his head ruefully, he had let her take control for a while, being the new man in town and star-struck. But her fake body and sloppy, drunk kisses had turned him off. *And I've managed to avoid her for months and now Marty wants me to shoot with her...hell, no!*

Heaving a sigh, he pinned Marty with his hard stare, wondering how the man was able to wear a suit in the California spring heat and still appear cool. "I'm going back to Virginia to connect with my family for a little while. I'll let you know when I'm available again."

A trickle of sweat beaded on Marty's forehead as his face turned red. "You can't do this. This'll kill your career...a career that I've spent the past couple of years building for both of us. You take the summer, you'll become a one-shot wonder. You'll be replaced before you can blink."

Without a backward glance, he walked out of the tent, Marty's threats still bouncing off, and slid his sunglasses on his face, weaving past the cars in the parking lot toward his rental truck. Driving toward his small efficiency, thoughts of his upcoming trip buoyed his flagging spirits.

3

Grabbing his bags from the conveyor, Rafe walked toward the airport exit, his heart lighter now that he was back in familiar territory. No matter the years spent in California, it was the Virginia soil that gave him roots. Breathing easier, he felt the tension loosening from his shoulders.

As he walked toward the exit, a familiar sight brought a grin out on his face. "Cael...good to see you, man," he greeted as he hugged his friend.

"Well, look who's finally home," Cael returned, back-slapping him. Reaching down to grab one of Rafe's bags, he added, "Looks like you're gonna stay for a while. Tired of all the adulation out in California?"

"You've got no idea how much I've been looking forward to being back here," he replied, following Cael out to his SUV.

The two men climbed inside and Cael easily pulled into traffic, heading toward a familiar destination.

"Everyone okay?"

Grinning, Cael nodded. "Zander's itching to get

married and, with Rosalie not having any family, I think they were just waiting for you."

Rafe grinned, remembering Zander begging him to come home so they would all be together for his big day. "Wouldn't miss it," he replied honestly. "Talked to him the other day...swear it's like talking to a new Zander. I think his grumpy ass just needed someone like Rosalie."

They laughed, the Richmond skyline fading into the background as they headed into the outskirts.

"How's your sister and her family?" As the words left his mouth, he could not help but notice the peaceful smile on Cael's face. Out of all of Miss Ethel's boys, Cael was the only one who had stayed connected with family after growing up in the foster system. He had a sister, now grown with a husband and daughter, welcoming Cael into their fold.

"Great, just great," the reply came. Shaking his head, he added, "My niece is six now and a total princess. Dolls cover her room and she lives in a dream world of castles, princes on white horses, and I swear she dreams of unicorns."

"You're lucky, man."

Cael nodded, his smile still on his face. "Don't I know it."

Turning down the familiar road, they passed the old homes. The trees were taller, the hedges fuller. A few homes had taken out the old gardens, planting just grass instead, drawing a frown from Rafe. As the house at the end of the street came into view, his heart leaped, seeing the well-tended flower gardens, neatly trimmed shrubs, and rose bushes beginning to climb their trellis'. Several cars and motorcycles lined the drive and street outside and he knew his welcoming party was about to begin. The thought struck him, once more, how this type of party was much more to his liking than the drunk-fest, hangers-on, parties back in California.

Parking in the driveway, they barely made it halfway up the front walk before the door opened and a group swarmed out, led by Zander with Miss Ethel on his arm. A light pink, belted shirt-dress hung on her thin, but strong, body, her fingers clinging to Zander. Her hair, now white, was still pulled back in a bun and her eyes, more grey than blue, twinkled just as bright.

"Oh, my goodness," she cried out, her hand already reaching for him as he rushed into her arms.

Towering over her slight frame, he inhaled deeply, the light scent of her rose water perfume filling his mind with memories, as he blinked at the moisture pooling in his eyes. She finally leaned back, peering up at him, her eyes assessing.

Before she could ask, he assured, "I'm good, Miss Ethel. Now that I'm back home, I'm good."

Patting his cheek, she nodded and said, "Well, let's not stand on the porch. Come on through. We've got a nice lunch for you...out in the back where there's some shade."

Rosalie tossed him a smile as she moved to walk with Miss Ethel toward the back of the house and into the kitchen.

Zander grabbed him in a bear hug, pounding his back as he said, "Good to see you, Rafe. Been too long."

As he stepped back, the twins, Jaxon and Jayden, welcomed him in equal fashion before Asher shoved them aside, gaining his hug as well. Zeke, one of Miss Ethel's later boys who now worked with Zander, was there as well. The men followed the women, making their way into the large kitchen, where platters of fried chicken, potato salad, coleslaw, baked beans, biscuits, and several pies sat ready to be taken outside.

They made quick work of transporting the food and soon everyone was settled at a long picnic table, Miss Ethel ensconced at the end in her comfortable wicker chair. The table was placed under a large tree, the spring leaves already providing some cover. Looking around, he was pleased to see the backyard had been tended, but knew it was time for fresh mulch. Casting his gaze around, he saw a few jobs that he could help with. Satisfied with that knowledge, he dug into his food.

"Miss Ethel, you make the best fried chicken I've ever tasted," Rafe enthused. "I've missed your cooking."

"Well, thank you, but I'm afraid you need to thank Rosalie. She did the chicken."

His eyes widened as he peered down the table at Zander's beautiful fiancé. "Seriously?"

Shaking her head, her cheeks pink with a blush, she said, "Well, Miss Ethel taught me her recipe."

"And, if I have anything to say about it, they'll teach me and we'll start having Miss Ethel's wings at Grimm's Bar," Zeke called out.

Whipping his head around, he stared at Zander. His best friend had opened his bar when getting out of the military and had been satisfied with just an old-fashioned, no-frills bar. "You finally adding some food?"

Zander shrugged, his lips twitching. "Not my thing, but if Zeke wants to take it on, we'll see."

"Man, it's only been a few months since I was last home and things are moving along," he said, digging into more of Miss Ethel's and Rosalie's food.

"So, how's California?" Rosalie asked, her sky-blue

eyes peeking around Zander as she looked at him. "I've never been to the West Coast."

Swallowing, he replied, "I was mostly in the mid to southern part. Beaches are pretty...they've got palm trees which we don't have here, but I prefer the beaches here in Virginia. Less crowded."

"Well, if you weren't Mr. Army July Hunk, then you woulda missed out on all that California sunshine."

Laughing on the outside, Rafe inwardly cringed. "Yeah, who knows what my life would have been like if it hadn't been for that calendar."

Looking around, he did not mind his friends' assumption that his modeling career must be a rewarding life, but as his gaze slid to the end of the table, he halted. Miss Ethel's eyes were focused on him. Offering him a small smile, she simply nodded and continued to eat.

"So how long are you planning on staying this time?" Asher asked, pushing back from the table as he patted his stomach.

Wiping his mouth, Rafe looked around the group before pronouncing, "I'm not going back for a while. I'm taking the summer off and spending it here."

Rafe looked at Miss Ethel, bent over with the hose in her hand, watering the newly planted flowers. He smiled, the memories of many hours spent in this yard assailing him. For the past two days, he had stayed with her, working in her yard.

"While I've been gone, it looks like the others have done a good job," he admitted, looking at the yard with a critical eye. The space was not very large, but when she stopped taking in foster boys she added a few more flower gardens along the fence, since there were no more impromptu baseball games to be had.

She pushed her white hair back into its bun and nodded. “Cael comes to mow and Jayden helps to keep the bushes trimmed. Jaxon always makes sure to keep the sidewalks clear and Zander, along with Asher, takes care of odd jobs. When I need some extra help, Zeke will come over as well.”

They worked side by side, in silence, for a little longer before she asked, “You want some lemonade?”

Grinning, he said, “I’ve never turned down your lemonade and don’t plan on starting now. I’ll take the tools back to the shed and meet you in the kitchen.” Taking the small spade from her, he headed off to the shed in the back corner, replacing the implements in their places. Stopping in the mudroom at the back of the house, he washed his hands, splashing cold water over his face and neck.

With a quick wipe with one of the towels, he headed into the kitchen, noting the plate of homemade chocolate chip cookies sitting on the dining room table next to two glasses of lemonade.

Waiting until she was seated and served, he sat and helped himself to several cookies. After a moment of companionable silence, he looked over, seeing her observing him carefully. Leaning back, he said, “You’ve been awfully patient, Miss Ethel.”

Cocking an eyebrow, she grinned, “Oh?”

“Now, don’t play coy,” he laughed. “You’ve got questions in your eyes.”

She patted his forearm, saying, “Do you have any gardens to look after in California?”

Her question caught him off guard, but he answered honestly, "No, ma'am. I live in a tiny apartment over a friend's garage."

"I would have thought a big-time model, like yourself, would have a house with a view...and maybe a yard to tend."

Leaning back, he shook his head slowly. "Believe me, I'm not nearly as big-time as you think and, while I could afford something larger, I guess I just never felt at home in California. Plus, I travel so much, it would have been hard to have a house with a yard."

"Do you think you'll go back? To stay?"

He fiddled with his napkin, his thoughts swirling in his head. "I don't know, Miss Ethel. I'm twenty-eight years old and you'd think I'd have this all figured out, but life just has a way of taking over."

"Yes, yes," she agreed. "When I first decided to take in a young boy, I had no idea that the next twenty years would be spent raising foster boys."

"You definitely found your calling."

"Do you think you've found yours?" she asked, taking another cookie, munching politely.

With a definite shake, he replied, "No. Not at all. The military was never going to be my forever career but I figured something would come along when I got out. Since I was a mechanic when I was in, I thought about working as one, but then...well, the Army calendar came out and modeling contracts started rolling in." Shrugging, he said, "Figured I'd do a few shoots, see where it went. But now, two years later, it's like my life isn't my own anymore." With a self-recriminating chuckle, he admitted, "You were right, you know."

"About what?"

"It doesn't matter what you look like, people are going to see what they want to see. When I was a kid, I couldn't wait to grow out of that awkward phase but, now that I have, I'm still being treated a certain way just because of how I look. You were right, you have to be proud of the person you are, because that's what really matters. That's how you find happiness."

"You have always been a good person, son," she smiled warmly at him.

"Thanks, Miss Ethel. I think it's about time I start surrounding myself with good people, too."

Easy quiet settled over them as they finished their treats. Rafe took the glasses and plates to the sink, washing and drying them while Miss Ethel moved to the living room. By the time he joined her there, she was in her chair, the ever-present knitting in her hands. He watched a moment as her fingers worked so quickly, the needles appearing to move of their own volition, making the strings of yarn into a shawl.

The motion was calming, and he thought back to the many evenings in this room, her spirit seeming to take the random strings of their lives and bringing meaning to them.

"I have a proposition for you," she said, startling him out of his musing.

His gaze jumped to her, but she was still staring at her needles.

"A proposition?" Intrigued, he could not imagine what she had in mind.

Laying the knitting down in her lap, she held his gaze. "I've heard about someone who needs help...a friend of a friend. You might not be looking for anything to do, but since you have a few months and appear to be at loose ends, I thought you might be interested, since you enjoy working outdoors."

She now had his complete attention as he leaned forward, his forearms planted on his knees. "Okay...I'm all ears."

"Well, one of the ladies from my church's knitting circle knows that there's a woman, a shut-in, living outside the city. Supposedly her house has a large yard and gardens that have now gone unattended."

"And you want me to work in her yard?"

"Well, as much as I love having you here with me, I feel bad knowing there's someone else who could use your talents and, if you're not going back to California for a couple of months, you'd have time to whip her gardens into shape."

He leaned back and said, "You said she lives outside of town. Sounds like quite a commute."

"Oh, goodness me, I forgot to mention there's a groundskeeper cottage on the grounds."

"Groundskeeper cottage? Grounds? How big is this place?"

"Well, I don't know, but I don't think it would be anything you couldn't handle."

"This woman has no family? Sons or grandsons to keep her yard up? Or hire a lawn service?"

Shrugging slightly, Miss Ethel said, "I don't believe there is family. I just hate the idea of someone coming in and taking advantage of her. But, please, don't feel obligated. It was just a thought."

He watched as she smiled pleasantly, picking up her knitting, the needles once more clacking. Rubbing his chin, he pondered the situation. *I've got the time. I've got the knowledge. I like the work. I'd have a cottage to myself for the whole summer...no agents, no photographers, no fans.*

"I'll do it," he announced suddenly, startling Miss Ethel.

She jumped slightly, laying her knitting down once more. "My goodness, you didn't have to make up your mind so soon," she exclaimed. "Are you sure?"

Nodding, he admitted, "I need a break, Miss Ethel. I think this just might be exactly the thing to help me figure out the next phase of my life. Even if I go back to California in the fall, at least I'll have had some time alone to be outside...to think, while helping an elderly lady."

Leaning back, he let out a sigh of relief, missing Miss Ethel's lifted brow and the slight smile curving her lips.

4

The dark, rain-filled sky inhibited Rafe's view, making the drive slow. After having turned onto a winding, narrow lane, several miles off the main road, he peered through the windshield as the wipers swished, slinging water to the edges of the glass. The drive was lined with woods on either side, thick and already green. The narrow lane would make it difficult for two cars to pass, but with a dirt shoulder on either side, he assumed it would be possible with caution, though he hoped he would not have to take that chance.

The drive wound back and forth, gently leading upward. Coming to a clearing, he slowed the truck to a halt, leaning forward to gain a better view. He stared at the scene in front of him, his mind having difficulty catching up to what his eyes were seeing.

The grass showed no signs of having been mown lately. The shrubs were overgrown and unshapely. The trees sported dead limbs amongst the ones bearing leaves. What was once flower beds, now lay in complete disregard. As his gaze continued up the continuing long driveway as it rose up the hill, his breath caught in his throat.

A dark, stone house rose from the edge of a cliff overlooking the James River, shrouded in overgrown trees. The foreboding building had an ominous appearance, almost castle-like with a rounded turret on one corner. For an instant, he wondered where he had seen the house before, then remembered a picture from Zander's storybook.

With a shake of his head, he continued up the drive, observing the turnoff for the groundskeeper's cottage. The gravel lane followed the curve of the wood, ending with the small, one-story cottage, created from the same dark stone as the main house. Sitting near the edge of the surrounding trees, the windows were covered with wooden shutters painted blue, metal latches securing them from the elements.

The sun was hiding, the rain pouring, and he longed to get inside. *Might as well get settled first, so I'm ready to go to work tomorrow.* Once he had decided to take Miss Ethel up on her offer to help the shut-in, it took a couple of days for permission to be granted, directions to be given, and instructions to be sent. He was to live in the groundskeeper's cottage, provide his own food, have full use of the tool garage, and under no circumstances was he to bother the owner. *Whatever,* he shrugged. *A spring and summer, in peace and quiet, working outdoors, not having to make conversation, and not being fawned over...heavenly!*

Parking in the front, he reached for the bag in the seat next to him, making sure to take out the cottage key sent to him. Jogging to the wooden door, he unlocked it quickly, stepping inside. Flipping on the light switch nearest the door, he moved his gaze around, a grin spreading across his face.

The living room was to the left, a dark blue, overstuffed sofa and striped chair taking up most of the room. A wooden coffee table sat in the middle, but his eyes were drawn to the opposite wall. Where most homes would have a large TV with an entertainment console, instead the wall was floor to ceiling built-in bookshelves, filled with books, surrounding a stone fireplace. A woven rug graced the wooden floor, making the room homey. A flash of living in a Hobbit hole flew through his mind as he swung his gaze around.

Immediately to the right sat a wooden table and two chairs, with only a short counter separating the room from the small kitchen. From where he stood, he viewed an older model refrigerator and stove. The only nod to modern conveniences was a microwave on the counter.

A short hall was in front of him, with only three doors. As he moved forward, he found the single bedroom, the bathroom and a room designated as a mudroom, containing a washer and dryer, sink, and hooks for coats and a place for boots near the back door. Peeking into the bathroom, he shook his head at the small space, wondering how his large body would fit into the narrow tub and shower.

He stepped into the bedroom, spying a single bed, dresser, and small closet. Dropping his bag, he turned and went back to the front door. The rain was still pouring, but he wanted to get his groceries in, so he darted back to the truck, unloading it in haste. Closing the door behind him, he shook his head, sending water droplets all about. Wiping his hand over his face, he moved to place the groceries into the refrigerator and cabinets. Walking into the living room, he stared at the fireplace, wondering how long it had been since it had been lit. Not cold, he still felt like a fire would be perfect in the storybook room.

Dropping his chin to his chest, he wondered what was coming over him. *Storybook room? Get a grip, man!* Moving to the window, he remembered the wooden shutters were closed on the outside. Opening the front door, he looked through the rain up toward the main house. Every bit as imposing as when he first laid eyes on it, he sighed, thinking of the elderly woman living in that monstrosity.

Checking the weather prediction on his phone, he saw the rain was supposed to end during the night, making tomorrow the perfect time to investigate the tool garage and begin reclaiming the gardens. Knowing there was nothing else to be done that day, he walked back into the bedroom and unpacked.

Later, after fixing dinner in the kitchen, he sat at the table eating spaghetti, garlic bread, and salad. He grinned, knowing the carbs would be worked off the next day out in the sunshine and not in a gym. Relishing his meal, he leaned back, patting his stomach when he was finished.

It felt odd being alone after years of rarely being by himself. He would disappear to his California efficiency at night, but his days were packed with people...lots of people. The incessant noise became background chatter, but without it, he heard every sound—the tick-tock of the clock on the wall and the rain hitting against the glass windows. But mostly, there was peaceful quiet.

Washing his plates and the cooking pans, he took the extra time to dry them, not having anything else to do. With the kitchen tidy, he moved into the living room, drawn to the bookshelves. Stuffed with hardbacks and paperbacks, he drew his finger along the spines as he studied the eclectic titles. Classics...British, American, French, and a few German. Mysteries. World studies. Religious. Hemingway, Dostoevsky, Wilde, Homer, Dante, Steinbeck, Twain, Dickens...the list went on.

Humbled that he was standing before a treasure trove of books, he almost dropped to his knees. Miss Ethel had instilled in each of them the power of the written word and he was awed at the fortune found in this tiny cottage. Upon closer inspection, he observed the books were not just someone's collection, left to gather dust, but they had been lovingly handled. Their spines showing the faint marks where they had been opened, it was not hard to image someone's fingers turning the pages as they read.

Coming to a section of hardback books, their bindings appeared to be leather and he gently pulled one out, eyes widening at the gold edged pages. Opening it, he sucked in a quick breath, seeing an author's signature in the first edition. More classics. Carefully replacing the book, he continued his perusal. Seeing a bound set of Grimm's fairy tales, he grinned. *Zander would be thrilled just to have a chance to see these books.* He decided to invite him to visit, but then thought better of the idea. *Not before checking with the owner.*

Pulling out a copy of Steinbeck's *East of Eden*, he moved to the chair, settling into the deep cushions, finding it much more comfortable for a man his size than he assumed. Flipping on the floor lamp near the chair, he opened the book, eager to delve into the words.

Eleanor moved to the window, peering out into the dark night, the sound of rain still pattering on the stone terrace.

The room was dark, illuminated only by the flames in the fireplace. Wrapping her arms around her body, she stared out the window, her mind wandering aimlessly down memory paths, leading nowhere.

A light at the edge of the woods caught her eye and she jerked her head to the side to gain a better view. Eyes narrowing as she attempted to focus, she saw the faint flicker of light coming from the area of the groundskeeper's cottage. Nodding to herself, she remembered that today was the day he was arriving. *Good,* she sighed in contentment. She hated the way the grounds had so quickly fallen into disarray after the last groundskeeper left.

Emitting an indelicate snort, she thought of the last man to work on the yard. Ancient. Good intentions, but so elderly he was barely able to handle the lawnmower...a riding lawnmower. Sighing, she thought of the man before that...a young man, eager to get his paycheck, but not so eager to do the work required. And the man before that...another young man, interested in the work but the intricacies of the gardens were beyond his scope and she had watched in horror, his pruning little more than butchering.

Her attention drew back to the cottage and she wondered who was now going to attempt to care for the grounds. She vaguely remembered reading the letter. Had been in the military. Looking for work. Miss Ethel's recommendation. A small smile slipped across her face. Well, if Miss Ethel recommended him, he cannot be too bad. *I hope.*

Turning from the window, she moved slowly through the room, banking the dying fire before leaving the room, walking slowly to her bedroom.

Rafe's head nodded to the side before jerking upward. Looking around sheepishly, as though someone would have seen him, he stood, stretching his tall body. Replacing the book onto the shelf, he stalked over to the door, opening it widely. The rain had stopped and he breathed in deeply, the fresh air filling his lungs. The night was black, but with the clouds moving past, the moon was able to cast a glow onto the world outside the cottage. The foreboding house on the hill still loomed larger than ever. Wondering when he would meet his employer, he remembered Miss Ethel's words...a shut-in, prefers her privacy, doesn't want to be disturbed. *Seems mighty lonely*, but then, at that moment, spending some time in solitude was exactly what he wanted as well.

Steinbeck's words came back to him. **"All great and precious things are lonely."**

Closing the door, he turned out the lights before heading to bed. A quick shower standing in the narrow tub, where he had to stoop to wash his hair, and he was ready to call it a day. Sliding into the bed, he positioned himself at an angle to make sure his feet did not hang off the end. Wondering if sleep would come, he soon drifted off into a peaceful slumber, in the little cottage at the edge of the woods, down the hill from the castle.

5

The early sunrise sent sparkling beams across the bed, causing Rafe's eyes to blink, taking a moment for him to remember where he was. Sitting up, he was unable to keep the grin off his face. The curtains were light blue. The antique, wrought-iron bedframe held an amazingly comfortable mattress and soft, cotton sheets. Picking up his phone from the small nightstand, he checked the time. *Shit! It's seven o'clock.*

Tossing back the multi-colored, patchwork quilt and sheets, he bounded from the bed, irritated that he slept longer than he had planned. Rushing into the bathroom, he quickly finished his routine and dressed in jeans and a t-shirt. Pulling on a flannel shirt to fight the early morning chill, he stalked into the kitchen. Soon bacon cooked in the microwave, scrambled eggs, toast, coffee, and juice fueled him for the morning. Giving the dishes a quick rinse before leaving them in the sink, he pulled on his boots from near the back door and grabbed his work gloves.

Heading out the door, he stopped short, the crisp

morning air slapping him in the face. Sucking in a deep breath, he felt invigorated in a way he had not felt in a long time. Another quote from Steinbeck's *East of Eden* flooded his mind.

"And everything changed color. And the world opened out. And a day was good to awaken to. And there were no limits to anything."

In the light of day, the view up the hill toward the mansion brought him up short, his breath catching in his throat. If he thought the house resembled a castle in the dark, it was even more so in the daytime.

A dark, river stone façade covered the three-story house and the roof was made from grey, slate tiles. Four chimneys rose from the roof, two in dark brick and two in stone. The windows on the upper floors, edged in granite, peeked out from the stone walls. On the first floor, many of the windows were surrounded by stone arches. Imposing, heavy, wooden, double doors graced the front, giving off the impression they acted more as a barrier than for welcoming guests.

The shrubs at the base of the house were unruly and overgrown. Ivy climbed, untrimmed, along one side, partially covering a few of the windows. The sun was still behind the trees, but he longed to view the mansion when the morning sun hit it full force. Snapping out of his awe of the building, he pulled his thoughts back to the grounds.

Walking along the path toward the tool garage, he viewed the tall trees with leaves and pine needles coating their bases. A woodland creature's mecca, he watched as squirrels and chipmunks raced in the undergrowth. As he continued, the forest floor was covered in moss and ferns. He kneeled, dragging his gloved hands through the wet soil, amazed at the dark, rich earth. The forest had clearly been here for a long time, renewing the earth around. He stood, letting the soil sift through his fingertips.

Lifting his head, he listened as the gentle breeze ruffled the branches overhead and inhaled the earthy scent before continuing to the large, wooden shed. Finding the door unlocked, he entered, his eyes taking a moment to adjust to the dim light. A dirty film covered the windows and he stalked to the closest one.

Taking a rag from a nearby table, he wiped the glass, partially smearing the dust, but allowing the sun to beam inside more clearly. Satisfied with the results, he moved to the other windows, performing the same task. Tossing the rag, he turned and scanned the now visible room. A large, riding lawn mower was parked in the middle of the room. Wooden tables and shelves lined the side walls, covered in bags of grass fertilizer, boxes of pesticides and, upon closer inspection, bags of bird seed, torn open and munched on by resident mice.

The back wall, covered in pegboard, held rakes, hoes, mallets, weeders, trowels, shovels, spades, saws, pruning cutters, and weed trimmers. Leaf blowers were in the corner, along with a tiller. Moving around the space, he appreciated the number of tools, knowing that with them at his disposal, his ability to reclaim and maintain the owner's yard and gardens would be much easier.

Walking back to the door of the shed, he looked over the span of the uncut grass. *First things first. Cut the grass.* That job would take all day, considering it would involve using the grass catcher the first time around due to the grass being so tall. *No worries, I've got nothing but time.*

Pulling back the heavy, velvet green draperies, laced with gold thread, Eleanor blinked at the light as it poured into the room. The sound of the lawn mower had drawn her to the window. The same window she peered out of last night but, now, the light of day illuminated the expanse of land extending from the house to the woods. Shifting her gaze back and forth, she was unable to see the new gardener, but the hum of the mower assured her he was at work. Nodding in silent agreement that the grass was the first thing that needed to be cut, she stepped away from the window, returning to her breakfast.

The dining room contained the original maple table, matching chairs lining the sides as sentinels to a time gone by. Tall, floor to ceiling windows lined the wall, framed with heavy brocade curtains pulled back with deep red ties, overlooking the woods. The floor was covered in Oriental rugs her grandfather brought back from India. Large, framed paintings covered the red, silk wallpapered walls. Dark wood wainscoting with matching chair rails completed the room.

Sitting alone at the long table, she ate in silence. Leaning back in her chair, she allowed her mind to drift back to when her family sat at the table. The cook would place the breakfast on the tall, oak sidebar and as they entered, each would fill their plates. Her father sat in his usual place at the head of the table, her mother to his right. She and her brother had loved that their table usually held her cousins as well, over to play.

Laughter would ring out, her parents not minding children acting like children even at the table, as long as manners were still observed. The smile slowly dropped from her face as she thought of how they had all faded away into the past, now leaving her alone with her memories. Finishing her coffee, she took the dishes to the huge kitchen and, after rising them, placed them in the dishwasher.

Picking up the essay she was reading, she retreated down a long hall, to a study on the far side of the house. A brick fireplace anchored the end of the room, flanked with two comfortable chairs in deep blue. A settee faced the fireplace, perfect for sitting and warming toes on a cold, winter night. The mantle contained silver-framed photographs of her family. The windows on this side of the house overlooked the ravine where the James River meandered below. Finding the view peaceful, she sat at the desk, opening the manuscript and began reading, the man working in her yard far from her thoughts.

The sun beamed down on his back and soon Rafe tossed his flannel shirt on the seat underneath him. The force of the sun had risen above the tree line, now sending its full illumination onto the house. He looked across the lawn, seeing the blue slate of the roof covering the grey stone, now lighter in the sun. The house appeared to rise from the edge of the cliff it was perched on and he marveled at the architecture, appreciating the way the design melded in with the surrounding area.

The house looked to be perfectly habitable, the grounds being the only unkempt part. The image of an elderly lady, living a life of leisure inside the fortress walls struck him and he could not help but smile. For some reason, Charles Dickens' description of Miss Havisham from *Great Expectations* came to mind.

"She was dressed in rich materials - satins, and lace,

and silks - all of white. Her shoes were white. And she had a long white veil dependent from her hair, and she had bridal flowers in her hair, but her hair was white. Some bright jewels sparkled on her neck and on her hands, and some other jewels lay sparkling on the table. Dresses, less splendid than the dress she wore, and half-packed trunks, were scattered about. She had not quite finished dressing for she had but one shoe on - the other was on the table near her hand. . .”

Giving his head a shake to rid himself of the fanciful notions, he turned back to the grounds, viewing what he had accomplished so far.

The grass was so tall, he had to mow with the blade on the highest setting and still needed to stop every twenty minutes to empty the grass catchers. To keep from having to take unnecessary steps, he set up a compost pile in the woods. Using a flat-bed trailer with a hitch he discovered behind the shed, he drove there and dumped the clippings. Shoveling the grass out at the base of the trees in the cool shade, he then raked it into the dead leaves and pine needles so it could decompose, making a rich mulch.

As he drove back to the shed to unhook the trailer, he began the task again. The acreage was so vast, he knew he would spend the rest of the day just completing the grass cutting. *Don’t rush things, Rafe. It takes time to cultivate a plant...time to cultivate a garden.* Miss Ethel’s words floated through his mind as he continued his mowing laps.

The sun, now fully on the house, gave him a chance to see it in all its glory. The light gave the slate roof a bluish tint, although the stone walls remained grey. The windows captured the reflection of light, lessening the foreboding appearance. He smiled his admiration for the architect and builder.

Taking a lunch break, he walked back to the cottage. At the door, he turned and stared over the expanse of yard, seeing almost half of the grass now cut, trim and neat. From this distance, he observed a few places where it needed to be mowed again to level the lawn. Satisfied with his morning's work, he entered the abode.

Pulling out slices of bread, turkey and ham deli slices, provolone and cheddar cheese, lettuce and tomato, he made two large sandwiches. With a pickle and potato chips piled on the side, he sat down at the small table, his lunch in front of him. Starting to dig in, his eyes shifted to the bookcase. Staring for a moment, he lay his sandwich back on his plate and grabbed a few paper towels. Wiping his hands carefully, he moved over to the shelves, eschewing the leather-bound volumes and choosing a hardback of Thomas Hardy's *Far From the Maddening Crowd*. Taking care to keep the pages clean as he ate, he read silently as he finished his lunch.

"I have felt lately, more and more, that my present way of living is bad in every respect."

Hardy managed to capture in one sentence the very thoughts that had plagued Rafe for months. Scrubbing his hand over his face, he vowed to spend the summer figuring out what he wanted to do with his life. *A change is necessary...absolutely necessary.* The thought of Marty flew through his mind, but he dismissed it quickly. Determined to do whatever was necessary to keep the agent off his back, he stood and, using a bookmark found on the end table, closed the book before washing up from his meal.

Eleanor's afternoon was spent much like her morning. After a simple bowl of soup, she continued to sit in the library, reading the manuscript, her red pen in her hand. After a while, she stood, stretching with some difficulty, and moved into the family room. The addition to the house had been completed for her grandmother, who enjoyed sitting in the comfortable informal room, viewing the gardens below in the winter. In the warmer months, the slate terrace just outside the doors provided a perfect place for afternoon tea. Her mother had added the trellis with climbing roses adorning the structure. With tall Magnolia trees on one side, the shade had been perfect for ladies who did not care for too much sun on their skin. A stone wall on one side overlooked the cliff, leading to the river below.

She stepped outside, ready to continue her afternoon in the shade, but the sound of the mower caused her to halt abruptly. Nervously casting her eyes about, she still could not see the new gardener. Even so, forgoing the pleasure of sitting on the terrace, she moved back inside. Not wanting to encourage contact, she walked back to the library. Placing her grocery order online, she decided to take care of some housekeeping.

Walking up the sweeping, front staircase, she moved silently over the carpeted hall toward one of the many unused rooms of the house.

By the time the sun had moved across the sky, casting long shadows over the grassy yard from the tall trees at the edge of the woods, Rafe had finally finished mowing. With a critical eye, he viewed the freshly mown lawn and discerned a few rough patches where he would go back over with the mower tomorrow. But, for now, he was pleased with his day's work.

Replacing everything in the tool garage, he shut and latched the door before walking back down the hill toward his cottage. The sound of a vehicle had him looking over his shoulder as a delivery van moved up the drive and to the back of the house. A young man, dressed in jeans and a t-shirt, alighted and opened the back, hefting a large box that he set outside the door. The sign on the van read, **Beskins Grocery**.

Rubbing his chin, he realized his employer was truly a shut-in. *No reason I can't shop for her. I'll ask as soon as I meet her if she would like me to take over the groceries. If I'm shopping for myself, I might as well shop for her too.* He hesitated in his steps, tempted to walk up to the main house to ask, but decided against it for now. His instructions had been clear: the owner of the house wanted seclusion. If he had a question or concern, her phone number had been given and he was to send a text.

That piece of information had surprised him. Texting did not mesh with his idea of the elderly mistress of the manor, but he assumed someone stayed with her and could handle the correspondence.

Having learned his cottage did not have its own Internet, he had been able to use the house's Internet, given a password when he was employed. He wondered about the lack of privacy for the owner, but was not going to turn it down.

Entering his cottage, he immediately pulled off his boots, leaving them by the door. Walking into the bathroom, he stripped and stepped over into the tub, turning on the shower. He washed the dirt and sweat from his body, pleased that hot water was plentiful. Dressing in cut-off sweatpants with a drawstring waist, he baked chicken for dinner, adding store-bought potato salad to the side and was thrilled with his indulgence of a large slice of pie for dessert. Eating for the pleasure of eating once more, he relished his food.

An hour later, he sat in a chair in the front yard, sipping a beer and listening to the crickets chirping. Fireflies danced across the long expanse of freshly mown grass between him and the main house. He wondered if the owner ever sat at one of her windows or on the terrace, looking down at the lawn, appreciating the fireflies as well.

As he moved inside, he opened his laptop, pulling up his email. Instead of looking at his computer, he first pulled out his phone, sending a text to letting the owner know he was available to shop for her when he went into town. Afterward, a quick look showed him that his mailbox was filling with emails from Marty and one from Cherelle. Deleting them all without reading them, he shut down his computer. Deciding to forgo finishing the Steinbeck book from the previous night, he chose Tolkien's *The Hobbit*. Grinning, he settled back into the chair, his long legs stretched out in front of him, ready to slide into a world of pure fantasy.

As was becoming a habit, Eleanor stood at the window, the heavy curtains pulled back, allowing her a view of the expanse of lawn in the moonlight. The fireflies danced across the freshly mown grass, seeming brighter than before. Smiling at the view before her, she flicked her gaze toward the cottage, seeing a light in the front room. Disturbed by his offer to shop for her, she had immediately sent a polite 'no thank you' text. Now, she wondered if she had been too hasty. *After all, I wouldn't have to see him if he brought groceries to the back door.* Shaking her head, she decided she had done the right thing. *He'll leave at the end of the summer. No reason to get used to someone doing it for me.* Inhaling in a deep breath, she stared out at the fireflies one last time before dropping the curtain back into place.

6

The next morning dawned sunny as Rafe rubbed the sleep from his eyes. Stretching diagonal across the bed, he felt the burn of muscles that had completed a hard day's work the previous day. Loving the feeling, it was different than the pain from a gym workout. A memory flash of his father digging in the garden flew through his mind. *"Nothing like hard work outdoors to really exercise the body as well as the mind."* It had not made sense to him when he was eight years old, but now, as those words came back to him, he recognized the wisdom of his father.

Sitting up in bed, he glanced at his phone, pleased to see it was only six-thirty. Finishing in the bathroom, he threw on a clean pair of jeans with another t-shirt and the flannel from yesterday. When he first moved to California, he thought about what he wore every day, even going to and from a photo shoot, kidding himself that the attention to detail might make a difference in his modeling career. *Hmph...modeling career. What a crock of shit! More like selling my soul.*

Moving into the kitchen, fixing breakfast, he had to admit that there was nothing wrong with modeling, per se, but the environment was conducive to building egos in a highly competitive business. *No wonder I began to feel as though I was losing myself.*

Checking his phone, in case his employer wanted to talk to him, he was surprised to see she had responded, but furrowed his brow as he read that she politely declined his offer to get her groceries.

Eating quickly, he filled a travel mug with coffee and a thermos of cold water, before heading out to the tool garage. Deciding to tackle some of the Boxwood hedges on the perimeter of the grounds first while the dew evaporated, he grabbed a wheelbarrow, placed the trimming shears into it, and rolled it toward the hedge closest to the driveway, but farthest from the house.

The trimming was also going to be a multi-day task, as overgrown as they were. They could be cut back to the shape they needed to be and, since new leaves could grow on old wood, he decided to trim at least eight inches all around. The gas-powered hedge trimmer made fast work of cutting the shaggy limbs, but having to continually stop, pile them in the wheelbarrow and take them to dump into the woods, cost him a lot of time. Finally, he decided to bring out the mower with the trailer hitched and haul the branches away just like he had the grass.

It was lunchtime before he made it halfway to the house on just one side of the drive. Walking back to the cottage, he looked over his shoulder, wondering about the occupant. Still bothered that she lived so secluded, he nonetheless thought it best if he worked his way from the woods toward the house in his lawn care. *Just in case she needs more time to get used to someone being here.*

Loneliness threatened to overtake Eleanor. *How long have I existed by myself in this house?* She knew the answer—one year, four months, and three days. Trying to remember what her life had been like before was becoming harder and harder.

She walked down the long upstairs hall, dividing the bedrooms, one on either side, each with their own private bathrooms. The largest, the master bedroom that her parents had shared, faced the river and included a private sitting room as well. The other wing of the house contained a hall, similar to this one, where her grandparent's master bedroom occupied.

The room she had claimed as a child, with the balcony overlooking the gardens, was across the hall. However, the balcony faced the sun most of the day, keeping her from enjoying the space. Since coming back, she had left it, preferring the bedroom next to the master, which also overlooked the river.

Situated on a high point, a straight cliff leading to the water, gave her a sense of privacy, as well as freedom. She could sit on her balcony, unseen by anyone and watch the water below rushing by. Occasional boats—commerce, fishing, and personal—would float by. The sun did not hit this side of the house until the late evening, giving her a perfect place to enjoy the view without any of the unpleasantness.

The doorbell sounded, startling a gasp from her lips. *The groundskeeper?* Remembering the family attorney was coming today, she immediately felt foolish. Hurrying to the door, she peeked out first, before opening it.

"Ms. Bellamy," he greeted, shaking her hand warmly.

"Mr. Thomas," she smiled, stepping back to allow him to enter. The older gentleman, always so precise in his dress, followed her. His uniform of a dark suit, paired with a crisp white shirt, and red tie that matched the red handkerchief tucked into his suit pocket, was familiar to her. His snow-white hair was neatly trimmed, as was his mustache. Small in stature, he nonetheless gave off an air of competency that had most men jumping to do his bidding.

"Where is Sally?"

Closing the door behind him, she led the way into the study. He was an old family friend and deserved to be comfortable in the study as opposed to the formal living room. Waving her hand, she replied, "She has this week off to go see her family. She's usually only here three days a week anyway, but I've come to rely on her so much, it feels odd not having a housekeeper around."

She poured a cup of coffee for both of them and they continued to make small talk before engaging in the business aspect of his visit.

He pulled out several legal and accounting papers for her to sign. "Make sure to read these carefully," he warned unnecessarily.

"Now, you know that my father always taught me to never sign before reading." Looking at him, she said, "I'll read these tonight and can have them sent to you tomorrow."

"That will be fine," he agreed. Leaning back in his chair, he asked, "How has your physical therapy been going?"

Her lips pinched as she answered, "Okay. Painful, but okay. I haven't been going in to see anyone lately. I decided it was just as easy to do the exercises here myself."

"Do you think that's wise, my dear?"

Offering a slight shrug, she said, "I find it easier...both physically and emotionally."

His warm gaze held understanding. Sighing heavily, he said, "Before I go, I have one other thing to bring up to you." Throwing his hands up, he added, "I already know what your response will be, but I have to ask, nonetheless."

She cocked her head in silence, waiting to see what business he had left to discuss.

"A buyer wants to make an offer on this property. I know it's not for sale, but he's willing to pay handsomely."

"A buyer?"

"A developer. Philip Hayden."

Her breath left her lungs in a rush. "A developer?" Nodding slowly in understanding, she said, "He wants to turn my home into a high-class hotel doesn't he? Well, you can tell him it'll be a cold day in hell before I sell my family home."

His lips twitched as he held back a grin. "My dear, I could not have said it better." Standing to leave, he reminded, "Don't forget, I'll need the papers tomorrow. Just have a courier bring them to me."

As they walked to the front door, arm in arm, he said, "Martha wants to have you over for dinner soon." Seeing her about to protest, he added, "Just you. It would be private."

Smiling as she kissed his cheek, she said, "We'll see. If not, I'll have you and Martha over here."

Watching him drive away, she stood on the front stoop for a moment before hearing the buzz of a gas-powered motor close to the side of the house. Realizing the gardener was nearby, she hastened inside, closing the door firmly behind her.

Sitting outside that evening, Rafe sipped his beer while enjoying the setting sun over the trees. The long shadows arched over the freshly mown grass and the long row of hedges banking the drive on one side, now neat with their new trim. He had run the mower over the few patches that needed a re-do and felt satisfied that the lawn would just need weekly mowing from now on.

Breathing deeply, the cool air with the scent of pine filled his senses, and he wondered when the last time was that he just sat for the pure enjoyment of the evening. The fireflies were darting around and he grinned, knowing he had not noticed such simple pleasures in a long time.

Turning his mind to the next day, the weather forecast called for rain and he considered cleaning the tools and mower since he would not be able to trim the tree branches. With his tomorrow planned, he finished his beer and then headed back inside. Moving to the chair in the sitting room, he picked up *The Hobbit*, determined to read more before turning in for the night.

Pacing in front of the fireplace in the study, Eleanor fretted, papers clasped in her hands. They needed to get into her attorney's office the next day, but when she went online to arrange for the courier service, she discovered they had gone out of business. Without being able to call upon Sally, she did not know anyone else she could contact.

Rubbing her forehead, she tried to focus. *I could call Mr. Thomas to come back.* She hated that idea, considering his office was thirty minutes away and he had just been to her house. *I could drive myself.* That idea was dismissed, knowing it would be difficult to drive that far. *Or, at least, I don't think I could.* Passing by the window overlooking the lawn, she stared down toward the woods, seeing a light beaming from the cottage's window. *The gardener...I could ask him.*

Not being able to come up with a viable alternative, she moved to her phone and composed a text, hoping he would read it before starting work the next day. Placing the papers in an envelope, she lay them by the table next to the back door. Sucking in a deep breath, she moved through the first-floor rooms, turning the lights off. As she walked up the stairs, her phone chimed an incoming text alert.

Checking, she saw it was from Mr. Walker, the gardener. *Probably should start thinking of him by name, not just as 'the gardener'.* Scanning the missive, she breathed a sigh of relief. He agreed to take the papers into the attorney's office. He also added that he would be stopping at the grocery store and if she changed her mind and wanted him to pick up anything, he would be glad to. *He's so kind, definitely need to think of him as Mr. Walker.*

Flipping off the hall light as she entered her bedroom, her lips curved in a slight smile. Even though she had not laid eyes on the new groundskeeper, she felt better knowing someone was nearby, especially without Sally around.

Later, settled into bed, she opened the book lying on top of her nightstand, reading to relax until her eyes grew heavy. Turning off the light by her bed, she slid down under the covers, longing for a dreamless sleep…or at least one without nightmares.

7

Rafe approached the back door, his footsteps slowing as he neared. This was the closest he had come to the main house and his appraising gaze wandered over the stonework in appreciation. The drive split into two directions, one side leading to the back where he knew the original owners would have had servants enter and received deliveries. The other side curved toward the front door where a wide portico would have accepted the family and guests, keeping them from the weather.

A three-story turret was built into only one front corner, facing the long expanse of lawn and gardens. Moving beyond the back of the house, he peered over the stone wall, seeing the drop down to the river. The view was breathtaking and he realized all the rooms at the back of the house would have that same view.

Bringing himself back to his task, he saw a small table by the back door with a large, manila envelope sitting on top with a note attached. Stalking over, he read the note.

Thank you for taking the envelope to my attorney. The address is enclosed. Please take the day off for your trouble. I

do not need anything from the grocery, but thank you all the same. Please call if needed. Ms. Bellamy

The handwriting was definitely feminine, the lettering strong and precise. He smiled at the thought of the elderly lady handwriting her correspondence while sitting at a delicate antique table overlooking the gardens.

Shaking his head, he turned and headed back down the drive toward his truck. With the day off, he decided to drive to Richmond first to take care of delivering the envelope before stopping to check on Miss Ethel.

An hour later, he entered the stately offices of Mr. Thomas and observed a distinguished, white-haired gentleman speaking to the receptionist. As the man finished, he nodded politely toward Rafe before turning to walk down the hall.

Stepping up to the desk, Rafe said, "I'm here to deliver this envelope of signed documents to Mr. Thomas from Ms. Bellamy."

Before the receptionist could take the envelope, the older gentleman turned on his heel and stared unabashedly at Rafe. He moved toward him, his gaze sweeping up and down, assessing.

"I'm Mr. Thomas," he introduced. "And you are?"

"Rafe Walker, sir. Nice to meet you." He stuck his hand out, noting the attorney's firm handshake. "Well, I'll be on my way."

"You are her new groundskeeper, I believe?"

Cocking his head to the side, he nodded. "Yes, sir. I'm working there during the summer."

"I understand you came recommended by Miss Ethel. That's the highest recommendation I can think of," Mr. Thomas said, a twinkle in his blue eyes.

Chuckling, Rafe nodded. "Then I consider it an honor

to have her think that of me. Actually, Miss Ethel raised me." If he thought that bit of information was going to settle uncomfortably with Mr. Thomas, he was surprised when the attorney smiled widely.

"Ms. Bellamy is not just a client, but a friend. You'll forgive my inquisitiveness, but I like to make sure she is well taken care of."

"I would expect no less from a friend of hers, sir."

Mr. Thomas nodded, a slight smile curving his lips before sticking his hand out once more. "It was my pleasure to meet you, Mr. Walker. I hope your stay at Bellamy House is a good one."

"Thank you, sir. So far I'm loving the work there."

"I'm glad you're there, especially now that her housekeeper is on holiday."

Eyebrow lifted, he nodded. "I wondered if there was no one to assist her."

"Oh, she gets around just fine, but has someone to assist a few days a week with the heavy cleaning."

"Good. Glad to hear that," Rafe replied, finding himself relieved at the information. With a nod, he walked back out into the late spring sunshine. Driving out of town, he called Miss Ethel. She picked up on the first ring.

"Rafe, dear, how are you?"

"I'm good. I had to run an errand for Ms. Bellamy and am in town. I thought I'd run by and take you to lunch."

"Oh, dear. Normally I would, but I'm going to a church mission afternoon tea today."

Disappointed, he said, "I'm glad you're staying busy, but I'll miss you. Maybe on my next day off we can make plans."

"Of course, Rafe. Just let me know. By the way, how is the job going?"

"Perfect," he enthused. "I've been outdoors every day this week so far. Got the lawn and drive hedges whipped into shape. Next I need to start on trimming the trees and flower gardens."

"Have you...uh...met your employer yet?"

"No, but we communicated by text if she needs something." Chucking, he added, "I'm glad she can handle a smartphone." Realizing he sounded patronizing, he hastened, "Not every older person is as adept at staying up on technology as you, Miss Ethel."

Her laughter rang out before she said, "You know, Rafe, life has a way of surprising you when you least expect it."

Disconnecting after goodbyes, he turned down the highway heading back toward the west, following the James River. Stopping in the little town closest to Bellamy House, he dropped into the local grocery store to stock up. Eggs, meat, bread, oatmeal, peanut butter, fruit, and cans of soup and vegetables. Shaking his head, he thought about how lean he ate while living in California. Now, not having to worry about his shape, he worked hard outside every day and burned off the calories he ate...and enjoyed eating.

Looking around the little store, he wished he could take something back to Ms. Bellamy, but had no idea what she would like. Passing the bakery, he noted a little plate of freshly made sugar cookies and stopped. Reminded of the millions of cookies Miss Ethel used to make, he snagged the plastic-wrapped platter, thinking no one would turn down cookies.

On the way to the checkout counter, he spied a

platter of fresh fruit. Grabbing that too, he added it to the basket. Smiling at the cashier, he noted her eying him up and down. Inwardly chuckling, he realized he had not been ogled in over a week. *God, that feels good.* Just a couple weeks home and he already felt the change.

"You new 'round here?" she asked, her eager face turned up toward his.

"Working for now at the Bellamy place," he murmured, wondering if she was old enough to drive, much less flirt with a man his age.

Her gasp drew his attention back to her face, lifting his eyebrow in surprise.

Wide-eyed, she shook her head while leaning in, whispering loudly, "You work for the witch?"

Unsure he heard her correctly, he stammered, "The... the what did you say?"

"She's a witch...everyone says so. Her family's all dead. The kids at school say she put a hex on them." Shaking her head derisively, she added, "You better watch out. They say she's scary ugly—"

"And I think you would do well to tend to your customers and stop repeating malicious gossip," he growled in response.

A man wearing a manager's badge walked over, his disapproving gaze lifting to Rafe. "Is there a problem here?"

"Maybe you should teach your employees to have respect for their customers," he bit out. "I believe Ms. Bellamy orders her groceries from here. Perhaps she needs to find a new place to do business."

Now the manager stared wide-eyed at him before swinging his gaze to the young cashier. "Carly, get in the back and work on the stock." Turning back to Rafe, he rushed to say, "Please accept my apologies, sir."

Nodding curtly, he strode from the store. As he placed the groceries in the passenger seat of his truck, he heard steps behind him and turned quickly.

The manager had followed, saying once more, "I am sorry about that. The teenagers let their imaginations and their mouths run wild."

"Why do they talk about her like that?"

Shrugging, the man said, "I've only been at this store for less than a year. When I first started, Ms. Bellamy's weekly delivery order had already been set up. She just orders online. I've never met her, but..." he shrugged, "talk in town is that she had been away and since she's come back, she's lived in seclusion. She doesn't have any family left. I suppose that gets tongues to wagging." With that, he nodded toward Rafe and hurried back inside.

His good mood now blown away, he climbed into his truck, his mind on the woman inside the stone castle. It was nice to spend his days working in her yard with no added agenda from her. *Miss Bellamy just needs my skills to care for her property...no other expectations.* He had been simply thinking of her as an older woman, perhaps shut-in due to her age, but now he wondered if there was not a physical ailment as well. *Then why the hell doesn't she have household help?*

Brooding as he drove back to her place, he flipped on the radio to a country station and found he looked forward to returning to his cottage at the edge of the woods.

Spying out the small window by the door, Eleanor saw that the small table by the door now contained a bag with a note attached. Curious, she stepped outside, glancing around first. Stepping into the sunshine, she picked up the bag, finding it heavier than she expected. Peeking inside, she spied a platter of cookies as well as fruit. Unable to keep the smile from her face, she walked back inside, opening the note after placing the bag on the kitchen counter.

Ms. Bellamy, it was an honor to run the errand for you. Mr. Thomas sends his regards. I hope you enjoy the fruit and cookies...I couldn't resist. In case you need me for anything, please don't hesitate to call. Yours truly, Rafe Walker

Rafe Walker. She had never known anyone with the name Rafe. Her eyes glanced toward the cookies and she smiled at the kind gesture. Unwrapping the plastic from the plate, she took one of the decorated sugar cookies, sinking her teeth into the sweet deliciousness. Deciding to fix a cup of tea, she let it steep before carrying it to her study. Settling at her desk, she smiled again, feeling less lonely knowing the kind gardener was out there, close by, turning the tangled lawn into its former stately beauty.

"Marty, I told you, I'm on an extended break." Rafe had finally answered his agent's call after ignoring multiple calls, texts, and emails. "I'm taking the whole summer. No modeling. No plans. And no more fucking calls from you."

"I know, I know what you said," the whiny voice replied, "but I just wanted to make sure to stay in contact."

"What the hell do you think *taking a break* is?"

"Just make sure you take care of yourself, get exercise

and stay healthy, so you can come back ready to go. I'm already lining up contracts for you. Great stuff, top-notch companies—"

"You forget, Marty, my contract with you is over. My time and my body are mine again."

"Rafe, man, just keep your options open so that when the time off gets boring, you can come back."

Chuckling, he replied, "I'm getting daily exercise in the sunshine, taking care of a beautiful gothic mansion overlooking the James River. I assure you, I am not bored."

"Fine, fine, but just remember—"

"No more calls," he interrupted before disconnecting. Breathing a sigh of relief, he returned to his book.

8

For the next two weeks, Rafe's days formed a pattern. He rose early, ate breakfast, and then headed to the tool shed. He had managed to shape the driveway hedge, keep the grass mowed, trimmed the dead limbs from the edge of the woods and along the drive, and had begun work on the shrubs that were next to the house facing the lawn. Azaleas, Rhododendron, Forsythia, Holly. All combined pleasantly to keep the deep green mixed with blossoms during the summer.

In the evenings, he returned to his cottage where he ate dinner, sat outside enjoying the view of the lawn and gardens leading up to the main house, and then read from the many choices of books until sleep claimed him.

His days were filled with fresh air and hard manual labor, and his diet was good, simple food. It had been a long time he felt so healthy...or content.

He never noticed anyone looking through the windows, but he refused to peer inside. If Ms. Bellamy wanted her privacy, he was determined to give it to her. The housekeeper had returned a few days ago but, much to his surprise, she only came three days during the week and did not stay at night.

Pleased that Ms. Bellamy used a smartphone, he had sent a message before going into town again, but only received a polite reply, thanking him, but informing him that she did not need anything.

Pushing all thoughts from his head, he was determined to work on the flower beds next, hearing of a summer storm coming that evening. With tools in the wheelbarrow, he rolled it up toward the corner of the house where one of the neglected beds lay.

Sally peered out the window she was cleaning and stared at the man on his knees at the edge of the flower garden nearest the turret. Leaning to the side to gain a better view, she lifted her eyebrows as he stood. A voice from behind caused her to jump.

"Sally, what on earth are you staring at?"

Whirling around, she placed her hand on her chest, crying out, "My goodness, Ms. Bellamy, you gave me a fright. And I was just looking at the lawn. It certainly has taken shape while I was gone."

Nodding, she replied, "Yes, it has. Mr. Walker has done a very good job. I found myself thinking the other day that it hasn't looked this good in years."

Sally cocked her head to the side, a speculative look in her eye. "Have you talked with the new gardener?"

Snorting, Ms. Bellamy asked, "Why on earth do you think I would talk to him?"

"Well, have you met him?"

"I don't need to meet a man to know that he's doing his job," came the short reply.

Sally grinned as she continued to prod. "Okay, well, have you at least looked out of the window at him?"

Glaring, she said, "I have no desire for him to see me staring out of the window at him and therefore, no, I have not been peeking out at him. When he is working, I stay on the river side of the house. When it is evening and the sun has gone behind the trees, I make it to the terrace to enjoy the view."

Nodding slowly, Sally continued to smile as she moved away from the window. "Well, I think you'll be pleasantly surprised when you finally do meet him." With that cryptic comment, she moved the vacuum cleaner into the dining room, leaving Eleanor to stand in the middle of the living room, her surprised gaze on the now-drawn curtain.

The wind was already picking up as Rafe rolled the wheelbarrow back into the tool shed. Cleaning the shovel, rake, and spades before hanging them on the pegboard hooks, he startled as the wooden door slammed open, hitting the outside wall as a gust sent it flying. Hurrying over, he pulled the door shut and fastened it then continued to take care of his evening chores before heading back to the cabin. He pulled his phone out of his pocket and checked the weather app once more.

High wind gusts, heavy rain, and severe storms were still predicted to come through the area tonight and a growing storm front was moving in a few days after that. He was glad he had trimmed the dead tree limbs around the property but knew that, due to avoiding the terrace, there were possible problems there. *Well, I can deal with it tomorrow if needed. Surely, she won't mind my being there if it's a necessity.*

Finishing quickly, he opened the tool shed door, hanging on as the wind tried to throw it back again. Pushing with considerable force, he managed to close it and get it locked. Looking over his shoulder he hustled down the hill to his cottage. Taking in the large house, dark and imposing against the clouds, it had stood the test of time and the elements this far so now should be no different.

Noting the outside shutters were functional and not just decorative, he made his way around his abode, shutting and securing the wooden frames. The outside chair he normally sat in during his evening respite had blown over. Grabbing it on his way inside, he placed it near the table in the corner. Locking the front door, he stood with his hands on his hips, wondering if there was anything else he needed to accomplish before the storm hit. Coming up empty, he moved into the kitchen to fix dinner.

Later, sitting in the comfortable chair by the fireplace, the floor lamp casting a glow over his shoulder, he read more from *The Hobbit*.

"You certainly usually find something, if you look, but it is not always quite the something you were after."

Closing the book, he thought back to Miss Ethel's very similar words. *"You know, Rafe. Life has a way of surprising you when you least expect it."* Wondering why her words and the quote stuck in his mind, he lay the book to the side, turning out the light as he stood. Unable to peer through the shuttered windows, he moved to the door, opening it slightly, hearing the wind as it roared through the trees. Looking up the hill toward the main house, he saw no lights. Hoping Ms. Bellamy was tucked in safe and sound, he closed his door and, after bolting it securely, went to bed.

As the wind whistled around the front corner of her room, Eleanor lay her book down, concern etched across her face. She felt safe but wondered how Mr. Walker was faring in the cottage. Climbing from the bed, she slid on a robe and walked out of her bedroom while belting the soft fabric around her waist. Opening the bedroom door across the hall, she moved to the window that faced the lawn. Peering out, she strained to see down toward the woods, but the moonless night made the world appear black.

No lights visible must mean he's tucked in safe and sound. Sighing, she dropped the curtain and padded back to her room, settling into bed once more. The rain beat a staccato against the window panes. Knowing sleep would not be coming for a while, she continued to read.

Rafe woke early, immediately noting the wind had dissipated and the rain was no longer beating against the side of the cottage. Hurrying through breakfast, he threw open the door and breathed in the clean, fresh air. Water droplets clung to every leaf and limb, glistening in the morning sunlight. As he moved around the perimeter of the cottage, opening the shutters, the forest appeared to come alive. Birds fluttered about, their songs filling the air.

Squirrels and chipmunks scampered through the wet leaves on the ground. At the back of the cottage, where the neat grounds and large main house were not visible, it was almost possible to believe he had entered a fairy world.

Shaking the strange musings from his mind, he walked toward the tool shed, assessing the damage as he went. Several large limbs had blown out of trees and the lawn was littered with leaves. Coming upon the shed, he noticed a small tree had toppled over, it's slender trunk lying across the roof.

Mentally calculating what needed to be done first, he decided to inspect the area around the main house to start, wanting to make sure there was no damage. Walking from the back door, where nothing more than windblown leaves and small branches lay on the driveway, he made his way around the side facing the lawn. Again, blown branches were the only problem for the most part. As he turned the corner by the turret, he came upon the flagstone terrace, still in the deep shade from the tall trees.

The patio furniture was overturned, some scattered by the wind to the corner wall overlooking the river. The shattered remnants of a glass-topped table were spread over the area. Wet leaves created a slick carpet on the stone surface. And, to his dismay, several large limbs had broken and landed on the terrace. Knowing this area needed his attention first, he walked back to the shed to gather the necessary tools.

Still dressed in her long robe, Eleanor walked to the terrace. The night had not been kind to her as sleep was elusive, but now the sun shone through the windows and she threw open the doors, stepping outside. Gasping, she observed the storm's wreckage. Overturned furniture, including a glass-topped table that had shattered, created a dangerous mess. Leaves covered every surface and a few large limbs, as well as smaller branches, littered the patio.

Sighing, she walked carefully to the stone wall in the shadows of the terrace to peer over into the ravine below. The river rushed by, the waterline high.

Hearing a noise behind her, she glanced back, startled at the sight of a large man stepping to the edge of the terrace, seemingly unaware of her presence.

Jerking around, so that her back was to him, she felt her breath rush from her lungs fast as the river below. "You...you're not supposed to be here."

"Oh, Ms. Bellamy, excuse me," he said. His voice was deep and rich, its timbre resonating through her. He continued, "I didn't mean to come where I wasn't supposed to, but this area isn't safe until I clean it up."

She nodded jerkily, realizing this must be Mr. Walker. She knew he was right, but was unable to make herself turn around to face him. Indecision rooted her to the spot, her heart pounding furiously.

"Ma'am, I'll step around the side of the turret, allowing you to enter your house in private. Once you're safely inside, I'll come back to clean the area. I'll...uh...let you know when I'm finished."

Nodding again, she now felt foolish. *He must think I'm a crazy ol' bat.* Clearing her throat, trying to regain control, she said, "Yes, please. That would be best."

She heard his steps retreating from the stone patio and, when she was sure he was gone, she limped toward the door, her legs strangely weak. Once inside, she closed the glass-paned terrace door behind her, drawing the heavy curtains.

Walking forward a few feet, she stopped, her heartbeat still racing. Swallowing deeply, she hurried toward the study down the hall, far from the terrace. Slipping inside, she slid into a chair before she allowed the tears gathered in her eyes to tumble down her cheeks. Dropping her chin to her chest, she hated the impression she had made on Mr. Walker almost as much as she hated the need she felt to be alone. *Life had been so different once...a long time ago.* As thoughts of her former life, and the life she had planned, moved through her mind, she wondered if a life of seclusion was all she had to look forward to.

9

Rafe stood to the side of the house, his heart racing as much as his mind. Ms. Bellamy had stood in the shadows, her body short and slightly built, but he could have sworn her long hair was dark, not the grey or white he assumed it would be. *That doesn't matter...anyone can dye their hair.* Her voice came back to him...soft and melodious, sounding young. Her body was encased in a long, flowing robe, covering her from neck to toes. She did have a cane leaning against the wall, as her body had been bent over the masonry, her hands holding her steady.

Wiping a hand over his face, he felt the warmth of the sun hitting his back. He gave her several minutes to make her way inside, but in truth, it took a few minutes for his legs to regain their strength after the unexpected shock of seeing his employer for the first time. *Well, seeing the back of her.*

He called out, "I'm coming now. Let me know if you need more time." Hearing no response, he cautiously peeked around the corner and, seeing the terrace empty, let out a deep sigh.

Moving forward he began to work. Deciding to cut the large, dead, fallen limbs first, he powered up the chainsaw and sliced through the thick limbs, deftly piling them to the side of the terrace. Walking back to the shed, he started the mower, with a trailer attached, and drove it back to the house. Loading the heavy, cut limbs, he took the wood to the side of the tool shed, deciding to chop it later for firewood.

Driving back to the house, he next picked up the smaller branches and piled them into the trailer, repeating his steps from earlier. After two hours, he finally had all the wood removed from the large patio. With a thick, long broom, he swept the leaves and glass into a pile before using a dustpan to collect the refuse. Unable to separate the glass from the leaves, he bagged the entire sweepings. Standing back, he cast a careful gaze over the surface of the terrace, going over every foot until he was certain all slivers of the glass had been removed.

The sun, now high in the sky, had burned off the last of the water from the crevices in the stone, leaving it dry and safe to walk on. He moved to each piece of furniture, righting it and placing it around the area, uncertain of its original location.

Satisfied he had returned the terrace to a safe place for Ms. Bellamy to enjoy, he took the broken table and loaded it up on the trailer. Pulling out his phone, he sent a text.

I am finished and leaving. You are now free to enjoy the terrace, remnants of last night's storm have been erased.

By the time he made it back to the tool shed, his phone vibrated. Pulling it out, he let out a held breath, reading her response.

Thank you. I apologize for my terse behavior this morning. I appreciate your hard work.

Sending another quick text, **No apology necessary - Have a nice day**, he smiled as he started the chainsaw, ready to tackle the next downed limb, over the shed.

Dressed, with her former tears now washed away, Eleanor pulled back the curtain, looking down toward the shed. It was too far to see clearly, but she could just make out Mr. Walker piling cut limbs onto a stack of wood next to the shed. He was much larger than she anticipated. *Why had I imagined an older man? Retired, perhaps?* This man appeared fit and able. Wondering why he would want the job of a groundskeeper when there were many more interesting jobs out there, she acknowledged that her reasons for desiring privacy were not necessarily obvious, leaving some to question her choices as well. *We all have our needs... some more secret than others.*

Forcing those thoughts from her mind, she moved back to the terrace doors, peeking through the curtains. A slight gasp left her lips as she surveyed the pristine patio. No debris. No glass. No leaves, branches, limbs. Her furniture had been righted and stood ready for her to enjoy. *He didn't have to do all that.*

Smiling, she carried her latest book outside and, staying in the shade, she sat in one of the comfortable chairs, placing her glass of lemonade on the stone terrace beside her. After a while, warmth seeped into her body, lack of sleep from the previous night causing her eyes to grow heavy.

Sometime later, jarring awake, she sat up quickly,

trying to ascertain where she was. Seeing she was still alone on the terrace, she calmed. While she was asleep, the sun had stretched across the yard, now casting beams over her chair. Leaning over, she grabbed her glass before standing. Uncertain how long she had been asleep, she moved inside, glancing out the window just as Mr. Walker walked up from the shed, the leaf blower in his hands.

Placing her empty glass into the sink, she smiled before sending a text.

Several hours later, Rafe had most of the storm's damage cleaned up. Firing up the gas-powered leaf blower, he moved by the side of the house, blowing the downed leaves away from the flower garden he had just worked in a week ago.

Finishing that task, he stood with his hands on his hips, turning in a slow circle, pleased with the scene that met his eyes. Nodding in satisfaction, he felt his phone vibrate.

Pulling it from his pocket, his smile widened as he read the text. **I will leave lemonade on the table by the back door if you would like some refreshment.**

Deciding to take Ms. Bellamy up on her offer, he walked around toward the back, spying a thermos on the small table, as well as a covered, plastic tub. Opening the container, he grinned at the sight of a piece of pie along with a fork.

Taking the treat to the wall overlooking the river, he sat on the stone, digging in, listening to the rushing water below.

Finishing, he washed the container out with the hose

connected to the outside spigot before setting it back on the table. He did the same with the thermos, before sending a text. **Thank you for the dessert. Just finished.**

A moment later his phone buzzed as he walked back down toward the cottage. **You're welcome. Thank you again for making my terrace safe.**

My pleasure. I hope you enjoyed some time on it today.

Yes - a nap, in fact. Have a nice evening.

You too. By the time he slid his phone back into his pocket, he had arrived at the cottage. His heart light, he realized that was the longest communication he had had with his employer. It felt good to be doing something that was appreciated and maybe she was beginning to trust him, even if just a little bit. *No one should be completely alone.*

After heating a pizza for dinner, he moved his spare chair outside to enjoy the early summer evening. The fireflies were back to dancing across the lawn. His eyes naturally drew upward toward the house, where a light shone in one of the downstairs windows. The faint sound of music could be heard.

Curiosity got the better of him and he stood, moving toward the melodious tones of a piano. Walking straight up the hill, uncertainty slowed his steps. Almost turning around to go back to his cottage, he hesitated, rubbing the back of his neck. *She wants her privacy. She deserves to live her life the way she wants.* He halted as a voice was added to the song. No longer able to pull back, he moved closer to the window.

Shrubs, now neatly trimmed, kept him from standing close but, with the draperies pulled back, he was able to see inside the room. The large room contained a formal sofa and settee flanking the fireplace. A family portrait hanging over the mantle caught his eye, but it was the baby grand piano in the corner that captured his attention.

The woman from the terrace, judging by her hair, was seated on the bench, her hands on the keys. She rocked back and forth gently as the music poured from her fingers. Not perfect, some wrong keys were played, but she kept going. Some passages appeared to be more challenging than others but she did not stop.

Her back was to him, so he was unable to see her face, but her long, dark hair hung in waves down her back. Dressed simply in dark pants and a blue, long-sleeved shirt she was still of indeterminate age, but was definitely not an elderly woman, like he had assumed she would be.

Her head lifted slightly as she began to sing again, causing his heart to stutter. The melody floated through the air, filling his soul with peace. Standing in the dark, the fireflies still dancing across the lawn, the sweet scent of early blooming flowers in the air, Rafe wondered if he had crossed into another world, one he thought was only in fairy tales.

As the song came to an end, she turned slightly on the piano bench and he caught a glimpse of the left side of her face. His breath caught once more, this time in awe of her beauty. Flawless, pale skin glowed in the light of the candles on the piano. No smile graced her lips, but it did nothing to detract from her profile. Her eyes closed as her head bowed, her hands now resting in her lap instead of on the piano keys.

Suddenly aware that he was trespassing upon her privacy, he ducked, beginning to hurry back down the hill.

Embarrassed to be sneaking away, he nonetheless hoped his presence had not been detected.

As he made it to the door of his cottage, he shook his head in derision. *What an ass I am. First, I sneak to the main house, then I stand peering into a window, then I run away like some child about to get in trouble.* Moving inside, he sucked in a deep breath. *What is this place doing to me?* Laughing out loud, he realized he felt freer than he had in years.

Lights now out, Eleanor walked up the wide staircase, a small smile on her face. It had been a long time since she played the piano. Or sang. She knew she had played a number of wrong notes, her fingers struggling to stretch over some keys, but the desire to feel the music flow again soared through her.

What has come over me? Why now? Halting at her bedroom door, she turned and walked into the room across the hall again. Pulling back the curtain, she peered down at the cottage. She lifted her hand, placing it flat against the pane, as though touching...something.

Jerking her hand back, she shook her head. *Stop being ridiculous. The time for fantasies is long gone.* Letting the material slide through her fingers, she walked into her bedroom. Finishing her nightly routine in the bathroom, avoiding the mirror, she moved to her bed, sliding underneath the covers.

With a slight smile still curving her lips, she fell asleep, her heart lighter than it had been in years.

10

Steadily walking along the back side of the house, Rafe continually moved his eyes over the area. Up, to see if there were any large limbs that the storm had damaged that might eventually blow onto the house, and down, because there was only a narrow path behind the house before the ground fell off into the ravine. The forecast called for another large storm system to come through the area today and he hoped to take care of the work before it hit.

He thought the storm the other night was fierce, but the predictions for this one were worse. A 'nor-easter' was coming, the wind velocity expecting to spin off several tornados, possibly in the central Virginia area.

Stopping for a moment at the back of the house, he marveled, yet again, at the craftsmanship of the structure, especially in light of its age. From the back edge of the cliff, the stone manor rose three stories. With the size of the trees clinging to the forested ravine, he knew many of them had been there when the house was built. The large, dark stones were the same color as the river rock below and he wondered if most came from the ravine, hauled up by workers long ago. The windows on the front would have the garden view, but he now appreciated the windows on this side of the house, the woods and river below providing an ever-changing panorama.

The air was fresh this time of the morning, dew still clinging to the leaves in the trees and the fern fronds on the ground. For a moment, as he stood appreciating God's glory all around, he felt a kinship with the man who built the house...who had the vision to place a home on the edge of the cliff so that on one side was the river below and on the other, the sloping lawn leading to the forest. The image of castles belonging to a time gone by, defending their walls and creating a safe haven for the inhabitants, moved through his mind.

A squirrel scampering through the underbrush rustled the leaves, drawing him from his musings. Turning back from his perusal, he continued toward the terrace side of the house. He had sent Ms. Bellamy an early morning text, letting her know that he would be on the backside of the house and near the terrace.

As he rounded the corner, he spied a large limb damaged from the storm, but previously hidden from his view on the other side. He knew it would only weaken with time and, when another storm came through, it would land too close, if not directly, onto the terrace. Worried that might happen when he was not around, he wanted to make sure it was safe for her to enjoy.

Walking back down the hill to the shed, he loaded the chainsaw and the ladder into the trailer hitched to the mower, and drove back up to the house. Once at the terrace, he walked around the base of the thick tree trunk, looking for the best place to secure the ladder while giving him optimum room to use the saw.

Once satisfied, he steadied the ladder's base on the stone floor, pulled the rope to extend the ladder, and leaned it against the trunk. With a few shakes, he confirmed its security before climbing.

Halfway up, he observed the damaged limb was larger than he expected, almost the size of a small, full-sized tree. Still, he was determined to cut the dead wood off. It would take more than one cut to complete the task, so he'd have to move the ladder halfway through the process.

With storm clouds brewing overhead, he fired up the saw and carefully began moving the whirring blade through the wood. Since the limb was damaged but not dead, the wood was firm, not easily cut. Leaning over, he was just about able to cut it off completely. Frustrated that it bent but did not completely break off, he accepted that he could not continue to lean at the dangerous angle to finish.

Climbing down, he placed the chainsaw on the stone and turned back to the ladder. First lowering it to a manageable height, he moved it around the base of the tree until it was on the other side of the heavy, now-dangling limb. Repeating the process, he pulled on the rope to extend the ladder, steadying it against the trunk. Once satisfied it was in place, he bent to pick up the chainsaw when he heard a loud crack. Looking up, he barely had time to cover his head as the massive, tree-sized limb came crashing down.

Eleanor groaned in frustration, the Internet going out

making her work more difficult. Inside, she was staying away from the family room, whose patio doors opened onto the terrace, not wanting to be seen by Mr. Walker. From the upstairs study, she gave in to temptation and peeked from the window, jumping back when she saw him close by with the chainsaw in his hands, his thick arm muscles straining with the exertion of the task.

Dropping the curtain, she stepped back a few paces as though he might see her, an impossibility with the thick drapes between them. His face had been obscured through the branches, but he was larger than she imagined. Blowing out a breath, she turned and moved back to her desk.

The noise of the saw stopped and she heard the squeak of the extension ladder being raised and lowered. The Internet had finally given up and she knew her phone landline was out as well. Continuing her paperwork, she found it difficult to concentrate, knowing he was just outside. Standing, she decided to move to a different part of the mansion so she would not be tempted to sneak another peak.

Gathering some files, she was walking toward the door when she heard an enormous crash. Startled, she stared toward the curtained window. Realizing what a large limb he had been working on, she wondered if he would be sawing it into logs for the fireplaces.

Standing in the middle of the room, she listened for the chainsaw engine to fire up again. No sound. Cocking her head to the side, she listened for the sound of the ladder being lowered. No sound. Curious, she moved past her desk, placing the laptop and files back on the top as she walked toward the window. Still no sound.

Placing her fingertips on the fringed edge of the material, she barely pulled it back, letting out her breath. He was no longer up the ladder, close to her. The large limb was now gone, it's space allowing sunlight to shine in a bit more.

Knowing the terrace was directly underneath the window, she sucked in a breath, wondering if the limb had damaged the trellis. Still not hearing any sounds from Mr. Walker, she pulled the draperies back an inch more, leaning forward until her forehead was pressed against the cool glass. The heavy limb was lying awkwardly on the partially destroyed trellis, but most of its mass was on the terrace below.

Mr. Walker had shown nothing but skill and finesse since he had begun working there, so the damage to the trellis was surprising. Still uncertain why she was unable to hear him moving below, and getting a bit concerned, she stepped closer to look down, her eyes focusing on the scene below. Gasping, she blinked to clear her eyes.

She could not be seeing what she thought she was. Mr. Walker was lying face down on the stone, his legs sprawled out, trapped underneath the massive wood...and he was not moving.

Whirling, she ran as best as she could out the door of the study and down the stairs, her slight hobble tripping her occasionally, but with her hand firmly on the railing, she managed to stay upright. Continuing down the hall and through the first-floor study, she made it to the terrace doors, gasping for air, before pulling back the draperies, blinking as the sun poured through the glass.

The view before her appeared more daunting than from the floor above. She could easily see Mr. Walker sprawled out, unmoving, on the flagstone terrace, blood streaming from a large gash low on his forehead, right above his eyes.

Without hesitation, she headed for him, stepping over limbs and branches in the way. The wind picked up, whipping her hair wildly about her face. Glancing upward, she spied dark, black clouds moving in quickly, the air was already moist with the impending storm.

Focusing her gaze back on Mr. Walker, she breathed a sigh of relief. The heaviest part of the limb was not crushing him as it was caught on part of the broken trellis, barely being held off his body. Grimacing, she stood in indecision for a moment, wondering how to get help for him, knowing the electricity was off and the phone line was dead. She had her cell but it was all the way upstairs and he needed help now.

Looking down at her blouse, she stripped it off as fast as she could, leaving her in a camisole. Stepping closely, she knelt, tying it around his head, making sure to tighten the ends around his gash. His chest rose and fell with each breath, giving proof that he was alive. *I've got to get him inside...but how?*

Knowing she would not be able to use the chainsaw to get him loose of the fallen branch, she stepped around until she was at his head. Bending, with her hands under his shoulders she gave a great heave, only managing to move him mere inches. He mumbled incoherently and she dropped to the cold stone, crying, "Mr. Walker...Mr. Walker, we've got to get you inside. Please...can you move?"

His eyes blinked open a few times, but the swelling kept him from opening them completely. He tried to sit up, but fell back immediately.

"If you can just help a bit...um...maybe push your

legs..." Immediately contrite, she wondered how injured he was. Perhaps using his legs was impossible. She felt desperate tears forming in her eyes. For someone who had once been so strong, she cursed her weak body.

He mumbled, groaning in pain, as he rolled onto his back, before lying still once more. A gale-force wind whipped past, knocking her over. A loud crash followed and she crawled to the edge of the terrace, looking out over the lawn. A massive tree at the far end of the drive had snapped, it's large branches now lying across the lane.

Terrified, she forced her mind back to the task at hand. Casting a glance over her shoulder, she estimated they had almost ten feet left to go, just to get to the door. Swinging her eyes up to the sky, she could feel the rain beginning to fall.

An idea forming, she stood and pulled the rope from the back of the mower parked to the side of the terrace. Bending over near his head, she pushed and pulled until she had the rope looped under his back and around his shoulders. After running back inside to get a thick blanket, she rolled him side to side, placing the material underneath his body. Dragging the ends of the now wet rope to the mower, she looked at the attached trailer. Biting her lip in indecision, she leaned over and found the trailer was attached with only a pin. Unclipping it, the trailer came loose easily and she pushed it to the side, her muscles screaming with the exertion.

Refusing to give in to her weakness, she grabbed the rope ends, tying them around the mower seat. Looking back, she shook her head in derision. *God, this is such a stupid idea.* Unable to come up with a better one, she climbed onto the riding mower and turned the key, keeping the blade from engaging. Pressing gently down on the gas with her right foot, she gave it a try. Blessedly, it moved forward slowly. As the rope lost its slack, she pressed a little harder on the pedal and his body on the blanket moved as well.

Inching along, she watched as his body slid from under the tree limb and along the stone patio. Turning the steering wheel as the mower approached the terrace doors, she moved it toward the back corner of the house, barely managing to get the mower under the downed trellis. Looking over her shoulder again, she could see his body had been dragged as close to the doors as possible. Tuning off the mower, she moved back to him.

Out of breath, she pushed thoughts of fatigue to the back of her mind as the rain began to pelt down harder. Swiping her long hair from her face, she cursed not tying it up this morning. Stepping to the terrace doors, she threw them wide and, with a great amount of heaving and cursing, she managed to get him just inside enough to shut the doors against the wind.

Leaning heavily against them now, her chest heaving with exertion, she stared down at the bedraggled, unconscious man lying on her floor. Sucking in a shuddering breath, she thought, *Now what?*

11

Looking wildly around the bathroom, Eleanor wondered what she was getting herself into. Having gone upstairs to change into dry clothes and check her cell—*no bars*—she grabbed extra towels, as well as the first aid box. Hustling as fast as she could manage on quivering legs, she re-entered the study. Rafe's prone body was lying just as it was when she had left a minute earlier.

Swallowing her fear, she hurried to him, kneeling at his side. It was not the first time she had been around someone injured, not even close. She checked his pulse... strong. She opened his eyes...not dilated. She carefully untied her shirt from his head and wiped the blood from his forehead, pleased to see the cut was not as deep as she first feared. Even small head wounds often bleed excessively.

Taking the washcloth, she cleaned the cut before closing the edges using small butterfly bandages. The gash went from one side of his forehead to the other and, even bandaged, she could see the bruising and swelling. It would probably scar but there was nothing that could be done about that. Her main concern was stopping the bleeding and she was pleased to see the bandages holding well. *Hopefully, he's not a vain man. At least he's a gardener and a few scars won't scare the plants.*

Standing she looked around the room. Knowing it would be impossible to get him to a bed on the second floor, she considered the sofa nearest the fireplace. Biting her bottom lip, she admitted to herself that even that would be difficult for her to lift him to, even if he would fit.

A shiver ran over her, despite the coming summer warmth. With the clouds blocking the sun, and the wind picking up speed outside, a chill slid into the room. Moving as quickly as she could, she started a fire, using the ever-present logs already in place and adding some kindling and paper at the base. In just a few minutes, the flames crept high.

Now, with a fire crackling in the fireplace chasing the chill from the air, she bent to her next task. Pulling a thick quilt from the back of the sofa, she placed it on the rug in front of the fireplace. Making another trip upstairs, she came back with an armful of more soft blankets, arranging them into a makeshift bed.

Moving to him, she placed her hands under his shoulders but, once more, was thwarted in her attempts to move him. "Please, please, can you help me," she begged, encouraged when he blinked his eyes open, rousing slightly before moaning. "Can you help push yourself forward?"

Giving a tug, and with his help, she managed to maneuver him to a position where she could roll him, carefully cradling his head, toward the fireplace. "I'm so sorry, Mr. Walker. I know this can't be pleasant, but it's the only way I can get you over here."

Huffing, she managed to roll him onto the blankets on the floor near the fire and plopped down next to him. Placing a pillow underneath his head, she checked the bandages, pleased to see them holding firm and no more bleeding coming from the wound.

His clothes were soaked, but she wasn't sure what to do. After a moment of indecision, she accepted the heat from the fire would never get them dry, so she shifted down to his feet, untying his boots. Pulling them off, she was glad to find his socks, at least, were dry.

His t-shirt rolled up easily, but maneuvering his arms out of the wet material proved difficult. Finally, she pulled it over his head, her eyes widening at the sight of his naked chest. His muscular chest and tight abs were distracting and she blinked several times, trying to bring her focus back to his wellbeing. *It's not like I've never seen this before*, she chastised herself. But, with a last glance down, she had to admit he was better built than most men she had seen. His arm and chest tattoos caught her attention and she wondered the meaning of them.

Covering his chest and arms with a thick blanket, she moved to his jeans. Unfastening and unzipping the denim was the easy part, but trying to slide the wet material was much more difficult. Eventually she managed to wiggle them down his thick, muscular thighs, tossing them to the side. Avoiding looking at his boxers, she wrapped his bottom half in more thick blankets.

With him finally dry and wrapped tightly in front of the fire, she leaned back against the sofa, while still sitting next to him on the floor. Exhaustion set in, the past hour having been more physically challenging than it should have been. Angry that she had stopped her therapy, she nonetheless pushed the thought from her mind. *I had my reasons.*

Placing her fingers lightly on his forehead, she gently brushed his dark hair away from his bandages. Leaning over, she whispered, "You're okay, now Mr. Walker. You're inside...warm and dry. Just rest now. Just rest."

She wanted him to awaken, but her heart pounded in fear of the thought of his eyes opening.

Eleanor was clutching the edge of the kitchen counter when the kettle on the gas stove began to sing. Swallowing her nerves, she lifted the kettle from the hot eye, turned off the stove, and poured the water into two teacups. Adding a dab of honey to both, she stirred before dropping the tea bags in. Reaching into the cabinet, she pulled out a bottle of whiskey, adding a generous spoonful to her cup.

A slight smile curved her lips at the memory of her grandmother, who never drank alcohol, adding a small amount of whiskey to her tea when she had a cold...*for medicinal purposes, of course.*

Placing the cups on a tray, she walked down the hall to the study, entering the warm room. Setting the tray on the floor, she sat next to him, checking his forehead. No bleeding...just bruising and swelling. His left eye was almost swollen shut but the right one appeared less so.

She leaned over his body to snag a few pillows from the sofa. Moving to his head, she managed to lift his shoulders long enough to slide two more pillows underneath him, before sitting back down at his side.

His hand lifted. "Wh...wh..."

"Mr. Walker," she said softly. "You're safe but please move carefully. I've checked you out, but am still uncertain what you may have injured in your fall." His hand wobbled toward his face, but she captured it in her own. "Don't touch your face. You hit your forehead when you fell and you have a large cut. I've cleaned it and bandaged it with butterfly bandages to keep the edges together. We need to keep your hands off of it for now."

Licking his lips, he moaned, "Where am...I?"

"You're inside the house...not the cottage. I brought you in here because it was the closest room to the terrace."

"I...damn..." his weak voice whispered.

"Don't try too hard to move. I promise you're safe. I need to ask you some questions though...just answer as you can." Not getting a response from him, she asked, "Can you tell me your name?"

"Ra..." he breathed. "Rafe Walker."

"Good, good. Can you tell me what day it is?"

"Uh...it's...uh...Wednesday."

"And, do you know what you were doing?"

"Tree...there was a tree limb...terrace...I wanted to clear the limb before the storm came."

"That's excellent, Mr. Walker. You do have a cut on your forehead, some swelling. I want to keep an eye on you. Unfortunately, my phone line is out and the Internet is out. The signal for my phone is also down."

"Phone...my cell phone," he said, moving his hand under the blanket to his pants...finding none. Wincing as he attempted to open his eyes, he croaked, "Pants?"

"You were soaked, Mr. Walker," she said, her face blushing hot. "I had to take them off to get you warm."

"My phone...in my pocket," he said.

"Oh," she cried, "I didn't think of that. Maybe you have a better signal." Crawling over to where his soaked jeans had been tossed to the side, she dug into his pockets. Keys. Wallet. Cell phone. Pulling it out, a sharp edge jabbed her finger. Squeaking, she drew back and saw a small drop of blood on her finger. Turning her attention to the broken phone lying on her palm, "I...oh, dear. I'm afraid it's smashed."

He groaned, "What about my truck?"

Twisting her fingers together, she said, "The lane is blocked by a downed tree. I'm sorry...I don't know what else to do. We're stuck, but I swear, I'll take care of you."

Moving back to his side, she said, "I've got some tea for you. It's not too hot, but it'll help to warm you. I'll support your shoulders and help you sip. As soon as you can swallow, I've also got some painkillers."

He nodded and she guided the cup to his lips. He slurped, dripping only a few drops on the blanket. "Too bad there's no alcohol in this," he tried to joke.

"Oh, I added some to mine," she confessed, "but you need pain medicine more than whiskey right now."

Managing a chuckle, he agreed. Taking the pills from her hand, he swallowed them with another sip of the warm tea before she assisted him back to a reclining position.

Feeling helpless, he said, "I don't even know who I'm talking to."

"I'm sorry...I'm Eleanor. Eleanor Bellamy."

Turning his face toward her soft voice, he said, "You sound so young. Are you the daughter...or maybe the granddaughter of Ms. Bellamy, the owner?"

Laughter met his ears. "Oh, no. I am the owner. Bellamy House is mine."

12

His head pounded. Rafe lifted his hand, feeling the gauze bandage wrapped around his forehead, low over his brow. His eyes felt puffy to his fingertips and the sting caused him to immediately drop his hand. He heard the wind howling around the corner of the room and the rain hitting the windows.

Ms. Bellamy had left the room after telling him she was taking the empty tea cups back to the kitchen. Ms. Bellamy...Eleanor...*the owner? My employer?* Miss Ethel had described her as a shut-in, so he assumed she was elderly as well.

Her voice was soft...melodious, in fact, and he wished he could see her face. *Was she the person who had been singing? They could just be related, and Ms. Bellamy, Eleanor, has a young voice. Of all the stupid, dumb luck...I finally meet her and I can't see her.* Hearing a noise, he turned toward the sound, wincing as pain sliced through his head. Soft footsteps, a little unsteady came to him. *Did he detect a limp?*

"Please, be careful," Eleanor warned, dropping to his side.

"How bad is the storm?" he asked, his mind clearer now.

"Before the electricity went out, the weatherman said that the nor'easter was bringing heavy rains and wind gusts up to sixty miles an hour. Plus, there's the possibility of tornados spinning off..."

"Jesus, we just had a storm," he groused.

"I know. The weatherman also talked about unusual weather patterns...or something like that, causing all kinds of unpredictable storms."

Heaving a great sigh, he said, "Ms. Bellamy, I am so sorry. Fuckin' hell—uh...I'm mean—"

"It's fine. You can curse. To be honest, with all that's happened this morning, I think that cursing is probably the most appropriate response."

He grinned, appreciating her acceptance. "Well, Ms. Bellamy, I do apologize for everything that's happened. I can't believe that what started as a simple trimming has turned into such a disaster."

"Under the circumstances, I think you should call me Eleanor."

Lifting his hand toward her voice, he said, "Nice to meet you, Eleanor. I'm Rafe."

She placed her hand in his, startling as warmth radiated from his fingers to hers. "I'm sorry that this happened to you...I know you were just trying to make the terrace safe for me. I feel terrible that—"

"No, no. It's my job...not your fault at all."

Silence fell between them and, with his eyes out of commission, he found his other senses alert. The wind whistling through the chimney, the crackling of the fire, the warmth of the blanket cocoon he was wrapped in, the feel of her soft hand in his, the sound of her voice as it curled around him, offering comfort. He began to feel woozy. The pain medicine was working, but also making him sleepy.

"Rafe," she said, her voice close to his face. "You need to rest. I'll be right here in case you need something, but go ahead and fall asleep."

He felt her gentle breath wash across his face and wanted to stay awake, if only to hear her voice more. But the warm nest he was cradled in made it hard to resist the call of slumber. "I'll just rest a minute," he mumbled, just before he drifted away.

Kneeling by his side, Eleanor reached out her hand, her fingers shaking as she lightly brushed his dark hair back. His forehead felt cool to the touch and he had been able to move all his limbs, so she felt relatively sure there was no spinal damage. The room was dark, the storm clouds hiding the sun. She studied his face, illuminated by only the flames of the fire. Square jaw, dark stubble of beard. Firm brow, now hidden by the gauze bandage. He was handsome...rugged...all male. A man who oozed testosterone.

He was the vision of a man who would look devastating in a tuxedo or at the head of a table in a boardroom. And yet, as she thought of him working on the grounds for the past weeks, dressed in a t-shirt or flannel and jeans, he was also the kind of man who did not mind getting his hands dirty.

Her father had been such a man. Born to wealth, his

parents had still taught him the value of hard work. He had spent time with the estate's groundskeeper growing up, had learned to cook from the housekeeper. He had served in the Navy, after college, before taking over in the family business. As a little girl, she remembered seeing him escorting her mother to an event, looking ruggedly handsome and thinking he outshone every man in the room. A prince of a man…

She blinked away her fanciful musings as she looked down at Rafe. Her eyes drifted to his blanket-wrapped body. It had been impossible to ignore the muscles in his chest and abs when she took off his shirt. Or the muscles in his arms. Or his thighs. Lifting her heated gaze, she shifted on the floor. *I'm such a fool. He's just a man…an injured man and, God knows, I've seen plenty of those.*

As he slept, she stood and walked back into the kitchen, her limp more pronounced from her earlier physical activity, opening the refrigerator to see what Sally might have left for her to fix. Finding homemade beef stew in a container in the freezer, she pulled it out. After thawing it in the microwave, she put it in a pot on the stove, figuring Rafe would be hungry when he awoke. Once bubbling, she turned the stove off, letting the fragrant meal simmer until they were ready to eat.

Moving to the bathroom, she looked into the mirror, stunned at her appearance. Her normally sleek hair was waving wildly over her shoulders, having dried from the storm-induced shower. Her pale complexion was now accompanied by pink-tinged cheeks from the exertion of the morning's activities. Turning her head slightly, she grimaced at the sight.

Running a brush through her hair, she tamed it slightly before halting, her ears perked as she heard a noise. She dropped the brush, hustling into the study, but Rafe must have been moaning in his sleep.

With nothing else to do, she settled back on the floor, near the fire, and opened the book she had been reading. Placing one hand on his, she began to read, her voice gentle against the raging storm.

The wind howled and the rain hit his body, each drop stinging. The black night closed in around him, the moon not able to pierce the darkness. The forest closed in around him, branches reaching out to snag his clothing as the roots rose to trip him.

He was running but, directionless, could not tell where he was going. The fierceness of the storm was upon him and, looking over his shoulder, growling wolves were giving chase, their sharp fangs snapping at his heels. Whipping his head back to the front, he swiped the rain from his eyes. A castle, dark and looming, came into sight, light glowing in a single window. He was not afraid of what lie in wait for him inside, only knowing he needed to reach the safety of the castle.

Dodging back and forth between the trees, he prayed his legs would carry him to the castle wall before the wolves reached him. A tall tree stood near the closed gate and with a heroic effort he leaped into the air, his hands closing around the lowest branch. Swinging his body upward, he clung to the tree feeling the wolves snarling just below. Scaling up several more branches until he came to the top of the wall, he hurled himself onto the stone, the wolves now at bay. Dropping down the other side, he leaned against the wall, his breaths coming in great gulps.

The castle loomed ahead, dark and foreboding. Walking

closer, he moved stealthily, wondering if friend or foe resided inside.

As he neared, he stopped suddenly, the sound of a piano halting his feet. The beautiful music continued, guiding him forward out of the darkness. Suddenly, the sound of snarling resumed and looking over his shoulder he spied a lone wolf had made it to the top of the wall.

Running toward the front door of the castle, he threw himself against the wood, landing inside on the stone floor, kicking the mighty oak door closed behind him and shutting out the frustrated roar of the thwarted animal. Lying still, heart pounding, the sound of music, louder now, met his ears.

Standing, he moved toward the sound but as he entered the room, the music stopped. The stone walls were covered in tapestries and thick rugs kept the cold floors warm. Moving further into the room, he walked past the furniture, heading toward the stone fireplace, the blazing logs sending out warmth. A pile of blankets lay nearby and he fell onto them, pulling the top one over his shivering body.

The music began again and he fell into a deep sleep, the soft sounds of a woman's voice lingering in his ears as the soft touch of her hand rested on his.

Sleep eased away as the words became more focused. A woman...*Eleanor*...was reading. Lying still, he assumed she did not know he was awake as her voice continued steadily. Her reading voice was as beautiful as her singing, because he was pretty sure that was her singing, and the sound pulled him in as the words swirled around him.

He tried to understand how such a young woman was a shut-in. She seemed able. He remembered seeing the back of her on the terrace the other day. Her body was straight, with no obvious impairment. She had managed to drag his large body out of the storm and into the warmth by the fireplace. *Where did she get that strength?* She had assessed his wounds as well, dressing them. *How did she gain that knowledge?* She was, even now, taking charge, sitting with her hand on his.

Bellamy House. He realized he could have investigated the history of the mansion with an Internet search but, he had felt no need to. He was just there for the landscaping.

She continued to read, her dulcet voice reaching deep inside of him.

"I can live alone, if self-respect, and circumstances require me so to do. I need not sell my soul to buy bliss. I have an inward treasure born with me, which can keep me alive if all extraneous delights should be withheld, or offered only at a price I cannot afford to give."

He recognized the book—Charlotte Bronte's Jane Eyre. *Live alone...is that what's she's doing?* He thought of how he had been living alone in the cottage for the past weeks, little contact with the outside world, and how restful it had been. So much more than the flash of the cameras, the plastic bodies in the plastic world. As he lay, warm and safe with the storm raging and the wind howling outside, he felt at peace, a feeling he had not felt in many years...if ever. Certainly not in the Army or in the modeling world. *Had I sold my sold my soul to buy bliss?* he wondered.

13

Eleanor felt Rafe's fingers twitch and she jerked her gaze from the pages of the book down to his face. Unable to see his eyes, hidden behind the bandage, she whispered, "Are you awake?"

"Yeah," he replied, his voice more like a croak. Clearing his throat, he said, "Sorry."

"No, no, don't apologize," she admonished. "Let me get your water." Reaching up to the bottle of water she had nearby, she unscrewed the top and placed a straw into the neck. Placing one hand underneath his shoulders, she lifted slightly as she guided the straw to his lips. "Here, suck."

Finally able to lift his upper body up, resting on his elbows Rafe took several long sips. Grateful for the cool liquid, he did not stop until the straw made a sucking sound. Grinning, he said, "I must have struck bottom."

Pushing himself up further, he sat up, pulling the blankets firmly around his waist, not wanting to flash his employer...or rather his rescuer. "Thanks," he said, not missing the touch of her hand on his.

"I've got some beef stew on the stove for you. I'll go get it and be right back—"

"Please, don't go to any trouble for me."

"Don't be silly. I need to eat also and it's no more trouble to serve two than it is to serve one."

He listened as her footsteps padded down the hall, sure now of her uneven gait, then inhaled deeply before letting it out slowly. Lifting his hand, he felt the bandage over his brow and the puffiness around his eyes. *Of all the dumbass things to do!* Chastising himself for getting out at the beginning of a storm to try to take down a heavy limb, he groaned as the act of shaking his head caused pain. *If I'd just left the fuckin' thing...even if it fell, I could have cut it into pieces to haul away after the storm. And now?* Until the swelling in his eyes went down in a couple of days, he would not be able to see, nor do his job.

Tilting his head, he heard Eleanor's footsteps coming back into the room, along with the scent of roasted beef and savory sauce with vegetables. His stomach chose that moment to let out an audible growl and she laughed.

"I guess you are hungry," she said, setting the bowl on the coffee table before kneeling next to him. "I made sure that the stew is warm, but not hot. It won't burn you, but I can feed you to make it easier."

He brought his hands up. "Oh, no. You're not feeding me," he protested, irritation at his limited ability swelling inside. "If you place the bowl in my hands, I can manage."

Frowning, she said, "You don't have to try to be macho, you know. It's okay to need someone—"

"Says the lady who hides away," he retorted, frustration filling his voice.

Eleanor jerked, his words a slap. Forcing her voice to remain steady, she placed the bowl in his outstretched hands, "Fine. I'll be back later to collect the bowl, or do you think you can find your way around without seeing?" Rising, she took her bowl and left the room.

"Wait," Rafe said, hearing her uneven footsteps move away from him. "Dammit!" Angry that he allowed his pride to snap at her, after all she had done, his hand shook with the desire to throw the bowl against the wall. Sucking in a deep breath, he knew Miss Ethel would never forgive him for giving in to that desire. Instead, he berated himself. Miss Ethel would be ashamed of his cutting comment to Eleanor.

Uncertain when Eleanor might reappear, if ever, he lifted the bowl with one hand while finding the spoon with the other. Dipping into the fragrant stew, he sipped it gently, finding it as she said—warm but not too hot. The delicious, thick broth filled with chunks of roast beef, potatoes, carrots, and corn, had him lifting the spoon quicker in an effort to satisfy his hunger.

As the spoon began to scrape the bottom of the bowl, he replayed how stupid his words to her had been. Not only had he insulted a woman, his employer, and rescuer, making her uncomfortable enough to leave the room, he was now alone, not knowing the inside of the house or how to take care of his needs. The desire for more water and a bathroom only fueled his guilt as he inwardly cursed his hasty, unkind words.

Hearing footsteps re-entering the room he hastened to apologize. "Ms. Bellamy, I'm so sorry...that was an unkind and completely uncalled-for comment to make. I'm not usually like that...I can only blame the unusual situation that I find myself in, but that's still no excuse. Please forgive me."

He cocked his head to the side, waiting to see if she

was still in the room. He knew it was her...the delicate scent of roses clung to her hair. He lifted his head, a slight intake of breath somewhere above him.

"Please...call me Eleanor," she replied, her words soft as she bent beside him, taking the empty bowl from his hands.

"Eleanor, I'm so sorry..."

Rafe's voice, laced with regret reached her heart. "You don't need to apologize," she said with a shrug, licking her lips in uncertainty. "I suppose we all have our triggers. You need to be independent and I need to be...uh...well, I guess alone is the best word."

"The stew was delicious, by the way."

She smiled, recognizing his attempt to lead the conversation to a less contentious topic. "Thank you. Sally made it, actually. I brought some more water." Placing the bottle in his hand, she allowed him to unscrew the top and take a large gulp.

Finishing, he replaced the cap and handed it back to her. "Thank you." Clutching the blanket with his hand, he said, "I guess I'd better figure out how to get back to my cottage."

"Not today, I'm afraid."

"But—"

"Well, right now your clothes are in the washing machine and then they'll have to go into the dryer. I've brought a pair of sweatpants for you to put on. They belonged to my father...I assure you they're clean and should be close to the right size."

Rafe felt the soft, fleece being placed in his lap and he smiled. "Thank you. I'll return these as soon as I get back with my other clothes."

"Rafe, I'm afraid you still don't understand," she said,

her gaze scanning his face. "The gale-force winds have died down, but there are still some gusts. Plus, the storm will continue into the night. Then they are calling for another two days of heavy rain."

His breath left him in a rush as he tried to think through the situation. "I…well, I'm not sure exactly what to do, in light of that information. I know I can't make it to the cottage myself, but then I don't want you out in the storm—"

"Is there anything in the cottage that you can't live without for a couple of days?"

Shaking his head, careful of the pain, he said, "No… not really. Well, truthfully, not at all."

"Then I think the only recourse is for you to stay here for now. We can't get out by car until the downed tree is removed. We have food, fire, a gas stove, and I'm pretty sure the electricity will be fixed by tomorrow. Internet? Um, I'm not so sure. That may take an extra day."

"Eleanor, that's really generous of you, but—"

"But what? You need time for your head to heal and for the swelling around your eyes to go down. You can't work until then. This house has six bedrooms, each with their own bathroom, so I hardly think you'll be lacking for privacy."

He heard the smile in her voice and chuckled. "No, from the looks of the outside of this beautiful place, I'd say privacy is not a problem."

Her voice caught in her throat at his words. "Beautiful? You think Bellamy House is beautiful?"

Shocked at her question, he said, "Absolutely. I think it's one of the most beautiful homes I've ever seen. But why would you ask? Don't you like it?"

"Yes, of course I do!" Eleanor cast her gaze around the

room. The thick, green draperies were tied back so she could see heavy raindrops sliding down the window panes. The stone fireplace, not as formal as the brick structure in the living room, gave this room a feel similar to the cottage. The plush, Oriental rug underneath them threw colors of green and red against the dark, hardwood floor. The floral, comfortable sofa facing the fireplace with matching deep-cushioned chairs flanking, continued the room's homey feel.

"I love this house," she confessed, her voice once again soft. "It's just a little...um...old world for this part of the country."

"The first time I came up the drive I was captivated by the architecture," he said, a smile on his face. Shifting slightly, he added, "I'd love to hear more about the house at some time, but I need to...uh..."

"Oh, my goodness," she exclaimed, her cheeks burning. "I'll turn my back and you can slip on the sweatpants. Then I'll show you to the bathroom. There's one just down the hall, across from the kitchen."

She stood and turned around, facing the fireplace and giving him her back. She heard the rustling of blankets and the sound of him moving around.

"You know," he said, his voice coming from behind her, but higher, indicating that he was standing. "Since I can't see, how do I know you turned your back?"

"I...well, I..." she stammered.

Laughing, he rescued her from her embarrassment. "I'm only teasing."

Her laughter peeled out, mixing with his. The sound felt unusual to her ears and she wondered when the last time was she had really laughed. Reaching down to take his hand, she said, "Well, you just better hope I take you to the bathroom and not to the top of a staircase!"

Relaxing with her teasing him as well, he nodded, linking his fingers with hers. "I'll just have to trust that you'll keep taking care of me."

Trying to ignore the way his body looked as he leaned slightly in toward her, the sweatpants loose on his waist and tight on his thighs, she carefully guided him out of the study and down the hall, continuing to smile.

Once in the bathroom, Rafe felt his way to the toilet, maneuvering with some difficulty. He never realized how much he used his eyes just to take a piss. Finishing, he felt his way to the sink and washed his hands. Assuming there was a mirror in front of him, he tried to force open his left eye after determining it was the less swollen of the two.

A slit of light shone through, but it was enough to cause him to shut his eye quickly as pain sliced through his head. "Fuck," he muttered.

A knock on the door brought his head around.

"Rafe? Are you okay in there?"

He felt his way to the door, fumbling for the knob, and swung it open. "Yeah," he grumbled. "Just feeling sorry for myself," he admitted. "I tried to pry my eye open so I could see what the hell I look like, but that just made my forehead hurt."

She reached out and took him by the hand again, pulling him gently forward. "Come on, grumpy. I've just put your clothes into the dryer, so you'll be more comfortable soon."

Walking along with her tucked up under his shoulder for guidance, he was careful to not lean on her, cognizant of her limp, and small stature. Inhaling the scent of roses again, he was unable to keep the smile from his lips. He found himself curious about the enigmatic Eleanor, especially now that he was certain she wasn't elderly. "Where are we going?"

"I thought we could go back into the study, only I think you'll find the sofa to be much more comfortable than the blankets on the floor."

"Hey, don't knock the floor. It was dry, warm, and surprisingly comfortable."

Eleanor smiled as they moved along the hall, Rafe's hand stretched out to the side, his fingers gliding along the wall for balance and orientation. Describing where he was as they walked, she kept up a running dialog. "We're going back down the hall that leads from the kitchen to the downstairs study. I suppose it's more of a family room than a study, but my parents didn't have a television, so the room was just always called a study. It was my mother's favorite room and is one of mine as well. My grandmother had it added to the house, loving the comfortable place to relax. The double doors lead to the terrace outside and, with a stone fireplace and comfy furniture, it's a nice place to hang out."

She backed him to the sofa and with gentle pressure on his shoulders, guided him to sit. He shifted around, settling into the deep cushions and agreed, "You're right. This is nice."

Rafe listened as Eleanor settled on the sofa also, but from her voice it sounded like she was several feet away. Twisting his body toward her, he said, "Now what?"

Pausing, she said, "Well, I guess we just have to wait out the storm."

14

The silence in the room was broken only by the crackling of the fire. After a little bit, Rafe heard Eleanor rise from the sofa and add some wood to the flames. "I hate that I'm helpless and that you have to do all of this," he grumbled.

Eleanor sat down, twisting her body so that it faced Rafe on the other end of the sofa and tucked her right leg under her body. She studied him for a moment, seeing the tight muscles in his face and the way he clenched his hands. "Why is that? It is because I'm a woman? Or your employer? Or do you just hate feeling helpless in general?"

Shaking his head slightly, his lips twitched. "You go right to the heart of the matter, don't you?" Sighing, he said, "I guess it's mostly that I like being in control. I mean, sure, I was taught to always take care of a lady, so it goes against my grain to have you build the fire...not that you can't handle the job, but it's just not how I was brought up."

"Um...Miss Ethel?" she asked, her voice filled with hesitation. He smiled and she breathed a sigh of relief.

"You know Miss Ethel?"

"Well, she was good friends with my mom. I think she still goes to the same church that they used to. That's how she found out I needed someone here, I suppose."

"You're right about her. She definitely taught me how to treat a lady. But, my dad would have been disappointed to think that you were building the fire for me."

"But, you're injured," she protested.

Nodding, he amended, "I guess I should have said that my dad would have been disappointed if there was any way I could have accomplished it myself." Chuckling, he said, "I suppose I could try it but I'd be afraid I might set fire to your curtains."

Laughing, Eleanor settled back deeper into the cushions, enjoying the repartee. Other than Sally and the occasional visit by her attorney and accountant, she rarely spent time with others...and certainly not just for the conversation.

"What time is it?"

"It's almost five o'clock."

Rafe visible startled, "Wow, I can't believe it's so late already. Is the electricity still out?"

"Unfortunately, yes. But I've got a gas stove and thought we could have some tomato soup and grilled cheese sandwiches in a little bit."

"Sounds perfect." After a moment, he began, "What about tonight...I...uh..."

"Don't worry, Rafe, I won't throw you out," she laughed. "Remember, Bellamy House has six bedrooms, each with their own bathroom, so once I get you upstairs, you'll have your own space. My room is at the end of the hall and I'll put you in the room across from me, in case you need something. And, it'll be farthest from the stairs, in case you decide to wander in the night."

His hand drifted to his forehead again, and she leaned forward, placing her hand on his knee. "Are you in pain?"

"A dull throbbing," he confessed.

Standing, she said, "I'll get our supper and another pain pill. We'll turn in early and hopefully you'll feel better tomorrow."

As Eleanor's voice moved away from him, Rafe hastened to say, "May I come with you? To the kitchen?"

A few seconds of silence passed and he readied himself for rejection but, to his relief, she replied, "Sure." He felt her take his hand and he stood, moving closer to her body.

She moved to his other side, taking his arm instead of his hand. Retracing their steps, they made their way to the kitchen and she gently deposited him in a chair. "Originally, my grandparents did not have a table in the kitchen, only eating in the dining room. But, with it just being me here, I had a small table added. You can sit and keep me company while I perform culinary delights making soup and sandwiches."

Laughing, he said, "Don't knock your culinary delights. Since I am completely at your mercy, a peanut butter sandwich would be a delight!"

He heard her moving about the room, the sounds amplified without visual cues. The can opener. Pouring of liquid. The spoon scraping along the pot. The whoosh of the flame on the gas stove. The scent of tomatoes and cheese filling the air.

Soon, he heard platters being set on the table in front of him, the warmth curling from the hot soup reaching his face. "Smells great," he enthused honestly.

"Here's your spoon," she said, placing the utensil in his hand. "The bowl is at twelve o'clock. The sandwich is on a small plate at ten o'clock, and your water is at two o'clock."

His brow knit, causing pain which he ignored, as he turned his head toward her voice. "I didn't expect military lingo from you."

Silence ensued again and he was afraid she was not going to talk to him. About to apologize, he released a held breath when she spoke.

"I suppose there are lots of things about me you don't know."

Unable to see her face, he instinctively knew she did not want to discuss that topic. Dipping his spoon into the soup, he leaned over the bowl to taste the warm broth. "Man, that's perfect. Thank you."

"Well, I can open a can of soup with the best of them," she quipped, sitting down at the table with her own bowl. "Just wait until you taste my sandwich. You'll think you've died and gone to grilled cheese heaven."

Barking out a laugh, he reached over, finding it just where she indicated, and took a large bite. The buttery, toasted bread housing the melted cheddar was perfect, and he grinned. "Yep, heaven."

They ate in silence until the simple meal was finished. As he scraped the bowl with his spoon, he leaned back in his chair, hearing her still munching. When it sounded like she had finished, he asked, "Tell me about Bellamy House. I'd love to hear about this fascinating manor."

"Bellamy House? Really?"

He heard the warmth in her words and knew he hit upon a favorite topic. "Yeah...I'd really like to know the history."

"Let me clear the dishes first and then I'd love to talk about my house." As she stood and gathered their plates, he silently vowed to take care of whatever he could for her as soon as he was able to see again. He heard her rinse the dishes before placing them into the dishwasher.

Eleanor washed the pot and pan, leaving them in the drying rack, thinking about how to describe her home to him. "The short version is that my great-grandfather built this house for his bride. But then, I can give you the long, wonderful version, if you like."

"Very much, please."

"For that, I suppose we should get comfortable."

"Lead the way, dear lady," he said, holding out his hand.

She walked over, her gaze on his outstretched hand and hesitated. His hand was strong. Long fingers. Short nails. It was beautiful. Sucking in a shuddering breath, she reached out her left hand and wrapped her fingers around his. The electricity in the house may have been out, but the zing she felt from his hand through hers could have lit the entire area.

Rafe cocked his head to the side, the slight pressure of her hand in his causing his breath to quicken. He cursed not being able to see her face. Her hand was soft...and yet strong...sure. He remembered the piano playing and it all made sense. If the hand that was holding his now was the same one that created the soulful music, there had to be strength in it.

"Come on," she encouraged, sliding her body under his shoulder again, leading him out of the kitchen.

"Back to the study?"

"No, this time I think we'll move to the library."

"That sounds impressive," he admitted.

"To be truthful, many of the rooms in this house are filled with books. My grandmother loved to read. There were bookshelves in the family room where we were earlier. My father's study had his books, and my grandmother and mother loved the library."

She once more talked as she guided him down the hall, explaining what they were passing along the way. "The entry foyer is on your right, the front door in the center. The main staircase is also on your right, but I usually use the one near the back, where we were. The formal dining room is directly behind the foyer, to our left. The formal living room is straight ahead."

"And the library?"

"Right here," she said, gently guiding him toward the left. "It can be closed off or opened to make the formal living room larger. My parents rarely did that, but my grandfather would do so when they hosted a large event."

He tried to imagine Eleanor's life, full of soirées, teas, dinner parties. *Different from mine, that's for sure.*

He knew as soon as they entered the larger room, her voice having a slightly different echo than in the large, tiled entry foyer. He felt soft carpets underneath his feet and the scent of old books filled the air. Inhaling deeply, he relished in the odor of old print, leather-bound books, and the rose from the woman next to him.

It was impossible to ignore the way she was tucked in, offering support...while at the same time feeling distant. Cursing that the dignified lady had to assist him, he tried to move slightly away but immediately stumbled on the edge of a rug.

"Careful," she cried out, moving in closer. "Here's the sofa. It's comfortable also, although I prefer the one in the family room. It's just that this room feels like the right place to begin the story."

Rafe settled back, sinking into the soft cushions. Hearing her sit close by, he smiled, longing to have her close. *I haven't seen her and I'm already getting attached.* Turning his face toward her, even though his eyes could not see, he prodded, "So, this house. Tell me all."

15

The room was quiet as Eleanor gathered her thoughts, the only sound coming from the grandfather clock against the wall.

Rafe respectfully waited, hoping she did not regret agreeing to tell him about the house, now afraid that old wounds may surface. Opening his mouth to assure her they did not need to talk, she began.

"My great-great grandfather immigrated, as a young man, from England in 1895. He was Richard Bellamy... younger son of a gentleman." She chuckled, saying, "A poor gentleman, I should add. At that time, the industrial revolution had taken hold and the options for a younger son were much more open than in previous times. Before, either the clergy or military would have been his only true choice of occupation. But, he was fascinated with machines and had spent time in Bristol near the docks, learning shipping. The new steamships were making world trade explode at that time."

Hearing the enthusiasm in her voice, Rafe turned his body fully toward her, amazed that she could relate her family history back that far. Not knowing much about his own, he listened with fascinated interest.

"He saw America as a place to expand his dreams so, with his family's blessing, he came over, ready to start anew."

"He must have been very brave."

Laughing, she said, "I like to think that he was. Or maybe just desperate with the times. Anyway, he was smart, tenacious, hardworking and, from a letter written by his ladylove that ended up in the family Bible, we know he was very handsome." A thought popped into her head and Eleanor stumbled with her words. *That description suits Rafe as well.*

Clearing her throat, she continued, "Due to his father's influence, he managed to secure a job with Tolsen's Shipping in Philadelphia. Within ten years, he had worked up to a managing partner. He and Tolsen's son, Carl, became business partners as well as best friends. And he met his wife, the beautiful Sonia Tolsen, Carl's sister. She was the one who wrote the letter."

"It's amazing that it was passed down through time."

"Believe it or not, my mother found the old Bible on a shelf in the library, hidden behind some other books."

His sense of hearing heightened, Rafe heard the excitement in her voice and smiled, wishing he could see her face. "Did Richard and Sonia build this house?"

"Oh no, they continued to live and thrive in Philadelphia. But, their eldest son, Richard Bellamy, II, who was of course my great-grandfather, moved to Virginia to attend the College of William and Mary. He met his wife, Cynthia, who was the daughter of a rival shipping magnate, and he started the branch of Tolsen and Bellamy Shipping in Richmond." Her voice became wistful as she added, "I would have loved to know more about their story. Can you imagine...their family as industrial rivals?"

"Sounds like a Romeo and Juliet story," he said, moving his hand to rest on the cushion between them, surprised when his fingers met hers. He felt her hand jerk, but she left it there, and he reveled in the simple touch. "So, what happened next?"

"Times were good before the Great Depression and Richard, II, began work on Bellamy House, having purchased the land rather cheap years before. He wanted it out of the city and on a hill, overlooking the land. According to my grandfather, his father wanted to build a manor house for his wife, re-creating the type of large homes that he saw in England when they traveled back to visit relatives.

"When he first started the building, the shipping industry was still doing fine, but then, when the Depression hit, money was tight and the house languished for several years."

"They didn't get to live in it at all?" Rafe asked, getting into the story, leaning forward slightly.

"He hired many local workers as contractors, but they were only able to complete part of it. His son, my grandfather, was born here in 1930."

"Another Richard?"

Laughing, she said, "It's kind of embarrassing, but yes, my grandfather was Richard, III. It sounds like the kings of England, doesn't it?"

He relaxed further into the cushions, stunned at the tone of her voice as she spoke of her family. Light, joyful, entertaining. He imagined her face, eyes bright as she told the stories to her children in years to come. He was not ashamed to admit, at least to himself, that he had done the math while she spoke and came to the conclusion that she must be around his age. Still, he felt a strange twitch in his chest at the thought of her with children. While his thoughts were swirling, she continued.

"After several lean years, the business took off during and after World War II and the company once again made fortunes. My grandfather could not wait to bring his bride, Helena, here. He made sure it was a place that he was proud of, that it completed his father's vision."

"So he finished building Bellamy House," Rafe said, his attention still riveted with her tale.

"Yes, Bellamy House became all that it is now because of my grandfather. He wanted to use the natural elements and, since it was built on a cliff overlooking the river, he used the dark, river stone from nearby. Of course, it gives the house an ominous appearance, as opposed to brick or granite that many more modern homes have. But, it was his vision." With a slight giggle, she added, "I think he secretly harbored the desire to have a castle. All we need is a moat to be defensible."

"If it keeps raining, you just might have one," Rafe quipped, loving the laughter coming from the other side of the sofa.

"So, my father was raised in this house and when he married my mother, they lived here as well. My grandfather died early...lung cancer." She sighed heavily, saying, "As so many people in that time, he was a smoker. It's funny, because my grandmother hated the habit and would only allow pipes or cigars to be smoked in the house. She made him smoke his cigarettes outside. Of course, that did not deter him. I rarely saw him without a cigarette or cigar in his hand."

"But you have your memories," he said gently, reaching his hand out toward her along the back of the sofa. He heard her shift around before placing her fingers near his. After a second, he realized he was touching her left hand, but her right hand would have been the closest. The thought flew out of his mind almost as soon as it entered as she continued her story.

"I do have wonderful memories. I was raised in this house as well. The school bus would come to the end of the drive and I would hop on, excited to go to school but, at the end of the day, I loved walking up the drive even more, coming into the clearing and seeing the large, Gothic house that was home."

Questions filled his mind, but he stayed quiet. *You were wealthy, but rode a school bus? You attended public school?* She was so multi-faceted that he wondered if it would be possible to discover everything, but he knew he wanted to try. Her voice called to him and he desperately wanted to learn all he could.

"And now?" he dared to ask, immediately contrite as he heard the slight intake of her breath.

"I think that's all for tonight," she said, her voice pleasant, but firm. "It's getting late and we should turn in." Standing, she moved toward him, reaching down to take his arm, assisting him to his feet.

He stood, immediately tucking her into his side, noticing her stiffen slightly before seeming to relax. As their feet left the plush carpet and were once more on solid marble tile, he grinned, claiming, "I know we're back in the entry foyer."

"Very good, Rafe," she encouraged. "We're going to take the front staircase since it is the closest to us. I've already put your clean clothes in the bedroom that you'll be using, but I also placed some pajamas in there as well. They're clean, I assure you, but did belong to my father. I hope that's all right."

"Absolutely," he agreed, not wanting to shock her with the revelation that he never wore pajamas. His hand grasped the rail she guided him to and, taking the steps carefully, they ascended to the second floor. By the sheer number of steps, he knew the first floor of the house was quite tall. Finding carpet underneath his feet again, he allowed her to guide him down the long hall.

"In the north wing, behind us, are three bedrooms, including one of the masters and two smaller ones. The same is on this side of the house as well. My grandparents had the master on the north side and my parents were in the one over here."

"Is that where you stay now?" As soon as the words left his mouth, he realized it was an impertinent question, but her quick response gave evidence that she was not offended.

"No...actually, I use the room across the hall from when I was a child." Laughing, she said, "That puts you in my old room, but don't worry, it has been redecorated. No frilly, pink, princess curtains, nor the purple, punk theme I had as a teenager. Once I left home, I ordered my mother to redecorate it any way she wanted as long as it was welcoming."

Stopping at a door, she explained, "The master is here, taking up the front of the wing. You and I will be just down there, across from each other."

He heard the sound of a door opening and she moved him into the room. He was beginning to get used to the uncomfortable feeling of stumbling blindly into the dark, but hated the sensation.

"Okay, here's the layout," she said. "With your back to the door, the windows are about fifteen feet ahead at twelve o'clock. They are actually French doors that open to a balcony, but it is locked now. The bed is at nine o'clock, the door to the bathroom is at three o'clock. I have pushed the two chairs and settee to the far corner of the room so you won't trip over them when you head to the bathroom. I've turned down the bed, but when you're ready to turn in, please let me know so that I can make sure you're in safely."

Unable to keep the grin off his face, he asked, "You gonna tuck me in?"

"Yes, I think under the circumstances, that would be wise," Eleanor laughed. Glancing toward the bathroom, she hesitated. "Uh...should I help with...uh...whatever..." She was glad he was unable to see the heat of a blush rising on her face.

Rafe hesitated, the quick quip of not needing any help taking a shower halting in his throat. First, because the idea of her hands on him, now that he was well acquainted with her soft body, had him wishing that they were sharing a shower for pleasure and not necessity. But, secondly, he wondered if he would be able to handle it himself.

Eleanor observed the play of emotions cross Rafe's face...from smug to sexy to uncertain. Realizing this was difficult for him, she took his arm. "Come on, I'll get the water going and then will just hang around out here while you shower and change."

Sighing, he dropped his chin to his chest and admitted, "I feel rather foolish."

"Don't," she said. "Honestly, it's not a big deal." She led him into the bathroom, calling out the location of the tub, shower, toilet, and sink. Leaving him standing next to the sink, she turned on the water in the shower, waiting just a moment until it was warm. Draping a towel over the top of the glass, she led him to the shower door. "Okay, I'll be outside. When you're finished, just use the towel up here and then when you step out, go to your right and you're at the sink. Your pajamas are folded on the counter."

Reminding him not to get his cut wet, she backed out of the bathroom, closing the door behind her with a click. She was torn between the desire to run to her room to get away from thinking of him just on the other side of the door naked and wanting to make sure he was safe. He was really throwing her for a loop. Sliding into a chair next to the bathroom door, she hoped he was managing. And trying not to think of his naked body in the shower. Dropping her forehead to her hands, she wondered what she was doing. *The swelling will go down and his eyes will be open. What then?*

Rafe washed quickly, the idea of Eleanor right outside the door making it hard to concentrate. Her voice was calm and melodious, whether talking, reading, or singing. She was short, her head tucking easily under his chin. Her skin was petal soft. He'd felt it when he linked fingers with her or leaned against her side. He wondered if she were left-handed, since she always kept him to that side.

Careful of his head wound, he allowed the water to caress down his back before finishing his shower. The towel was located exactly where she indicated and, once dry, he found the pajamas to the right, on the sink counter.

She had also given him a toothbrush, which he used. Standing at the sink, he again attempted to open his eyes but the swelling still kept him from seeing. Sighing, he felt his way over to the door.

As soon as his hand landed on the knob, she opened it from the other side.

"Feel better? I've got another pain pill to help you sleep."

"Thank you, yes." Swallowing the pill with the water she provided, he allowed her to lead him to the bed.

"Now remember, if you get up during the night, go straight from the end and you'll walk right into the bathroom."

He crawled under the sheets, feeling foolish once again, unable to see her. "I'll be fine, Eleanor. Thank you for everything today. Hopefully, I can see tomorrow and if the rain will just stop, we can see how to fix the terrace mess."

"No worries," she called out. "It will be there when you're ready for it." Walking to the door, she said, "I'm just across the hall, if you need anything. See you in the morning."

"Good night," he called out, his body sinking into the comfortable mattress. As sleep claimed him, he hoped tomorrow would bring his vision so he could finally view the enigmatic Eleanor Bellamy.

Across the hall, she was hoping for the opposite.

16

Rising early the next morning, Eleanor hustled out of bed faster than she usually moved. She had not heard a peep from across the hall, but wanted to check on Rafe anyway. Wrapping a robe around and tying it at her waist, she stepped quietly into the hall, still hearing nothing. She stepped to his door, peeking inside, seeing a large lump under the covers. Tip-toeing over toward the bed, she listened intently, but only the deep breathing of sleep met her ears.

Making her way even closer, she could see his face in the faint light coming in the window, the bruising extending above the bandage and his eyes still swollen. Inwardly chastising herself for being glad, she couldn't deny it relieved her to have another day to enjoy his company.

I didn't think I was lonely...maybe it had just gotten so easy to be alone. Just one day with his company and someone needing her and she felt more alive than she had in a long time.

His body shifted slightly and she jumped, backtracking quickly. Moving into her room again, she dressed in comfortable yoga pants and a lightweight cotton, long-sleeved t-shirt. In the bathroom, she brushed her hair, braiding it into a long braid that draped down her back. Moisturizing her face, she slipped on her sneakers and was walking out her bedroom door when she heard Rafe moving around on the bed.

Knocking loudly on the door frame, she called out his name. "Rafe? It's me, Eleanor. Are you awake?"

Grunting, he sat up in bed, his hands instantly going to his face. "Damn," he grumbled.

Stepping into the room, her gaze was drawn to his naked chest, all corded muscles and sinew. Tattoos down one arm like a sleeve. Swallowing deeply, she asked, "How do you feel?"

"Like I was hit by a tree," he joked.

"Oh..." she groaned, a slight giggle slipping out.

"Actually, my face feels less tight, so I think the swelling went down." He turned his face toward her voice and asked, "Does it look better?"

"Uh...well," she hesitated, "it kind of looks worse." At his groan, she quickly added, "The bruising. The bruising looks worse." Moving closer, she said, "But your eyes are a little less puffy." She tried to sound happy, but felt her stomach drop. "If you want to get dressed, I can check the cut before we go down for breakfast." She walked over and handed him his clean jeans and t-shirt from the previous day. "I'll just wait outside."

After a few minutes, Rafe was dressed and sitting on the edge of the bed. He felt the gauze being taken off and heard Eleanor's sharp intake of breath.

"What is it?"

"It actually looks good. I know that if we had been

able to get to the hospital, they would have probably given you stitches, but the butterfly bandages have done a good job holding. There will be a slight scar just above your eyebrows, but that'll be all." Joking, she added, "It's a good thing you work with your muscles outdoors and don't have to worry about a little scar."

Her words jarred him. *She doesn't know what I really do.* Stomach clenching, he reached up to feel the slightly puckered skin. She gently pushed his hand away.

"Stop," she ordered, "you don't want to get the wound infected. I think we can leave the gauze off today to give it a chance to heal more rapidly."

Nodding, he reached for her arm again, pushing down any feelings of nerves. *I didn't want to model forever*...but the idea of not being able to have it to fall back on caused his feet to stumble as he got up. Recovering as they made their way to the kitchen, he commented, "This feels different. These stairs have carpet."

"I'm using the back stairs that are closer to the kitchen," she explained. As they entered she sat him at the table again and, a few minutes later, plated scrambled eggs and bacon. Handing him a cup of coffee, she gave the coordinates of his food and they began to eat.

Cocking his head to the side, he said begrudgingly, "I still hear the rain."

"Yes, it's supposed to last for a couple of days."

"I know," he admitted, taking a sip of coffee. His mood matched the gloom outside, though the coffee instantly warmed him. "Man, that's good."

"I like my coffee strong," she admitted. "Thought you might also."

They finished eating in comfortable silence. As

Eleanor rinsed the dishes and pans, she looked over her shoulder. "So, what do you want to do today?"

Slumping slightly, he rubbed his chin. "You've probably got things to do…I can just…sit somewhere."

She watched as he took another sip of coffee, his face dark with his unshaven beard, and felt a sense of longing she had not felt in a long time. "I don't have anything I need to be working on today. We can spend it together…if you like."

The smile spreading across his face at her suggestion caused her heart to skip a beat. *Dangerous…this is a dangerous game I'm playing. One where I know the outcome.* But for once, playing it safe no longer felt right. Filling her lungs with a deep breath, she stood up straight and reached out to take his hand. "We can just hang out today. You learned all about Bellamy House yesterday…I'd like to learn about Rafe Walker today."

"I'm afraid my history isn't nearly as interesting as this manor's," he said, "but I'd love to hang out with you. Where shall we go today?"

"How about the formal living room? After all, my parents always received guests of honor in the living room."

Standing, Rafe took her arm as she led him down the hall, recognizing the feel of the marble tile of the entry foyer under his feet. "Oh, so I'm an important guest now, am I?"

"Absolutely," she enthused, as she led him into the large room, formally decorated with brocade sofas, conversational arrangements of chairs, a massive brick fireplace in the center of one wall with floor to ceiling windows flanking. At his request, she described the room for him, right down to the pieces of art and the formal painting of the family over the fireplace. "And in the corner, is the baby grand piano."

"Will you play for me sometime?" he asked, sitting on the sofa with her next to him. "I heard you play one night and thought it was beautiful. That was you right?"

"You…you heard me? I mean, yes, it was."

Nodding, pleased to finally have a face to pair with her voice, he turned toward her. "It was enchanting," he said, longing to have her play and sing for him. "I can't think of anything I'd like more."

Sucking in her lips, she confessed, "I haven't played for anyone in a long time—"

"You've already played for me. Unwittingly, I admit. But still, I hope you'll consider it. Just think of it as playing for a friend."

A warm ribbon began to curl around her heart when Eleanor heard him call her a friend. Swallowing deeply, afraid the ribbon would turn to ice, she breathed easier as the warmth spread throughout her body. Every sense was heightened. She wanted to cup his face, sweeping her thumb over his stubbled jaw. His arms, so thick with muscles…she knew what they felt like as he leaned on her as they walked. *But to have them wrapped around me in caring.* She realized in that moment that she lived alone by choice and had tried to convince herself she was not lonely. *But I am. Lonely to my bones.*

"Hey, you don't have to play, if you don't want to."

His face, filled with concern, hurt her. Leaning over, she placed her hand on his arm. "No, no, it's fine. I'd like to play for you later. But first, I get to have a chance to know you. Remember?"

Hating that he could not see her face, Rafe wondered about the sadness in her voice. Pushing that aside, he shifted on the sofa in an attempt to get closer, but hoped he disguised it as just getting comfortable. Pleased when she did not move away, he settled back, placing his large hand over hers, holding it gently.

"You already know that I was one of Miss Ethel's boys, as she liked to call us. My parents were killed in a car accident when I was eight. There were no relatives to take me in, so I went into the system."

He felt her fingers flex on his arm and he offered a rueful smile. "I was lucky...Miss Ethel was the first, and only, foster home I was placed in. She's wonderful...actually, she's the best."

"My mother always had the utmost respect for her."

Nodding, he agreed. "I didn't realize it at the time, but after hearing some stories from a few of my friends, I realized how lucky I was."

"Can you tell me about your parents?" she asked.

Her melodious voice slipped around him like a blanket, secure against the cold, making him want to tell her everything. "Sure," he agreed, linking his fingers with hers, loving the connection. "My dad was a hard worker. He did not have a formal education, but began cutting grass as a teenager and then eventually started his own lawn care business with over twenty employees working full time for him."

"Wow, so you come by your skill naturally."

Nodding, he said, "I used to ride around on his lawn tractor and listen to him talk about trees and plants. He knew when to cut and when to prune. He'd talk about plants that grew on new wood or old wood and how to take care of each variety. He knew if a plant needed alkaline or acidic soil. As a kid, I thought he was the smartest man I knew."

"And your mom?"

"She worked with my dad. She'd keep the records and handle the bookings. I remember she was always there when I got off the school bus."

"They sound wonderful, Rafe."

"They were the best, that's for sure," he agreed. "I used to ask for a brother or sister and I know they would have liked a big family. It seems my mom had some complications when she had me and they didn't want to chance any other children. With their jobs, they got to work from home, so they were always around and I got to spend a lot of time with them. During the winter, Dad's business did snow plowing."

Sighing heavily, he said, "That's when it happened. The winter when I was eight. We'd had a big snow and Mom needed to go to the grocery store, so she went out with Dad since he was going to be plowing a parking lot anyway. I was playing with a next-door neighbor when the police came by."

He heard her sharp intake of breath, but he kept going. "Seems a large dump truck skidded through an intersection and hit them straight on. They were killed instantly."

The room was quiet, the tick-tock of the tall grandfather clock interrupting the silence. He felt her gently rubbing his hand where their fingers were linked and wished he could see her face.

"I'm so sorry, Rafe," Eleanor said, her voiced laced with sadness as she scooted closer to him so their legs were touching, wanting to provide comfort.

"It was a long time ago, but I can still see my dad out on his tractor in the summer sun, his ball cap on his head and a big smile on his face when he would see me."

Clearing his throat, he continued, "I had no living relatives, so I was taken to a foster home."

"Were you scared?"

"Shitless," he laughed. "But, Miss Ethel lived in this big house at the end of a nice street. She already had a couple of boys there and I fit right in." Thinking for a moment, he said, "I now realize what a gift she has. She took frightened boys and made us into a family. She made sure we did well in school. She taught us manners. Strange as it sounds...that sweet, older lady taught us how to be men. We were truly brothers...still are. They're my best friends.

Still smiling, he continued, "Zander's the oldest in our group. He owns a bar and recently found the love of his life...getting married soon. Cael and I are the same age. Then there's the twins, Jaxon and Jayden. Asher was the youngest for a while, but then Zeke came along. There were some others that came and went but we were the closest and have stayed that way."

"That's so lovely. I wish...well, that's lovely."

"Anyway, I grew up and after graduation, I joined the Army. Did a couple of tours and got out."

"You were in the Army?"

He noted her voice sounded strangled, but he nodded. "Yeah...I was a mechanic...did a tour in Kabul and Kandahar."

"You were in Afghanistan?"

Wishing he could see her face, he leaned closer, feeling her shoulder now against his. "Hey, what is it?"

A long sigh ensued. "I was a nurse...Army Reserve. I was in Kandahar also, but only for a short time."

"Wow, small world." They were both quiet for a few minutes, before he asked, "You aren't a nurse anymore?"

"I...no...I...uh...don't practice now. Not directly. I edit manuscripts...from home."

Wanting to know more, he remained quiet, hearing the hesitation and heartbreak in her voice. Uncertain how to proceed, he was grateful when she asked him more about his childhood, since that topic seemed to take the sadness from her voice. Grinning, he settled back, making sure to keep her close as he began to regale her with tales of Miss Ethel and his brothers' antics.

"Zander has always been the fearless one," he began. "He had a rough background and by the time he landed on Miss Ethel's doorstep, he was used to taking care of himself. I guess it would be easy to assume he was only out for himself, but he seemed to relish having the rest of us to take care of as well."

Eleanor relaxed deeper into the cushions, smiling at the animated way he talked about his friends, trying to imagine him as a young boy.

"Cael actually has a family...well, a sister. She was a teenager when they needed help and wasn't old enough to take care of him. But they're close and now he has a niece to dote on. Then there are the twins, Jaxon and Jayden." Laughing, he said, "They were a mess. They'd always try to trip Miss Ethel up, but she could tell them apart instantly. I don't know how she did it, but she never got them mixed up. All of their teachers did, but not her."

Eleanor laughed at the idea of twin boys, seeking attention, trying to confuse their foster mom. "And Asher?"

"Asher was the youngest for a while. He was quiet...I guess he was in awe of the rest of the gang." Letting his mind rove back over their childhood, he said, "Now that I think about it, Asher was quiet but not a pushover. I think he has natural goodness about him, he's certainly the voice of reason more often than not now that we're older."

"How on earth did Miss Ethel do it? Raise all those boys?"

"Oh, that's not all of us. Don't forget Zeke. He came along a few years before Zander and I left to join the Army. Plus, she had others coming as well. We were just her first group." He was quiet for a moment and then added, "And as to how she did it? God only knows, but we're thankful she did. I remember the social workers and our teachers all saying how she was the best foster mom."

"It's a gift, don't you think?"

Nodding, he agreed. "Absolutely. She used to say that God gives each of us different gifts and it's up to us to find out what they are and use them. Hers was definitely giving love to a bunch of rowdy boys who needed it more than anything."

"And your gift, Rafe?"

Chuckling, he said, "I guess I got mine from my dad. I love working with growing plants. The forces of nature bend and twist them, but they always come back. Like the little flower that comes up between the cracks in the sidewalk or the tree that clings to the side of a rocky mountain. Miss Ethel always told me that plants can teach us a lot."

Her voice tremulous, she said, "You're right. And how wonderful for you that you've found your gift and it's become your passion."

He wanted to ask what her gift was, but did not want to halt their easy conversation. Her soft sigh broke the quiet of the room and for the millionth time he wished he could see her face.

17

The heavy rains finally slowed to a drizzle after lunch, but Rafe and Eleanor continued to stay warm and dry, enjoying each other's company. Settling in the family room again, this time with no fire, they sat closely facing each other. He found his hand continually drifting toward her, nervous until he felt her fingers link with his.

"So, what now? A game of blind man's bluff?" he joked.

"Oh, God, your jokes are awful," she laughed.

He liked hearing the sound of her laughter. A flash of memories from California hit him, the parties where people laughed too loud, too often, too drunk, or too ingratiating. Her laughter came from the heart, a sweet melody, not trying to impress anyone. Real. Genuine. "I'd like to learn more about you. I've been given the amazing history of Bellamy House, but not much about the amazing Eleanor."

"I...there's not too much to tell," she stammered. His silence told her that he disagreed, so she tentatively began, "You know I was raised in this house. I went to VCU for nursing and when I graduated, I joined the Army

Reserve. After their training, I worked my time at a veteran's hospital in Richmond. I had previous experience in an ER from school and, when the opportunity came for me to go overseas with the Reserve, I jumped at the chance."

"And you're no longer with them?"

"No."

"And, you don't work as a nurse anymore—"

"No."

Her short answers gave him pause and, unable to observe visual cues, he hesitated, not knowing what to say. He heard her sigh heavily before feeling her lean back against the cushions.

"I'm sorry," she began.

He felt her pull away and hastened to say, "Eleanor, you don't have to tell me anything. If I could see your face, I'd know when to shut up."

Barking out a laugh, she said, "You don't need to shut up, Rafe. I'm the one who brought it up." Rubbing her finger on the back of his hand, she admitted, "It's hard. I suppose I owe you honesty."

"Only what you want to share," he assured. The feel of her fingers on his hand gave him the push to add, "I know this is crazy...what happened yesterday and what I'm feeling right now, but I really want to know you."

Her voice, soft as a whisper, asked, "You feel it too?"

Inching forward, he nodded. "Yeah."

Inhaling deeply, gathering her courage, she said, "When you're able to see, there will be a lot you'll discover, so I suppose there is no reason to stay silent." Observing his rapt attention, even with his swollen eyes and patched cut, she said, "The family portrait over the fireplace is one of my most treasured possessions. It was taken the year I graduated. My mother is sitting in her favorite chair in the living room. My father just to her left. I'm standing next to him and my..." She halted, swallowing deeply in an attempt to dislodge the boulder that always stuck in her throat when she talked of him, "My brother is sitting on the arm of Mom's chair."

Rafe's heart pounded at the pain in her voice. He wanted to ask, but knew the answer would not be a happy one. Instead, he clutched her hand tighter, hoping to offer her strength.

After a moment of silence, she let out a long, tortured breath before continuing, "My life was so good...so wonderful...and then...I landed in hell."

"Can you tell me," his voice, soft as a whisper, pleaded.

Clearing her throat, she said, "I flew with my platoon to Kandahar. My parents pleaded with me not to go, but you know the drill, you go where the military tells you to go. And, for me, the chance to use my skills in a war zone was exciting. I wanted to make a difference. We were scheduled to be there for a month and I worked in the hospital there. I admit, it was horrible, the things I saw, but I knew every time I helped save a life, I had a meaning...a purpose that went far beyond anything I had ever experienced. In the ER stateside, we dealt with life and death, but also a lot of non-emergency cases. This was non-stop medicine and I loved it." She looked at him, watching him nod his understanding, knowing his attention was riveted to her. "It was our last weekend and I volunteered for a call out."

His ears perked, straining to hear the intonations in her voice, wanting to suck up each nuance. Pulling her slightly closer, he nodded, wanting, and dreading, for her to continue.

"The details aren't important," she said, her voice losing it melodic sound, becoming robotic, "but, suffice it to say, our convoy ran over an IED."

"Fuckin' hell," he breathed, his heart clenching.

"Flames everywhere. My door was stuck...the only way out was through the back. Over people...some still alive...others not."

"But you got out, Eleanor. You got out."

"Yes, I did...but I was on fire."

Her fingers left his hand and he felt cold as her body moved away. Her uneven footsteps resounding as she left the room, the limp not as prominent as before, but still leaving him cold to his bones, alone on the sofa. His heart lodged in his throat as he considered what hell she had endured...and still endured.

Eleanor stood in her bathroom, her left hand gripping the counter as she looked down into the sink. The solid surface held firm but with her knuckles turning white, she wondered how she did not crack the marble.

Practicing deep breathing, learned over months of pain management, she counted slowly. *Pain management... another word for how the hell we manage torturous pain without losing our minds.* Reaching twenty, she shifted her gaze to her right hand, the reddened scars puckered over the skin. Counting to another twenty, she lifted her gaze slowly, halting at her neck. Perfect skin on the left... marred, tangled skin on the right side, reaching up to her ear and across her right jaw. Another twenty, deep breathing. She pulled off her shirt and ran her eyes over her body. The burn scars scattered over her entire right side, from hip to shoulder and down her arm. She did not need to strip further to know they continued down her leg. Every scar was memorized, imprinted on her brain.

She remembered the stares…the whispers…the taunts. Some real and some in her mind. *Beast.*

Sitting so near to Rafe, his handsome face and spectacular body leaning closer, had given her a hint of what could have been. If life had been different. Having escaped to her bathroom upstairs, she felt a pang of guilt over leaving him abandoned in the den, unable to see. But she knew he was fine and she needed… *a moment to myself. But, then, haven't I had plenty of those?*

Sighing, she pulled her long-sleeved t-shirt back over her chest, covering all the scars other than the ones on her hand and neck, which he was unable to see. *For now. But when the swelling goes down and his vision is normal? I'll be reduced to the poor, reclusive employer once more.*

Counting to twenty a final time, she smoothed her hair back into its braid and left the bathroom.

Rafe sat, his heart pounding, his stomach knotting at the thought of what Eleanor had gone through and was currently experiencing. Cursing his inability to even do something as simple as go find her, he sat, his hands clenching into fists.

The idea that she had been injured gutted him. Her words reverberated through the room. "*I was on fire.*" He had been thinking of her as the princess in the castle when she had, in fact, selflessly served her country.

Burned. He had seen a few burn victims during his time in Afghanistan and the agonizing hell had broken bigger men. His mind cast back to the thoughtless words of the young grocery cashier. Had Eleanor been taunted? Cast off? *But what of her family? Surely, they cared for her?* The questions swirled in his mind, each possibility worse than the one before.

Minutes passed and he wondered what he should do. Cocking his head to the side, he listened carefully. He heard soft footsteps coming closer. Uncertainty filled his being as he leaned forward, perched on the edge of the sofa, ears trained to every sound.

"Eleanor?" he called softly. Feeling the sofa dip beside him, he held his breath.

"I'm sorry," she said, her voice barely above a whisper. "I just needed a moment—"

"There's nothing to apologize for," he assured. "I'm the one who's sorry. We don't have to talk about anything. In fact, the rain has slowed, so I'm sure I can get to the cottage." He felt her hand on his arm.

"Don't be silly, Rafe. I want you here. And you have nothing to apologize for either. We were getting to know each other. It seems we both have difficult pasts...you appear to have a better grasp on your situation than I do. Mine still...well, I haven't talked about it in a very long time."

"Honey, you only have to tell me what you want. Not one thing more. I want to know about you, but only as much as you are comfortable sharing."

The endearment slipped from his lips and, while Eleanor knew it might be a throwaway, it wrapped around her heart. It had been so long since anyone had used an endearment with her...especially a virile man. She stared at his face, unable to see his eyes but noting his attention was all on her. "I'd like to talk to you...I think it might be good for me to talk to you." Sighing loudly, she added, "Plus, it's not like you won't know once you can see."

"I promise when I can see, I'll see the beautiful woman I know you are," he said.

A rude snort emitted and she admonished, "Please don't make promises you have no way of knowing if you can keep."

Knowing his growing feelings would not change, Rafe kept quiet. She was so different from everyone else he had experienced over the past several years. Her conversations were about real issues, not the latest developments in botox injections. She listened to him, not just hearing what she wanted to hear. She sat near, but did not try to wrap herself around him, hoping he could get his agent to work with her. He listened carefully to what she said, hearing her fears in her voice, but he knew when he gained his sight, she would remain as beautiful to him as she was right now.

Eleanor continued her story, her voice full of regret. "I managed to escape the burning vehicle and was tackled by one of the uninjured squad members. He body slammed me to the ground, but he managed to put the fire out. I was stripped and they got another medic to immediately work on me. They had me back to the hospital as quickly as they could. On heavy-duty painkillers, I don't remember much about the next few days before I was flown to the base hospital in Germany."

Rafe's hand snaked out to find hers, once more linking their fingers.

"I didn't even find out who had died or was injured along with me until much later...that's how drugged I was. By then, it seemed like a nightmare—caught between sleep and reality."

"I'm so sorry," Rafe said again, feeling inadequate, remembering Zander had spent time in the military hospital in Germany as well.

Eleanor stared at Rafe's face, his poor swollen eyes still shut, and yet, she could see honest emotion in his expression. Her voice dropped to a whisper. "That's not the worst."

Rafe's heart seized at her barely-there confession that more was to come. It clearly devastated her more than her body being burned. Suddenly, his thoughts shot to the family portrait she mentioned. *Mom, dad, brother. Where are they?* Unable to ask the question, he just squeezed her fingers.

"My parents, who never wanted me to be in the Army Reserve and certainly not serve overseas, hopped a charter jet to come see me in Germany. My brother begged to come and at the last minute they agreed. He was seventeen years old."

Leaning back in the deep cushions, Eleanor turned away from Rafe's intense face and stared toward the cold fireplace, the flames from yesterday long burned out. "It was weeks later, when they were sure I was going to live, the chance of infection lower, and I had had three surgeries that the Chaplain finally informed me. My family's plane crashed in France on their way to the base in Germany. All killed."

"Jesus Christ," Rafe breathed. "Oh, fucking hell." Unable to hold back, he moved forward, his arms fumbling wide to encircle her body. Unable to see what he was doing, his arms crashed against her, but she moved in, melting into his embrace. Holding her close, he breathed in the rose scent from her shampoo as her small, soft body leaned into his. He felt her trust and silently vowed to uphold it.

A tear slid down her cheek as Eleanor allowed him to engulf her in his strength. *How long has it been since someone held me? Offered me more than an awkward pat on the back.* Sally had hugged her, but Eleanor had stiffened at times, knowing that the embrace had been motherly, but not wanting that substitute for the real thing—*or not deserving that substitute.*

"It's okay, Eleanor," Rafe cooed, feeling her body shudder as a tear wet his shirt. "Let it out...let it all out, honey."

Her confession continued, as she said, "I know it's a sin, but if I had been able to commit suicide, I would have."

He jerked in response, even knowing that was not uncommon with burn victims. He said the only thing he could think of. "I'm glad you couldn't. You're so strong."

"Hmph," she disagreed, leaning back up, grabbing a tissue from the end table. After blowing her nose, she shrugged, saying, "I didn't feel strong at the time. Looking back, I realize it was just my family's resilience flowing through my blood that kept me going. Recovery, therapy, more surgeries and the cycle began again."

"When was that?" he asked, wondering how young she must have been.

"I was twenty-four years old. It was three years ago."

"What happened? When you got back?"

A pause was followed by a sigh. "I came here. There were things that needed to be done. Thank God, I had Sally, my housekeeper, who had maintained the home while I was gone. Our family lawyer had taken care of my parents' company holdings. My parents wanted to be cremated, so that happened and it was much later, when I was able, that a private memorial service was held for them and my brother."

He felt her body stiffen and tensed in anticipation of what would come next.

"That's when it started," she whispered, "and I found out I wasn't as strong as I thought." Swallowing the lump in her throat, she said, "Some of my parents' friends were wonderful, but it only took a few words to send me into hiding. You see, a few thought I should never have gone overseas...instead of returning to condolences or thanks for my service, a few said that my actions led to my family's death."

"You're shittin' me, right?" he bit out, anger flowing through his body.

Shaking her head, she said, "Oh, no. Their condemnation rang through my mind and I started staying home. I was home, but had no family. Thoughts of suicide filled my mind once again. Antidepressants probably saved my life, along with counseling.

"At first, I thought of continuing my nursing, but the scarring made it difficult for complete range of motion and I can't be outside in the direct sunlight for any length of time. So, it became easy to just hide away here. Even when I went to town, I heard the taunts of some children, calling me a *beast.*" Sighing, she added, "Their parents would shush them, of course, and most of the residents knew what had happened to me and my family, but it became easy to just stay away from everyone."

"And probably the longer you were away, the easier it got?"

"Yes, exactly," she admitted, glad that he understood.

"I know it was partially due to depression, but I just didn't want to be around anyone."

"But lonely..."

Heaving another great sigh, she nodded. "Yes...very lonely."

18

The rest of the afternoon was spent with little talking, both exhausted from their emotional confessions. The words, once out, could not be taken back. The shame and anger that had choked her for so long was still there, but Eleanor felt freer having shared, as though holding onto the negative emotions had given them weight. Rafe spoke, interrupting her thoughts and drawing her attention.

"I'm so glad you told me your family history. I loved hearing about this beautiful manor house."

"You know, I've had an offer to sell Bellamy House," she said, as they sat in the study. "Philip Hayden of Hayden Development Company wants to turn it into a luxury hotel."

Shocked, Rafe whipped his head around toward her voice, wishing for the millionth time he could see her face. "No!" he said vehemently, "You're not even considering it, are you?"

"No, no," she assured. "I have no intention of selling my family home. Anyway, I have no idea what I would do or where I would go."

The idea of her being alone in the world hit him and he wished to reach out to hold her in his arms again. Before he had a chance to speak, she suddenly stood, saying, "Let's go into the kitchen and I'll fix some dinner."

Understanding her desire to move away from the heavy conversation, he nodded, allowing her to lead him down the hall. After another sandwich dinner, the electricity came on, but the Internet and phone lines were still out.

Rafe convinced her to take him to the living room and play the piano. At first self-conscious about her mistakes due to her hand being unable to stretch to its fullest, she soon became lost in the sound of the notes moving through her. She began to sing as she played, and he was convinced it was even more lovely than the first time he heard her.

Casting his mind back to what she had endured caused his heart to clench again. Her strength awed him. Her courage humbled him. Her determination inspired him. But, her pain had him wanting to be her champion, fighting her fights and battling back her fears. He hated that narrow-minded people had taken away her spirit and caused her to retreat.

Leaning his head back, he breathed deeply as the music flowed between the two of them, swirling around and connecting them in ways that words could not. He reached his hand up, gently touching the gauze bandage over his brow and eyes. The skin around his eyes felt less tight so he lifted the bottom edge just a bit. A sliver of light came through and he almost yelled out in excitement. The movement sent a slight pain through his forehead, but not nearly as bad as before. Looking over, he could just see Eleanor's body rocking back and forth as the music filled the room.

Not wanting to interrupt the moment, he lowered the bandage back into place and stayed quiet. *Hopefully, tomorrow I'll be able to see her.* The desire to hold her close while looking into her eyes was overwhelming, but he wanted to have his vision fully back before he surprised her.

Relaxing into the cushions again, he allowed her music to fill his soul.

Eleanor lay in bed that night, the thought of Rafe across the hall filling her mind with visions of his perfect body... and what she knew would never come to pass. Him holding her. Kissing her. Loving her.

Rolling over, punching the pillow, she used all the tricks she had learned to fall asleep. When in pain, she would empty her mind to find rest. But tonight, sleep was elusive. Flopping to her back, she stared at the ceiling, counting all of the things the fire had taken from her.

When in such a dark mood she always thought of her family, for if they were not traveling to visit her in the hospital they would still be alive. She thought of her inability to be in the sun, her burn scars too tender for the heat, therefore giving up her outdoor pleasures. She thought of giving up her career, unwilling to face the stares from others. And, she thought of her lost beauty, but knowing vanity was a sin, she tried not to dwell on her appearance.

But, tonight, it was the loss of the chance of a relationship that ate at her the most. A handsome man was just across the hall, but would never be hers. A silent tear slid down her cheeks, the loss of what she had never known causing her heart to ache.

Light pierced Rafe's vision as he blinked in the pale morning light. He remembered pushing the gauze bandage from his eyes during the night, the material irritating. And now, the rain had stopped and the morning's sun was beginning to peek through the clouds, filling the room with a slight glow.

Jerking up in bed, he looked around the large room, thrilled that his vision was back, thanking God for the gift of sight. He was sitting in an oak, carved-poster bed, covered with a maroon, down comforter. The tall windows to his left allowed the sunlight to shine through, matching maroon curtains pulled back with brocade ties.

A settee and chair were placed near the window. A tall chest of drawers was to the right, the oak matching the bed. Wood floors were covered with a plush, navy rug, edged in maroon leaves. Paneling covered the lower portion of the walls with ivory paint above to the ceiling. Ornately carved wood created the chair rail and crown molding. Elegantly framed pictures covered the walls, giving evidence of having awakened inside the walls of great house.

Desiring to take it all in, mother nature called instead. He hurried into the bathroom, the bright lights almost blinding. After using the facilities, he moved to the mirror, studying the cut on his brow. There was still swelling around his left eye making it difficult to open it completely. The edges of the cut were mending, but there was no doubt a small scar would remain, a reminder of his time here at Bellamy House.

Smiling, he could not wait to surprise Eleanor with his now open eyes. Quickly dressing in his jeans, he figured he'd get a clean shirt when he got back to his cottage. Stepping across the hall, he rapped his knuckles on her closed door.

"Rafe? What's wrong?" The door flew open, Eleanor's hair waving wildly about her head, a sleep crease down her cheek and a light blue robe hanging off her shoulder, as she jerked her eyes to his.

"Hey gorgeous," he said, his smile wide, arms thrown out to the side. Thrilled to be able to see her, finally, his eyes devoured her face. Her porcelain complexion was pale against her dark, silky hair. Her lips were full and he imagined them as she sang, her voice pure. She was a foot shorter than he, her body slight, but definite curves hit his gaze, her robe barely covering her matching nightgown. Her eyes were the deepest brown as they met his, unfocused at first before flying open wide.

A sudden intake of breath met his ears. She held his gaze for an instant, before whirling around, presenting her back to him. "I...I thought something was wrong."

He placed his strong hands on her shoulders, feeling them tremble beneath his touch. "Please, Eleanor, don't be upset. I've been dying to see you." He noted the burn scars on the side of her neck, from her ear down, disappearing underneath the robe.

"Why?" she choked out.

"Because...you're special to me. Someone I want to know...spend time with. The past few days have only sparked my desire to get to know you more."

She turned slightly, her unblemished side facing him.

"I…I'm not ready for this, Rafe. I wasn't prepared for you to see me."

"Your scars don't scare me, Eleanor. They're part of you…part of what makes you an amazing woman."

Eleanor lifted her sideways gaze to Rafe as she wrapped her arms around her waist in a protective stance. Swallowing deeply, she stared into his gorgeous face, his piercing eyes only making him more handsome. "I…I can't do this now. I'm sorry." With that, she stepped back into her room, closing the door and locking it with a resounding click.

Heart heavy, Rafe walked over the wet grass toward the cottage. *Has it only been two days since I was last here?* It seemed much longer. He knew he needed to look around, see what downed trees would need to be taken care of, but all he could think about was how things had ended with Eleanor.

He had stood at her closed door, pleading with her to talk to him. She had…from the other side of the door. Her honesty touched him.

"I've loved the past days with you, Rafe, but this is too much, too soon. I'm just not ready."

He knew that to argue with her feelings of insecurity would only make things worse, so he left, vowing to her that he would give her time to accept his friendship. He stopped at the door of the cottage, his feet almost stumbling. *Friendship and, hopefully, more…but she's not ready to hear that.*

Throwing open the door, he entered, breathing the familiar woodsy scent in deeply. He stripped and climbed into the shower, the hot water sluicing over his body. Finished, he looked into the mirror at the healing cut, swiping some antibiotic cream across it. Grateful to pull on clean clothes, he fixed a bowl of oatmeal, planning his day.

First, cut away the downed tree from the driveway to make it passable. He had glanced at the terrace on his way out of the house and knew that might take some help. He also needed to buy a new phone and check in with Miss Ethel and his brothers. Rinsing his bowl, he formulated his day's plans.

Eleanor stood at a window overlooking the grounds, watching as Rafe walked through the wet grass toward his cottage. She noticed every nuance of his body. His broad shoulders, his trim waist, and his dark hair. The way his jeans fit snugly over his thighs and cupped his firm ass. The way his biceps bulged from the t-shirt. A perfect masculine specimen.

Drawing in a shaky breath, she hated the way she hid from him when he had been so excited to have his vision back. Dropping the heavy drapes, she turned from the window. *But I need time...time to get used to him. He wants to become a friend and I want so much more.*

Walking down the stairs, she entered the kitchen and, soon, with her fingers wrapped around a cup of strong coffee, her cold hands began warming. After only two days of his company, the room seemed too quiet, too empty. Sitting at the table with a bowl of cereal, she sighed, the loneliness no longer comforting but, instead, threatening to choke her.

In the distance, she heard the familiar sound of a chainsaw and jumped up to see what he was doing. Moving through the foyer she opened the front door and spied him in the driveway, his truck nearby while he sawed the downed tree. Even at a distance, she could see the muscles in his arms and back move as he bent and flexed in his task.

Maybe...maybe...I could learn to have him look at me. Maybe a friendship with him would be okay. At least I'd have him in my life. Sucking in a deep breath, she determined to approach him when he finished the driveway, to ask him to come to the house for lunch.

She watched as he moved the logs to the side of the drive and placed the saw in the bed of his truck. But, instead of getting in and driving back to the cottage, he started the truck and headed down the drive until he was out of sight. Gone.

Her knees buckled and she landed in a heap at her front door, a sob wrenching from her chest. She had thought that him seeing her, with all her scars, would be the worst thing that could happen, but the idea of him leaving caused her heart to ache in a way she had not felt in a long time.

It was all too much. The emotional roller coaster she had been on for the past few days careened off the tracks. With no strength left she slumped over, her arms wrapping around her bent knees, the sob coming from deep within. She cried aloud, knowing there was no one to hear her pain.

19

“Why didn’t you tell me?

Rafe sat in Miss Ethel’s living room, staring at the beloved woman standing in her kitchen, her delicate, but strong, hands busy working bread dough. She glanced his way before looking back down at her task.

“Come on, Miss Ethel, don’t you think that I could’ve handled things better if I had known about her injuries? I thought my employer was an older lady, shut-in due to age or something. If I’d known about Eleanor, I could have...I don’t know...been more prepared.”

Miss Ethel turned from the counter, her sharp gaze landing squarely on him. “And if I had...would it have made any difference to how you performed your tasks?”

He opened and closed his mouth several times, unable to produce an answer.

“That’s what I thought,” she said, her eyes warm on him. “Oh, Rafe dear, you must know that Eleanor’s story was for her to tell...in her way and in her time, if ever. For all I knew, you would never meet her, simply work on her grounds for the summer and then leave. You did not need to know the particulars of your employer."

Shoulders drooping, he knew she was right. He had been satisfied doing just that...*until I heard her sing.*

Turning back to the dough, she rolled it out and busied herself making it into biscuits. "What do you think of her?"

He leaned his hip against the counter, scrubbing his hand over his face, wincing when his fingers hit his cut. "She's...she's remarkable. She could have easily become a society woman, but she became a nurse. And a nurse with the Army Reserve for goodness sake. Still, to have served in Afghanistan..." His mind traveled across the ocean to his time in the Army. While the Hunk Calendar might have publicly defined his time over there, he knew the horrors of war as well as anyone.

Sliding the rolls into the oven, Miss Ethel washed her hands before wiping them on a dishtowel. Turning around, she walked over to him, reaching her hand up to gently touch his face. "She did a good job patching you up without stitches. I don't think a small scar will mar your handsome face."

The cocky reply that would have normally slipped out, caught in his throat. Shaking his head, he said, "Nah...this is nothing."

Patting his cheek, she said, "I think your brothers are here. You want to go greet them and then you all can set the table?"

He bent to kiss her cheek, her papery skin warm underneath his lips. "Yes, ma'am." Just as he turned, hearing the front door open and Jaxon calling out his greetings, she held him in place with her hand on his arm.

"Rafe? You'll find a way to make things better. Remember, roses take a long time to cultivate...but when they bloom, it's worth the wait." With another pat on his arm, she turned back to the stove.

Within a few minutes, the house filled with the sounds of the men greeting one another, catching up on their lives. Rosalie's soft voice cut in through the masculine bantering as she cooed in concern over Rafe's injury. Miss Ethel soon called them to lunch, and the large gathering settled around the table. After saying the blessing, they dug in.

Rafe told them about Eleanor, as much as he felt he should share, and as the meal ended he looked around. "Guys, I have a favor, but only for anyone who can spare the time."

His announcement quickly gathered everyone's attention. "The cleanup of the grounds I can handle...and want to. But the terrace that she is able to sit on and be shaded from the hot sun is a mess, the trellis is in shreds from the storm. I want to get it made right as soon as I can—"

"What do you need?" Jayden interrupted. "Name it and we'll help."

The others voiced their agreement, drawing a sharp intake of breath from him. Rafe knew they would help but he was uncertain of their willingness to drop everything at a moments notice for someone they did not even know. Glancing at Miss Ethel's smiling face, he said, "The large limb that fell on me needs to be cleared out. My plans were to take it down in sections but when the whole thing fell, well...you know how that ended. So, it needs to be cut up and hauled away. It also fell on her trellis, which was the very thing I was trying to prevent. It's totally crushed and I'm not going to be able to build it by myself."

"When do we start?" Zander asked, his smile wide as he winked at Rosalie.

"Soon as you can," came his quick reply.

"Nothing like the present," Cael said. "I've got nothing going on this afternoon."

The room resounded with agreements and Miss Ethel stood, saying, "Well, it looks like we have an afternoon full. Rosalie, will you help me pack up some of my cookies and we can take them when we visit?"

"Uh...Miss Ethel," Rafe jumped in, his brow knitting, causing him to wince. "I don't think that's a good idea—"

"Nonsense," she replied. "You all will be outside working and perhaps Eleanor would like a little female company."

Knowing Miss Ethel would not be deterred, he nodded but his stomach twisted nervously at the possible disaster coming.

Eleanor was sitting in the study attempting to read, but her mind was not on the book. The vision of Rafe's truck as it drove down the long drive, disappearing through the trees, stayed on her mind. Her heart still ached with a sense of emptiness and she wondered if it would ever be filled. *How can I feel this way after only knowing him a couple of days?* No answer came to her, but she knew something had shifted in her while in his presence. A feeling of dread had mingled with a glimmer of hope, and now it felt like that hope was lost.

The sound of vehicles roaring closer caught her attention and she moved to the window to peer outside. Several trucks and SUVs, along with two motorcycles, sat in her driveway. A group of men, led by Rafe, and all nearly as handsome as he, walked toward the back of the manor, tools in their hands, smiles on their faces.

Dropping the drapery, she stepped back quickly as though they would see her with x-ray vision. Wrapping her arms around her waist, she sucked in her lips, heart pounding. *He came back*...but he brought others, sending panic crashing into her world. Her head swung around as they made their way to the terrace, exclamations over the mess ringing out. Hearing the sound of chainsaws whirring, she slipped to one of the windows nearer the terrace and peeked out. Rafe had tossed his shirt to the grass, his upper body muscles and tattoos flexing with each movement. Unable to tear her eyes away, she barely noticed the other men as they worked, her focus entirely on the man who had held her thoughts all day.

The doorbell sounded, jerking her attention from the man candy outside. Unable to fathom who would be visiting, she suddenly felt as though her quiet, ordered world was coming unglued. Moving down the hall, she walked through the foyer to the front door, looking through the peephole to see who was there. *Miss Ethel... and another woman.* The desire to pretend to not be home filled her, but knew that would be taking the easy way out. *And Miss Ethel knows I never leave, so she'd know I was lying.*

Swallowing deeply, pulling her hair over her right shoulder to cover as much of the exposed scarring as she could, she opened the door and angled her body out of habit to show her unblemished left side. "Miss Ethel, what a surprise. Please come in."

She stood back, allowing the older woman to enter before pressing a kiss to her cheek. Looking anxiously toward the other woman, now visible and clearly beautiful, she nodded her greeting.

The young woman offered a broad smile and, much to Eleanor's shock, pulled her into a deep hug.

"I'm so glad to meet you. I'm Rosalie, Zander's fiancé. He and Rafe are best friends," she gushed.

"Uh..."

Rosalie didn't seem to notice Eleanor's discomfort as she continued, "Miss Ethel and I wanted to bring you some cookies while the men work."

"Uh..."

Patting her arm, Miss Ethel assured, "Don't worry, my dear. We won't inflict the group on you. The men are perfectly happy working outside to reclaim your terrace, while we women have a chance to chat."

Nodding her head in a jerky motion, she finally remembered her manners. "Please, come on back. Uh... we can sit in the—"

"Oh, the kitchen will be lovely," Miss Ethel said, moving down the hall. "I remember sitting in the kitchen a few times with your mother and grandmother. We always said that tea among friends was better served in mugs over a kitchen table instead of fine china in a formal room."

Unable to stop the smile from crossing her face at the thought of her mother and grandmother sitting at the table with Miss Ethel, she led them into the kitchen, placing the kettle on the stove. Within a few minutes, they were all ensconced at the table, her two guests talking to her as though they were old friends.

She nervously patted her hair down her right side until finally Miss Ethel reached her hand over and touched her gently. "My dear, you are beautiful...just like your mother. A few scars only enhance the woman that you have been and still are."

Her gaze darting between the two, the looks on their faces gave evidence to their acceptance. "I...it's hard." Shrugging, she explained, "I'm not vain...at least I try not to be, but...the world sees the outside of a person."

Heavy silence stretched between them before Rosalie whispered, "Then, damn the world, Eleanor. Just be you."

"I try," she whispered. "It's hard to be brave when you're all alone."

"Of course, it is, dear. But being alone is part of your choice. There have been a great many things that happened to you that were not your choice. But for the things that are, you have the freedom to change that decision."

Miss Ethel's words filled her chest, swirling inside, reaching to the far corners of her heart. "I've been so angry, Miss Ethel. So angry at everything that happened. My family..." As tears pricked at her eyes, the older woman took her hand in hers and gave it a squeeze.

"Then I think its time to let that go. Let people in and you'll find it's not as hard as it feels right now to let the anger and pain go."

With a warm smile, Miss Ethel and Rosalie stood, carrying their cups to the sink to wash them out. She followed them as they walked toward the front door to say goodbye.

Hugging them both, heartedly this time, she thanked them for visiting. "I hope you won't be strangers," she said. "Please come to visit anytime."

"The same to you," Miss Ethel smiled, as Rosalie grinned.

Closing the door behind them, she walked toward the

family room, peeking through the curtain to see what progress had been made. Gasping, she saw that the massive, damaged tree limb that had crashed upon her terrace had been removed, all traces of it and the broken trellis gone. In its place stood the bones of a new trellis, sturdy and beautiful. Rosalie and Miss Ethel had walked around and were admiring the progress as well.

She fought the desire to go out and join them, meeting Rafe's friends and thanking them in person for their work, but her feet remained glued to the floor. Miss Ethel's words rang in her head and she knew them to be true, but not now. *One step at a time...I'll make my choices one step at a time.* For today, meeting the two women had exhausted her and, to be honest, she still feared meeting the men, the thought of seeing their stares at her scars too overwhelming.

Dropping the edge of the drapery, she walked back to the sofa, taking up her book. A slight smile curved her lips at the realization that Rafe had not left her permanently. He only went away to get help. Reminding herself that she only had him till the end of the summer took the edge off her happiness. *But I can reach out of my self-imposed exile... for a little while.*

20

Rafe stood in the shower of the cottage, the hot water washing the dirt, grime, and sweat from his body. The day's clearing and building activities had been fun with the guys, but he was reminded of his days in the Army, where by the end of a day of hard labor all he wanted was a hot shower. As he scrubbed his hair, he considered the difference between this job and his work as a model. Grimacing at the idea of spending his day flexing his muscles for a photographer as opposed to using his strength to help someone else, he turned off the water.

He wished, not for the first time, that his father had not died before giving him the benefit of his wisdom. Dressing in jeans and a clean shirt, he headed into the kitchen to heat some of Miss Ethel's leftovers. A knock on the door startled him.

Throwing it open, he jerked in surprise. Eleanor stood before him, the dark evening sky encircling her in shadows as the light from his cottage illuminated her face. Her dark hair, pulled over her right shoulder, framed her pale face, a highlight of blush on her cheeks. Other than the scars on the side of her neck that crept upward toward her right ear, her skin was flawless. Large, expressive brown eyes stared back at him, uncertainty in their depths. Sucking in a quick breath, he stared at her, bewitched. Wearing blue jeans, a green, long-sleeved shirt, and flat shoes, she was as beautiful as any model he had ever escorted.

As his gaze dropped, he saw she had a covered platter in her hands. Smiling, he stepped aside, waving for her to come inside.

She entered hesitantly, her eyes darting around before moving back up to his. "I…brought some…uh…dinner." Shrugging, she said, "If you haven't already eaten."

Taking the platter, he sniffed in appreciation, saying, "I was just about to fix something. Please join me."

"I've already eaten," she confessed. "You, and your friends, all worked so late, I thought you might work through the night."

Smiling broadly, he said, "We wanted to keep working until we were finished. I've got a little more to do myself tomorrow but, for now, it's a perfectly usable terrace for you."

Ducking her head in embarrassment, she finally inhaled deeply before piercing him with her gaze. "I owe you an apology—"

"No, Eleanor, you don't," he interrupted, placing the platter on the counter.

Her uplifted hands quieted him. "Please, Rafe. I need to say this." Seeing his nod, she continued, "I should not have turned you away this morning. I loved spending time with you, but confess it was easier when you couldn't see me. You weren't just being nice because you felt sorry for me or continually trying to avoid looking at my scars. It was freeing for me...freeing for me to just be myself. So, this morning when you could suddenly see me, I felt... naked...exposed. As though everything that had passed between us was over. And, I reacted badly."

Standing so close to him was still giving Eleanor the sensation of fear so she turned and moved into the small living room, noting the coziness of the space. Perching on the edge of the chair, she watched as he followed, sitting on the sofa.

"This room reminds me of the manor's family room," she commented, looking at the stone fireplace, comfortable furniture, and abundance of books.

"I thought the same thing," he agreed softly.

"For someone who enjoys reading as you do, this must have been a delightful addition in the cottage."

He nodded, his gaze moving to the books scattered around the room.

Clearing her throat, she said, "But anyway, I want to thank you for not leaving me and for bringing your friends to help. That was very kind of them."

"They were glad to do it."

She looked into his face, seeing the sincerity in his eyes. "I should have thanked them myself, but it was... well, spending time with Miss Ethel and Rosalie was lovely and probably all I could handle in one day."

Rafe nodded silently, allowing her the opportunity to unburden herself, but could not resist reaching over to place his hand on hers. Her right hand.

Eleanor stilled, her chest heaving until she realized the world had not come to an end because someone held her scarred hand. Battling tears, she lifted her eyes from their linked hands to his face. "Thank you."

Rafe knew the toll of the action and those words had

taken on her. Giving her fingers a little squeeze, he said, "Sit with me while I eat and then I'll walk you back to the house."

Eleanor opened her mouth to decline, but closed it quickly, finding she wanted that very much. Smiling, she allowed him to lead her to the small table in the corner.

Thirty minutes later found her curled up on one end of the sofa, he in the chair reading aloud from *The Hobbit*. She giggled at one point, exclaiming, "I can't believe you were reading this."

Waving his hand out toward the room, he said, "And what does this cottage look like?"

She swept her gaze around and giggled more. "You're right...it's like a hobbit hole."

He continued reading and she settled deeper in the cushions, observing him. He was so handsome, it almost hurt to look at him. Everything about him called to her. His face...his body...his voice. But he was so much more than just a perfect physical specimen. His friendship was reaching into the dark corners of her being, shining a light where she forgot it had once glowed. Closing her eyes, she allowed the words to swirl around her.

"There is nothing like looking, if you want to find something. You certainly usually find something, if you look, but it is not always quite the something you were after."

He stopped reading as she sat up straight, her eyes on him. Cocking his head to the side, he waited for her to speak.

"Do you believe that?" she asked. "That sometimes what we find isn't what we were looking for?"

Rafe silently considered the passage for a moment, thinking of his own life. *Wasn't that why I went into modeling? Searching for something, only to find what I really needed was back home with Miss Ethel and my brothers?* He looked into her face, so earnestly staring at him. *And what I found here? Searching for answers and finding them right here, sitting next to me.*

Nodding slowly, he replied, "Yeah. I think sometimes we do go searching but what we find is often not what we were looking for."

They sat quietly, both lost in their own thoughts. After a few minutes, Eleanor stood, a shy smile gracing her face. She hesitated for a few seconds before reaching out her right hand to him. "Thank you, Rafe, for a lovely evening and for...well, just thank you."

He took her hand in his much larger one, his eyes never leaving hers. "I should be thanking you," he admitted. "But, then, I suppose we've both gained from each other." Standing, he said, "I'll walk you back." Seeing her about to protest, he insisted. Offering his elbow, he grinned, "Come on."

She tucked her hand into the crook of his arm and they walked back up the hill, over the grass, fireflies dancing around, until they came to the terrace door. She hesitated as he continued to hold her hand. Looking up, she stared into his face, the faint light coming through the door casting his features with shadows. But she knew his eyes still pierced hers. Unable to move away, she stood rooted to the stone patio, her heartbeat pounding.

Bending low, Rafe stopped a whisper away from Eleanor's lips, giving her the opportunity to stop him, but no such halt came. "Eleanor," he whispered, his breath warm against her face. His lips caressed hers, a hint of a kiss, but one he felt reverberate through his entire body. Bringing his hands up, he cupped her face, his fingers grazing over her neck. Feeling her tense at the touch, he deepened the kiss to get her mind off her scars, angling her head so their mouths connected fully.

Eleanor felt the protest ready to bubble forth when Rafe's fingers touched her scarred neck, but he slowly licked her lips and she heard a moan, seconds before realizing it was from deep inside her. His tongue slipped inside, tangling gently with hers. Her body responded, the electricity moving from her mouth to her breasts to her core. It had been years since she had been held... caressed...kissed. Gasping for air, she moved back slightly before immediately clutching his shirt, pulling him back down.

Rafe slid one hand around her back to press her tightly to his chest, the feel of her breasts against him causing his cock to stand at attention. Not wanting to alarm her, he tried to angle his crotch away but, like a magnet, her hips followed.

Finally, with every ounce of strength he possessed, he pulled back, almost undone by the slight mewl of discontent coming from her lips. Her eyes opened, dark and wide, as she stared up into his. Seeing a sliver of doubt creeping into their orbs, he shook his head. "Don't go there, Eleanor. Stay with me...right here...right now. This is real. This is us."

Eleanor licked her kiss-swollen lips and gave a swift nod. Not knowing what *this* was, she was willing to find out.

"See you tomorrow," he promised, stepping back, the cool night air filling the space where only warmth had been.

"Yes," she breathed, unsure her legs would carry her inside, but knowing she needed to pull herself together. Smiling, she moved through the door, locking it behind her. As he turned and began walking back down the hill, she hastened upstairs and into the bedroom overlooking the grounds. Pulling back the draperies, she saw his shadowed form moving toward the cottage.

Placing her heated forehead against the cool windowpane, she wondered what she was doing. *He has the power to break my heart.* Turning and walking back into her bedroom, she crossed the floor and headed directly into the bathroom. Staring at her reflection, she realized she did not have to count to twenty before doing it. The scars were still there. The reddened, puckered skin still covered her neck and shoulders. Stripping off her shirt and pants, she viewed the continuation of scars covering her entire right side, from the side of her breast to her stomach and hips, her leg down to her ankle. They were still as visible as always.

But, for once, she did not stare at just the scars. Instead, what she noticed were her still tingling, kiss-swollen lips. And she smiled.

21

Rafe looked up, a smile on his face as Eleanor walked toward him, a tall glass of lemonade in her hand. He had been working in the rose garden. After she told him it was her mother's favorite he wanted to restore it for her as soon as possible.

He glanced up at the sun that had just gone behind a cloud. Her hair was not flowing over her right shoulder, but instead was pulled away from her face. Looking at her apparel, he noted the short-sleeved shirt, exposing the scarring along her neck and arm. Today was the first time she wore something so revealing and he knew it had taken a lot of courage for her to feel so exposed around him. Remembering what she said about sun exposure on her scars, concern shot through him. "Should you be out in the sun?"

Her smile met his and she shrugged. "I won't be out long and then I'll go sit in the shade on the terrace and stare at the gardener working in my yard."

He threw his head back, belting out a laugh. Dropping

his head, he leaned forward, planting a kiss on her lips before taking the glass from her hands.

Eleanor watched Rafe take a long sip, fascinated by the way his throat worked as he swallowed. *How can a swallow be sexy?* Not caring about the answer, she nonetheless enjoyed the view.

The past three days had passed in similar fashion. They had breakfast in her kitchen before he went to work. She worked on the papers until lunch, when they both met at the terrace for a simple picnic. She would spend the afternoon in the shade, occasionally joining him in the yard for short sojourns in the sunshine before moving back indoors. Dinner was in the cottage where they would finish the day, one reading to the other. Her favorite part of the day was when he walked her back to the manor, kissing her under the stars until she was wild with desire.

She wondered if he would take it further, but so far, he seemed content to explore her lips with his arms wrapped tightly around her. She had become accustomed to his fingers trailing little patterns on her scars, to the point she no longer noticed when he was doing so.

"Eleanor?"

His voice jolted her from her musings. Blinking, she looked up in surprise at the huge grin on his face. "What?"

"You just had a contented look on your face and I was hoping I had something to do with it."

Tapping her chin as though in great thought, she said, "Hmmm, I suppose a certain handsome man has me enthralled."

Laughing again, Rafe bent to kiss her, loving the way she was blooming for him. Each night when he kissed her goodnight, it was getting harder and harder to not pick her up and carry her to the large bed upstairs. But, wanting her to be completely comfortable and ready was first on his mind.

A breeze blew her hair back from her face as she continued to smile up at him. He leaned in, kissing her lips, her smile too tempting.

Staring into his eyes, she said, "Seriously, Rafe, you could be in a magazine with your face and body. You're so much more handsome than most men."

His breath caught in his throat as the confession of his career came to the surface. But the idea of making her self-conscious halted the words. *And I might not be going back to that career...so there's no need to say anything.*

Reaching his free hand to her waist, he bent to kiss her lips. "You're a goof and I'm sweaty. Go back to the shade, babe, and I'll come up as soon as I get finished with the roses."

Her eyes dropped to the roses, their buds ready to burst forth in color. She had been certain that they were doomed for this blooming season, but he had brought them back from the dead. "I love what you're doing here, you know. My mom would have been so happy."

"I'm glad I'm here too, but not just for the roses. They pale in comparison to you."

She grinned as she lifted on her toes to offer him another kiss before walking away. He watched her, knowing his heart had been captured.

That night, as Rafe sat on his sofa with Eleanor curled up next to him, her head on his chest, he read from *Jane Eyre*, having confessed to hearing her read the first day he had been injured.

She smiled, listening to the deep timbre of his voice, with her ear pressed closely, able to hear the reverberations of each word. She adored the classic story of love lost and love found.

"I ask you to pass through life at my side—to be my second self, and best earthly companion."

At those words, Rafe stopped, his breath coming short. He listened, but it was as though Eleanor had stopped breathing as well.

She twisted her head up to look at him, an unfathomable spark in her eyes. Finally speaking, she said, "Those words are beautiful. I think that if I was ever lucky enough to be asked to be someone's wife, those are the words I'd want to hear."

Not wavering, he nodded slowly, thinking the same things. "Yeah..." he whispered, his voice hoarse to his own ears.

The world still turned outside the cottage, but to the two inside, time slowed to a crawl as they stared into each other's eyes. Suddenly, she reached up, grabbing the back of his head, bringing his mouth to hers.

This was a kiss of sweet surrender, but one of all-consuming flames. Tongues tangled, noses bumped, teeth clashed. In a flurry of arms reaching for each other and fingers flying toward buttons, their lips never left each other's.

Rafe leaned back, just enough to see the unadulterated desire in Eleanor's eyes. "Babe?"

"Rafe...I need you...now. Please..."

"You don't have to beg," he promised. "You never have to beg." Standing with her in his arms, he stalked toward the bedroom, laying her on the soft comforter.

Their lips, still desperate for each other, nipped and

licked, as she slid her hands underneath his t-shirt, the skin of his back warm against her fingertips. She dug her nails in slightly, pulling him closer.

He pressed his weight into the mattress next to her, his right hand moving underneath her shirt, skimming her skin until he cupped her breast over her bra. The fullness of it filled his hand and his lips left hers to nuzzle her shirt up, kissing her stomach as he went. He felt her tense and realized he was near the puckered scars along her side. Refusing to back away, he continued his ministrations. After a moment, he felt her relax and he smiled against her belly before moving higher, latching onto her lace-covered nipple.

Moaning, Eleanor reveled in the sensations Rafe's lips were wringing from her body. She had not been with a man since before her accident. She had convinced herself for years that sex was overrated and nothing to miss, but now knew she had lied. At least, with the right man...it was everything.

She was fascinated by the play of muscles moving under her fingers as her hand continued to rove over his back. Her other arm curled around his neck, fingers gliding through his hair as she pressed him closer to her breasts. All thoughts of him discovering her scars faded to the background as he licked the top of them, spilling over her bra.

Desperate to discover more of his body, she grasped his shirt, attempting to tug it upward but their reclining bodies kept it trapped. The movement brought his head up, and realizing what she wanted, he stood, grabbing the back of his shirt and pulling it over his head in a smooth motion, dropping it to the floor.

Leaning up on her elbows, she watched his chest

heave, awed at his physical perfection. It was as though an Adonis had dropped into her life and she could not believe he was here with her. As his hands moved to his belt, her sudden intake of breath brought a smile to his lips. Sliding it out of the loops, he dropped the heavy leather to the floor, the clink of the buckle jolting her into action.

Sitting up, she grabbed the bottom of her t-shirt and, like ripping off a band-aid, she pulled it over her head. He stared at her heaving chest, her breasts barely contained in her bra. She hesitated as her hands reached for the front clasp and he watched as they shook slightly.

"Babe," he said, sweet emotion poured into the one word.

She shook her head, holding his gaze, and said, "If you want me, Rafe, I have to know that you know what you're getting." With that, she unsnapped the bra, letting it drop behind her, exposing the reddened, rough scars along her right side from her hip to her shoulder, including the side of her breast.

He moved his gaze along her body before landing on her eyes, a smile playing about his lips. "Jesus, babe. You're beautiful."

Her fears slipped away at the sincerity in his eyes, his words sliding through to her heart. Still smiling, she leaned back, slipping her fingers underneath her waistband and slipping her pants down her legs, before she lost her courage. Tossing them to the side, she lay back down, completely naked for his perusal.

Rafe's breath stuck in his throat at the beauty laid bare before him. He towered over her, suddenly unsure, dragging his hands through his hair. "I..." Seeing the flicker of pain in her eyes, he hastily said, "I'm afraid of hurting you. You're so petite..."

Eleanor looked at the anxiety etched in Rafe's tense jaw and smiled, reaching her hand out toward him. "The only thing that would hurt me is you walking away."

Holding her gaze, he nodded and dropped his jeans, kicking them to the side before crawling over her body, a grin on his face. Once more exploring her body with his hands, he latched onto a nipple as his hand slipped between her legs. Her slick folds welcomed him and as he slid a finger into her channel, her hips bucked upward in an involuntary seeking of more.

She felt his chuckle against her breast and clutched him tighter to her. Close to the edge already, it only took his finger dragging inside while his thumb pressed against her clit to push her over the edge. Throwing her head back into the mattress, she groaned out his name while her inner core pulsated with her release. Quivering from her orgasm, she gasped as his warm lips left her nipple, moving back to her mouth.

Rafe's soul shook as her body melted into his, her trust in him overwhelming. Sliding his hand from her core, he fought to hold on as he skimmed upward to cup her face. Finally lifting his head, he smiled down at her, his heart pounding as the light in her eyes beamed warmly.

"Please," she whispered.

"Anything, babe. You only have to ask."

"I want you, Rafe. I need you. All of you."

His reply was rough with need, "God, yes. You've got me." Moving away to grab the condom in his wallet, he rolled it on, his fingers shaking. "Hell, I haven't felt like this...ever."

"What are you afraid of?" Eleanor whispered, her fears snaking around her heart.

"You...you're perfect," Rafe whispered in return, crawling back over her body, nestling his aching cock against her folds, the warmth almost unmanning him immediately.

His words shocked her but, searching his eyes, Eleanor observed only truth. He watched as her brow knit and added, "Babe, you are more than the sum of your scars. You are all that is individually you. Strength, character, beauty."

A tear formed, sliding down the side of her head and she watched as his eyes traced its path before coming back to hers.

"I'm just happy," she said, her voice still a whisper, reaching her hands up to cup his strong jaw. "I never thought that I'd...well..."

Rafe stopped her thanks with a kiss, not wanting her gratitude. Soft and slow, he explored her warmth, moving his hips slowly against her core. She widened her legs and he shifted his cock to her entrance. Without lifting his lips from hers, he mouthed, "You sure?"

Her nod, along with her hands clutching his back, was his answer. Sliding in, careful at first before plunging in to the hilt, he hissed through closed teeth at the heat hitting him. Her core closed tightly around his cock and he looked down, hanging on to his sanity long enough to make sure she was comfortable.

"Move," she ordered, her eyes closed, her fingers digging into his back as her heels dug into his ass.

"Yes, ma'am," he grinned against her lips, thrusting his tongue in tangent with his cock as he rocked in and out.

Wanting her to come again, he ground his pelvis against her clit, eliciting moans from her he felt in his chest.

Eleanor's body felt alive, tingling in ways she had forgotten. His muscles corded and flexed underneath her fingers, his chest rubbed against her nipples, his lips teased and taunted hers. The coil starting deep inside wound tighter until she thought she would go mad with longing. Shifting slightly, his penetration hit a place deep inside, causing her orgasm to jolt through her body, ripping his name from her lips.

As Eleanor's slick walls clenched around him, Rafe threw his head back, his neck muscles straining as his own orgasm rushed over his body, pumping inside of her until drained. Falling, barely moving to the side as he crashed to the mattress, he kept his arms around her, pulling her in tightly, not wanting an inch of space between them.

"Thank you," she said, her face tucked into his neck.

"Whatever for?"

"For not treating me as though I was broken."

Pulling her tighter, he said, "Baby, you're not broken. You're the bravest person I know."

Eleanor felt his sweat-slicked body tucked into hers and reveled in the delicious feeling of bliss. As they cooled, their ragged breathing slowing. They clung to each other, the outside world kept at bay, as they lay in the tiny, fairytale cottage at the edge of the woods.

22

Eleanor lay in her bed, the morning sun peeking through the curtains. *Those aren't my heavy draperies.* Blinking several times, she tried to discern where she was. *The cottage!* Memories of the previous night flooded her mind and, unable to keep the grin from her face, she stretched her body. The normal tightness of her scars was still present, but easily eclipsed by the slight tingling between her legs. It had been a long time since she had had sex and never with someone like Rafe...handsome, huge, and oh, so caring.

Rolling over, the smile dropped from her face as she realized she was alone in his bed. Like a punch to the gut, she gasped with the knowledge he had slipped out earlier. She lay for a moment, uncertainty filling her being. *Do I go?* Looking around, she spied her clothes on the chest, folded neatly. Dropping her chin to her chest, she grimaced. *Oh, God. How embarrassing. He gets up to leave and I'm out like a rock.*

Tilting her head to the side, she listened to see if she could hear him in the cottage or the lawn equipment running, but no sounds met her ears. Even though she knew she needed to get back to her house, she hesitated for a moment, sighing deeply. *My first walk of shame...and with an employee that I have to see every day. No—not see. I'll just go back into hiding and pretend he doesn't exist.* As she stood and moved toward the chest, her eyes locked onto the mirror. Her upper chest was pink from his day-old beard. Her nipples were hard with the memory of his head on her breasts. Her hair, normally sleek, was wild and untamed.

Staring into the mirror, her scars were just as stark as always, but latching onto the reflection of her eyes, she finally accepted that there was more to her than just scars. She was a woman. A woman who once more felt alive, even if it was just for a few hours.

Turning away, she reached out, plucking her panties from the chest when the door suddenly opened. Gasping, she jumped back, trying to cover her nakedness with her hands.

Rafe stood in the doorway, his jawline even darker from not shaving, his smile wide and white against his tan face, and his eyes searching first the bed and then darting over to where she stood. "Hey beautiful," he greeted.

Holding her panties in a pathetic gesture, trying to hide behind them, she ignored the tray in his hand and said, "I thought you left."

Cocking his head to the side, he asked, "Why would I leave?" Scowling, he added, "And why would you think that I would?"

Blushing from head to toe, she said, "Please turn around so that I can dress."

Stalking into the room, he placed the breakfast tray onto the bed and walked straight to her, not stopping until his toes were directly in front of hers. "Babe, I've already seen you naked and I thought we established last night that I think you're gorgeous." He placed his hands gently on her shoulders, watching her swallow nervously, her eyes darting down. Acknowledging her uncomfortable stance, he snagged a blanket from the bottom of the bed and threw it around her shoulders, but instead of letting her wrap herself completely in it, he pulled her forward slightly so that her front pressed against his, the blanket snuggly covering the rest of her. Lifting her chin with his fingers, he repeated, "But I want to know why you think I would leave."

"I woke alone," she replied. When he did not comment, she continued, "It wasn't a poor, pity-me moment. I just figured it was a one-night kind of thing."

"That tells me what you thought, but if I made you think for one second that it was a one-night fling, then I must have done something wrong."

Her gaze jumped up to his, her head leaning way back now that they were so close. Shaking her head, she whispered, "You didn't do one thing wrong. It was perfect. I just know that it didn't have to mean anything."

"Then you don't know me. I assure you, it was not just sex."

She sucked in her lips, uncertain how to respond.

He bent his head, his lips meeting hers in a feather soft kiss. She melted into his body, his arms now encircling her. One hand pressed her back and the other cupped her head. Not hiding his erection, he pulled her closer so that his aching cock was tight against her belly. Sliding her hand between them, she cupped his shaft, feeling the pearl drop of precum on the tip. Hearing his gasp, she smiled, feeling the power in her simple touch.

"Baby," he croaked before clearing his throat, "are you sure, 'cause I only want to do this if you're sure—"

"I'm sure," she interrupted, lifting on her toes to kiss him again. His warm breath washed over her face as she whispered, "This means something to me too."

With a growl, he picked her up in his arms and laid her back on the bed, rattling the plate of fruit he had on the tray. Sliding down her body, he kissed each inch as he disappeared between her legs.

Eyes wide, Eleanor gasped again, this time with the sensation of his breath on her clit. She widened her legs, forcing her scarred hip to stretch.

He halted her with his hands on her thighs, mumbling, "This is for pleasure, babe, not pain. Don't force your leg. Just relax."

Smiling, she let each muscle relax as his tongue worked its magic. Soon, clutching the sheet, her body bucked into the air as her orgasm rushed over her, sending waves of tingles through her core. Lifting her head, she watched as he kissed his way back up her body until his lips latched onto hers.

Pulling back slightly, he grinned down. "Now that's what I call a great wake up."

"What about you?" she grinned, her smiling lips moving over his.

He pressed his cock between her legs, against her warm core, and continued to show her a great wake up call. It was another hour before they had the fruit he prepared.

"Here, try this."

Eleanor looked askance at the jar of goop in Rafe's hand, before looking back at his face, seeing his enthusiasm. "Uh...what is it?"

"Miss Ethel has pale skin and yet, she likes to be out in the sun working on her flower beds in the yard. So, for years, she has used this to help protect her skin."

Lifting her eyebrows, she leaned over the proffered jar and sniffed.

Laughing, he said, "It won't bite, I promise."

"What's in it?" she asked, her nose wrinkling.

He bent over, kissing the tip of her nose. "I asked her and she wrote it on the jar. It's got lavender, pomegranate oil, coconut oil, zinc oxide and shea butter. She swears by it. And," he added, pulling out another jar, "here is something for the scar tissue. It can help as well."

Smiling, she dipped her fingers in the first concoction and smoothed it on her face and neck. Still wearing long sleeves and long pants, she did not worry about her arms and legs, but rubbed some of the cream on her hands.

"Thank you," she said, beaming up at him.

"I like having you out here in the yard with me sometimes, but want you to be careful." Handing both jars to her, he kissed her lips before nodding toward the terrace. "Go on and work there where you're somewhat protected. I'll be in the rose garden for a while."

She watched him walk away, his confidence shining in the way he carried his body. Looking down at the jars in her hand, her heart warmed at his caring gesture. Inhaling a deep breath, the scent of flowers in the air, she turned and walked over the vibrant green, freshly mown grass, admiring the landscape. The thought of how much her parents would love the way the gardens were tended, flitted through her mind. *They would have liked Rafe.* That realization jolted her, but instead of tears, she smiled. Walking up to the shaded terrace, she settled onto the chaise lounge.

That evening, Eleanor rubbed her sweating palms on the thighs of her jeans, her eyes pinned on the sign above the door. **Roberto's Mexican Grill.**

"Are you sure? We don't have to do this, you know."

She looked over at Rafe, observing the concern etched on his face. When he first suggested they go into town for a meal, she turned him down flat. Then, guilt set in, and she decided she could not have a relationship with him and continue to hide away. Now, sitting in the parking lot, she let out a long, slow breath in an attempt to steady her racing heartbeat.

"No, no, it's all good," she said, her words more convincing than the tone of her voice. "I can do this. I need to do this."

He reached over and took her hands in his much larger ones. "I'm right here. Right here by your side."

She stared into his eyes and her tremulous smile focused on him. "That's the only way I could do this…with you by my side."

With a squeeze, he climbed down, hurrying around the hood to the passenger door, assisting her from his truck. With his arm protectively around her, he escorted her to the door. For their first foray, he chose a Tuesday night, thinking the restaurant would not be very crowded and the almost empty parking lot proved that theory correct.

The dim interior gave her a sense of privacy and, as

the hostess showed them to a booth in the corner, she looked around in interest. Spicy scents, mixed with grease, filled the air. Pictures of turn-of-the-century Mexico lined the walls. A bar took up the right side of the restaurant but only a few men sat at one end.

Breathing a sigh of relief as she looked around, she realized there was no threat here. Leaning over, she said, "Now, I feel rather foolish."

"Why?"

"I haven't been to a restaurant since before I left to go to Afghanistan. In protecting myself, I also denied myself."

He reached across the table and rubbed his fingers on her hands. "No more denying whatever you want to do."

The teenage waitress' eyes dropped to Eleanor's neck scars a few times, but she took their order without any hesitation. As she walked away, Eleanor leaned back, exhausted from her wariness.

A group of men sat at the bar, one who kept turning around to look at her. She noticed, but since he was behind Rafe, she remained quiet. After a few minutes, their appetizers were served and they dug into the pile of loaded nachos.

Focused on their food, she startled when a shadow crossed their table. Looking up, she stared, wide-eyed, at the man who had been watching her. He was an older man, but his scraggly, grey beard and motorcycle jacket with chains rattling gave him an edge. Before he had a chance to speak, Rafe was on his feet.

"You need something?" Rafe growled, his eyes pinned on the man staring at Eleanor.

Ignoring him, the man asked, "You the Bellamy girl?"

Rafe, stepping between the man and her, said, "You need to back away. Now."

Much to her surprise, the man ignored him once again and repeated, "You the Bellamy girl?"

Suddenly so tired of hiding, she tossed her napkin down to the table and jumped up from her seat, putting her hand on Rafe's back as she peered around him to stare back at the man. "Yes. I'm Eleanor Bellamy."

The old man grinned and nodded. "Nice to meet you. I used to do some work for your dad. Heard what happened to you and just wanted to say I was real sorry. Both about your injuries in the line of duty and for your loss."

Stunned, she opened and closed her mouth several times, her hand automatically reaching for his outstretched one. Two fingers from his right hand were missing. He grasped her right hand gently, giving it a little shake. Rafe stepped back, no longer concerned for her well-being and wrapped his arm around her shoulders, pulling her into his side.

The man's eyes jumped up to his and he said, "John Parker. Former Army Sergeant."

Rafe nodded as he replied, "Former Army Sergeant Rafe Walker. And it seems you know former Lieutenant Eleanor Bellamy."

John shook Rafe's hand as well before sliding his attention back to her. Leaning in, he said, "Miss Eleanor, you're just as beautiful as your mother was. God rest her soul. Your daddy was real proud of you."

She gasped and Rafe immediately wrapped his arm tighter around her for support. "He was?" she asked in a breathy whisper.

"Oh, yes ma'am. I worked on one of the Richmond shipyards that used to be in our county and would see your dad about once a week. He always talked about you with such pride." Rubbing his whiskers, he added, "Your daddy was a quiet man...not given to much talk. I think he used to speak to me about you 'cause I'd been over there myself."

John stared at her for a moment, his eyes moving over her face and neck, a slow, sad smile forming on his lips. "Darlin', you wear your scars proudly. You earned 'em and anyone who says different doesn't appreciate the freedom we fought to give them."

Two other men slid off their bar stools and stepped up as well, thanking her for her service and offering condolences, before turning and walking back to the bar. She smiled a wobbly, watery smile at them, the warmth from earlier now spreading throughout her being.

John's gaze drifted up to Rafe's and he gave a short nod. "Y'all enjoy your meal, now."

Plopping back down into the booth, her legs finally giving out, she found herself scooted over as Rafe sat on the same side as her, his arm still wrapped tightly around her shoulders.

Twisting her neck to look at him, she nodded. "I confess I'm a little shaken, but I'm good, honey. It's all right."

"I know, but I'm still going to make sure it stays good." Bending to place a quick kiss on her lips, he reached over to snatch more nachos.

Warmth flooded her from her heart throughout her body, a smile on her face as she focused on their meal as well.

23

After dinner the next night, Rafe linked his fingers with Eleanor's and led her from the kitchen into the living room. As he turned to sit down on the sofa, he caught her curious expression. Smiling, he tugged on her hand, allowing her to fall down near him on the comfortable cushions.

"What are you doing?" she asked, her face beautiful with a wide smile.

Suddenly nervous, wondering if he were about to do the right thing—or make a terrible mistake—he rubbed his hand over hers, offering comfort for himself as much as her. With a pointed look at the portrait above the mantle, he said, "Introduce your family to me."

Eleanor's gaze shot to the portrait as her eyes widened. Her mouth opened and closed several times before she wheezed, "Introduce..." Clearing her throat, she stared into Rafe's eyes, seeing longing in their depths. Dropping her gaze to their joined hands, she tried to still her racing thoughts.

"Baby," he said softly, drawing her attention back to

him. "If they were here, you'd invite me over…for dinner. I'd get to meet the wonderful people that made you and the brother that always made you smile…or made you crazy. But the point is, I would have met them."

She held his gaze and for a moment she was filled with the knowledge that her injury had taken something from her that she had not yet acknowledged—the opportunity for her family to meet Rafe and for him to meet them.

A gasp left her throat and he immediately moved in, his arms encircling her body. "Oh, baby, I shouldn't have asked. I'm sor—"

"No, no," she rushed, pulling back just enough to grasp his cheeks, holding him close. Her eyes were teary, but she blinked several times to keep the tears at bay. "You're right. You would have met them and they would have been so happy to meet you too."

Rafe said nothing as he held Eleanor, allowing her the chance to gather her thoughts in peace, hoping his body would offer her strength. After another moment, she appeared to have relaxed slightly and he loosened his grip, allowing her to lean back.

She looked up at the portrait for a long time, a smile curving her lips. "My father, who was actually *not* named Richard—"

"I'm surprised," he grinned, shaking his head.

Meeting his grin, she said, "I think my grandfather, the third Richard, would have kept it going, but my grandmother put her foot down. So, my father was Jonathan." Settling deeper into the sofa, she continued, "He was born here, but my grandfather was exceedingly specific about raising his son the way he had been raised…honor God, family, and hard work. And in that order. My father went to the University of Virginia and that was where he met my mother, Alice. Once graduated and married, they moved into Bellamy House as well, and he worked for the family business."

"What was he like?"

"He was..." she leaned forward, her hand on his leg, her eyes now gaining their sparkle once again, "larger than life to me when I was a little girl. He was a big man, right about six feet tall. He liked to eat, sure, but he swam and played tennis to keep in shape.

"I always wanted a pony but we found out I was allergic to horses, so I was never able to take riding lessons. I remember he would sometimes scoop me up and plop me on his shoulders and jog around. I also remember him getting onto the floor, on all fours, and letting me ride him like a pony."

She thought some more before saying, "He was funny...could tell a joke at any occasion and had a big, hearty laugh. Just hearing him laugh would always make others around him start laughing. He always had a big hug for me and I especially liked it when he came in to say goodnight. My mom would gently fuss, because she would get me all calm for bed and he'd come in and crack a joke or tickle me and I'd be ready to jump out of bed and play some more.

"I know he was smart and Granddad said it was easy to turn the business over to him. Dad used to say that if I wanted to go into the family business, I could, but that he wanted me to be happy and to major in any career that suited."

"Did he still feel that way when you studied nursing?"

Nodding slowly, she said, "Yes. He was proud. He told me that I had entered a noble profession and God would bless my choice." At this, she blinked furiously again. "He used to say that he married the smartest, prettiest woman he had ever met and considered himself to be the luckiest of men."

"Tell me about your mom," he encouraged gently.

She held his gaze, a soft, but sad, smile on her lips. "My mother was beautiful. She had some Native American in her heritage and it showed with her long, black hair, dark eyes, and high cheekbones."

They both looked up at the portrait at the same time, and he recognized the traits she had just described. The same traits Alice Bellamy had passed on to her daughter.

"They were such opposites. My father, large and gregarious. My mother, dainty and quiet. She had such a genteel quality...soft-spoken, kind, with a loving touch." Smiling, she added, "My dad was the one you could hear coming into a room, but my mother's quiet nature was the one you obeyed."

She looked at him, a sweet smile curving her lips. "In my teens, when most of my friends talked about their parents in not so flattering terms, I adored my mother. She was my best friend and I could tell her anything. She knew when my heart was broken, when I was happy, when I was mad. She could calm me with a gentle touch or even a look."

Silence coated them in the room for a few minutes, each grappling with what all she had lost.

"I really miss her," Eleanor said then, her voice barely above a whisper. Rafe's arms encircled her once more and she relished the feel of human touch—comforting, strength-giving, loving. Closing her eyes, she could almost imagine her mother's arms around her again. After a moment, she pulled back, staring into his eyes as he bent to place a sweet kiss on her lips.

"That's enough, baby," he said, gently. "I don't want this to be too hard on you."

"It's been a long time since I've spoken of them," she admitted. "Mr. Thomas and Sally knew them, so I haven't had to vocalize my memories. But with you, it's like...well, just like you said...I'm introducing them to you. And, honestly Rafe, it's good. It feels really good to do this. I'm just so sorry that you could not meet them in life, because they would have so liked you."

Smiling at this tidbit of information, he squeezed his arms around her. She leaned her head on his shoulder, her eyes drifting back to the portrait over the mantle.

"My brother was younger, of course, and I remember being so excited to hear that I was finally going to have a younger brother. He was so much like my father...I swear, I think he came out talking and laughing. At least, that's what Mom always said. He was a big teen and would have been a big man. I think he was already about six feet, two inches when he was seventeen. He loved baseball and even though I was already out of college and working when he was in high school, I made it to a few games. He was such a natural athlete. He and my dad loved to play tennis and, while they always tried hard, they weren't competitive. They just enjoyed sports and spending time together."

"Would he have gone into the family shipping business?"

"Oh yeah," she quickly replied. "He was looking forward to it and I know my dad was as well. He'd been accepted to the Business School at UVA, and Dad had big plans."

She shifted to face him again and with a scrunched brow, said, "You know what's weird? Even now, I can't believe they're really gone. It's like I just expect them to walk through the door, having been on a long trip, and greet me as they all pile back into the house." Letting her breath out slowly, she shook her head. "It still doesn't seem real and yet, my heart is so broken, I know it must be."

Rafe held her, knowing she had lost the battle of hanging on to her tears, feeling his shirt becoming moist, her breath hitching several times. He rubbed his hand up and down her back, making soothing noises, allowing the emotions to flow from her.

As she calmed, she leaned back again, this time a tremulous smile dancing on her lips. "If they were here, I'd get to tell them all about you."

Grinning widely, he nuzzled her nose before sliding his lips to hers. "And what would you tell them?"

"That I found a man...strong, hard-working, well read, smart, honest, true. A man so perfect, I could never have dreamed anyone better. And they would be so thrilled for us."

Her words hit him, taking his breath away while filling his heart.

24

Rolling to the side, Eleanor smiled at the sight of Rafe's body curled into hers. A week. A week of sweet, good morning kisses before he went to work on the grounds. A week of stolen minutes in the shade of the trellis...or under the Magnolia trees...or in the rose garden. A week of nights spent making love, either at his cottage or up at the manor. A week of neither caring about the outside world, only the world they were creating together.

He stretched and she watched in fascination at the play of muscles as they rippled under his tan skin. Lifting her finger, she traced the intricate tattoos on his arms and side. He snatched her fingers, kissing them one at a time.

She stared, mesmerized, as he continued to kiss each one, not seeming to mind, or even notice, the scars. The heavy weight she had been carrying around for years seemed to slowly dissipate with each kiss.

He looked from her fingertips to her face, her beautiful smile aimed at him. "You sleep okay, sweetheart?"

"Yeah," she whispered. "Perfect. Can I ask you something?"

"Sure."

"Will you tell me about your tattoos?"

Chuckling, he said, "Zander and I used to talk about what kind of tattoos we wanted to get when we were old enough." Hesitating, he added, "I know it'll sound stupid, but when I was growing up in Miss Ethel's house, we listened to him read fairy tales all the time. When we decided to get tattoos, we told the artist to design something from the pages of the book we showed him. We both got sleeves and this is what I choose."

Her finger traced the intricate picture covering his arm muscles. "It's beautiful," she breathed.

He stared at her, a smile playing about his lips. "What have you got planned for today?"

"Sally is coming today, so I'll spend time with her. What about you?"

"I'm heading into town this morning. I told Zander that I'd stop by Grimm's. Also, I've ordered some natural fertilizer and something else. I'll go pick them both up today. Then, after I mow, I'm going to keep working on the terrace."

Her brow knit as she queried, "What else do you need to do to the terrace?"

Grinning, he planted a kiss on her lips once more before saying, "It's a surprise."

Rolling out of bed, he stalked into the bathroom, leaving her watching his delectable ass in retreat, wondering what he was working on.

Rafe walked into Grimm's, and waved at the servers. Joe, one of the bartenders, jerked his head toward the back and with a chin lift in reply, he headed down the hall toward the office. The door was open so he rapped on the doorframe, smiling as Zander's head lifted.

The men greeted each other with back slaps before sitting down. "You look happy," Zander said, his gaze piercing Rafe.

"Feeling happy," came the simple reply.

"Seems like hard labor agrees with you."

Rafe barked out a laugh. "You saying my modeling wasn't hard labor?"

Zander rolled his eyes, then asked, "Have you decided what you're going to do at the end of the summer?"

He rubbed his chin in thought, sighing heavily. "To be honest…I don't know. I mean, I don't want to go back to California. That life was getting old before, and now, after spending time with Eleanor, I have no desire to return to that."

"But…" Zander prodded.

Snorting, a rueful sound, he said, "I'm not sure what I'd do instead."

"What do you want to do? Really want to do?"

He leaned back, rubbing his hand over his face before lifting his gaze to his friend. "Would you believe me if I told you that I'd like to start my own business?" Seeing Zander's raised eyebrow, he explained, "My dad owned a lawn care business. Sure, it was small, but I'd like to do the same. I'd hire people to run the office and others to take most of the contract work, but I'd like to be able to do what I'm doing at Bellamy House…reclaiming gardens that have fallen into ruins."

"So, what's stopping you, man?"

He leaned forward, resting his forearms on his thighs. "Never thought I was the kind of man who was afraid.

Now, I sometimes wonder if I haven't always searched out what was safe."

"What the hell are you talking about?"

"Safe. You know...I let you fight my battles when we were kids. I joined the military because I couldn't think of anything else to do. You were doing it, so it just seemed like the thing to do also. I fell into modeling because it was just offered to me, and I never had to really work for it."

Zander nodded, saying, "Never thought of it that way."

"But, now, I'm creating on my own. Working on my own. Designing the gardens on my own. I'm using skills that I know my father used, plus all that Miss Ethel taught me. It feels like I'm doing something that I want...not just something that I fell into."

"And Eleanor?"

A slow smile spread across his face at the thought of her beauty and strength. "What would you say if I told you I'm falling in love with her? She's beautiful, smart, strong, a fighter. And becoming more important to me every day."

Zander grinned in return, shaking his head. "I swear it wasn't that many months ago that you questioned how I could fall in love with Rosalie so fast."

"I was an idiot!" he exclaimed, falling back in his chair with a huff. "And so glad you didn't listen to me!"

"So are you going to tell her how you feel?"

Nodding his head, he smiled at his best friend. "Yeah... just as soon as I can."

The sound of feet running down the hall had both of them swinging their heads toward the door. Rosalie rounded the corner, rushing into the office, her face flushed, blonde ponytail whipping around her head, her hands clutching a newspaper.

"Babe," Zander called out, jumping up from his chair. "What's wrong?"

"Rafe!" she cried, breathing heavily, ignoring Zander and rushing straight to him. "This...in the grocery store... you've got to see this!"

Surprised, he looked down at the gossip paper from one of the grocery stands. "Huh?" he said, taking the paper from her hands. Reading the headline, he paled, sucking in a deep breath. "Oh, no. Fucking hell, no!"

Eleanor stood from the family room sofa, stretched her back and walked down the hall toward the kitchen. Sally was expected soon and she wanted to make sure she had the coffee ready. Sally might have been the family's long-time housekeeper, but she was also a friend and Eleanor always made sure to have the coffee on.

Just as she entered the sun-filled kitchen, she heard the front door open. "Sally?" she called out. "I'm in the kitchen."

Sally walked in but instead of putting her bag down, she immediately moved straight into Eleanor's space and grabbed her shoulders, pulling her in for a deep hug. Eleanor patted her back, but wondered about the gesture —it had a desperate feel to it. Before she had a chance to speak, Sally jumped in.

"Is Rafe here? Is he still here?"

Opening her mouth then closing it quickly, she tilted her head to the side. "Uh...Rafe?" At Sally's intent stare, she shook her head. "No, he went into town. Why? Do you need him?"

Sally's face twisted into a grimace as she took her by the hand and dragged her to a kitchen chair, gently pushing her down before plopping heavily into the closest one. "Has he talked to you? Told you who he is?"

A sweet smile crossed her face as she nodded. "I told you we were getting closer, Sally. We've shared. I've told him all about the family, my time in the Army, my injury... everything. I've held nothing back."

"But has he talked to you as well?"

"Yes, of course," she said, defensively. "He's told me of his family, being raised by Miss Ethel. Sally, you know all of this...why are you acting so strangely?"

"Because he hasn't been honest with you, that's why!" Sally bit out, her voice filled with pain. She bent to retrieve a newspaper from her satchel, unfolding it to the front page and smoothing it out with her hands before sliding it across the table to her. Tapping the picture on the front, she said, "Here."

Eleanor's stomach dropped with dread as her eyes moved from Sally's tortured face to the gossip rag on the table. She stared in horror at the close-up picture of her in the rose garden, a smile on her face, her scarred neck, shoulder and arm exposed to the camera's zoom lens. She was looking up into Rafe's face, which looked every bit as handsome as she always thought it did. And at the top screamed the headline...**Beauty and the Beast.**

Gasping, her fingers involuntarily clenched, wadding the paper under their grip. Forcing them to relax, she read the article.

International model, Rafe Walker, discovered after appearing in the Hunks of the Army Calendar, is seen

with a woman, whose appearance is unlike most of his famous dates. This comes as a surprise, seeing as his most recent relationship with actress Cherelle Parkinson is said to be ready to resume, as the two will soon be working together again. The woman, Eleanor Bellamy, certainly doesn't look like his usual partners, as he is usually seen in the company of Los Angeles socialites, actresses, and models. It is rumored she lives, secluded, in a Gothic castle in Virginia, far from the eyes of the public. According to Rafe's agent, the superstar chose to spend his summer performing community service for the shut-in, spreading his appeal from one end of the country to the other. One look at his face and it appears Ms. Bellamy was willing to brave the public. Who knew his sex appeal and beauty had the power to heal the Beast?

Eleanor stared at the words, for a moment unable to process what she was reading. Her eyes moved back to the picture and the headline. *Beauty and the Beast*. She was the beast. They were labeling her the beast. Her gaze dropped from the picture of the two of them, showcasing Rafe's handsome physique, to a series of pictures below the article. In each one, he was paired with a drop-dead gorgeous woman, though most were with the known actress, Cherelle Parkinson. A bevy of women, dressed to kill, all on the arm of the man she thought of as her friend... lover...and she had hoped more.

"Oh, sweet girl, I'm so sorry," Sally said, her face filled with regret as her eyes filled with tears, her hands reaching out to clutch Eleanor's. "I didn't want to show this to you, but you had to see it. I couldn't let you go on thinking he's something he's not."

"But he...we...what he's told me. You don't know what

we have, Sally. He wouldn't lie to me..." *But he did. It's right here in black and white.*

Eleanor was no stranger to pain. The pain of her burns. The pain of losing her family. The pain of her scars. But the pain ripping at her heart at that moment was just as devastating. A sob wrenched from her chest, an animalistic growl from deep inside breaking free as she fell into Sally's arms.

25

"I don't give a fuck! Look it up!"

Rafe yelled into his phone, taking the curves on the road at a high rate of speed, his truck tires squealing as he rounded each one.

His attorney's secretary's harried voice came back on the phone. "I've got Mr. Washburn here." He heard her relief at being able to turn him over to the man in question.

"Rafe, I've got your contracts and you're good. You finished your last contractual obligation before you headed to Virginia."

"I want his balls on a pike, Carlton. If I was there, I'd rip them off myself and shove them down his throat. I want—"

"I understand, Rafe," Carlton assured. "You're not the only one who is tired of Marty's shenanigans. This rag's article is going to blow up in his face. His entire client list will jump ship, seeing how he can fuck up their PR."

"You bet your ass it will. And one more thing, get your

PI on this. I want to know who the fuck got those pictures. They were trespassing, and I want their balls as well."

Disconnecting, he turned the corner into her drive, not slowing until he careened to a stop at the end of the drive. Jumping out, he ran to the front door, twisting the knob, finding it locked. Ringing the doorbell to no avail, he began pounding with his fist against the wood. Nothing. The manor was quiet.

Darting toward the terrace, he peered through the glass door, seeing the room empty. "Shit!" he cursed, dragging his hand through his hair. He ran back to the front, once more banging his fist against the door.

This time, he heard the lock click and the door swung open to Sally standing in the slim opening. One look at her face and he knew he was too late. Eleanor must already know.

Going against his upbringing, he gently pushed past Sally despite her protestations. "I've got to see her. I've got to explain—"

"She's not here."

Halfway to the stairs, he whirled around, disbelief pounding through him. "Not here? Where would she go?"

Arching her brow, Sally retorted, "You think she has no one to turn to at all? She may have chosen to live a private life, but I assure you she is not friendless. The poor waif you think you saved is a strong woman in her own right."

Stalking toward her, he towered over the older woman, his gaze hard. "You think I don't know how strong she is? You think I don't care? I'd give my life for her, so if you care for her so much, tell me where she is."

A flash of uncertainty passed through her eyes, but before he could push his point, she shrugged. "I honestly don't know where she is. She said she was going somewhere safe. I just finished cleaning and was getting ready to leave. So, if you'll please go, I can lock up."

"Sally, please," he begged, his voice hoarse, his words ragged. "I need to see her. I need to make sure she's all right. Please."

Her hands twisted together as she held his gaze. "I think I misjudged you and you truly do care, but Rafe, she needs space. She needs time. And I truly don't know where she went other than she was going somewhere safe. She did send me a text letting me know she had arrived and I'm to lock the house when I leave today." Looking down, she hesitated before adding, "And she told me to make sure you knew to vacate the cottage. She is terminating your services since they are no longer needed."

The verbal punch to his gut was real, doubling him over as he gasped for breath. He felt her hand on his shoulder, but he shrugged her off. Tears stung his eyes as he whispered, "If she calls, tell her I'm sorry. That not everything in that article was true. I would have you tell her that I love her, but that's for me to say when I see her." With that, he staggered outside, barely making it to his truck before slumping against the seat.

Agony turned into anger and he picked up his phone, dialing, not surprised when it picked up on the first ring.

"Rafe, my man. You ready to head back to sunny California?"

"Marty...you've fucked up. Big. You're fired as my agent and according to my lawyer, you're gonna be getting a lot of calls like this."

"Rafe? Seriously? That article alone is worth a fuck-ton of press. I've got calls galore, all wanting to book you.

They love the idea of the handsome man spending time with the—"

"You say it and you're a dead man, Marty. You're already dead to me, but swear to God, you say one more thing and you'll be drinking through a straw and your balls will be somewhere lodged in your throat."

"But—"

Disconnecting, he completed a rough three-point turn and headed back down the driveway. Not having any idea where to go, he made another call.

"Get everyone together. Your place."

Rafe slumped on the sofa at Zander's apartment, surrounded by Cael, Jaxon, Jayden, Asher, and Zeke. Their faces resembled his—pissed with an undercurrent of scared.

"Do you think if Miss Ethel talks to the housekeeper, she'll tell her where Eleanor is?" Asher asked, hope in his voice.

"I don't know," he confessed. "I sure as hell know she's not going to tell me."

"I just don't get what this Marty guy got out of the article," Jayden said. "It's so negative…why the hell would he want you in something so vile?"

Rafe leaned back against the sofa cushions, anger still coursing through his veins. "It's how they work. Agents love publicity. Any kind of publicity. Don't be fooled into thinking that the headlines you see on the grocery store rags are not staged. There's no such thing as bad publicity, as far as they're concerned. He was pissed that I was out of the spotlight for the whole summer and finagled a way to get me back in the public eye. The picture of me with Eleanor was a stunt used by him to make the big model look like a hero, being all nice to the unfortunate girl. He didn't give a fuck about her or how she would feel about it."

"The last time my niece was at the hospital, some athletes showed up," Cael said. "Most looked like they cared, but honest to God, a few only smiled when the camera was on them."

Nodding, Rafe said, "Yeah...same fuckin' thing. What's crazy is that the fucker actually thought I was going to be happy."

"You fire his ass?" Jaxon growled.

Barking out a snort, he nodded. "And my attorney is working on getting him to lose a bunch of his clients. Hit him where it hurts...although I'd still like to nail his balls to the wall. And I've got a PI on retainer that's gonna find out who took the photographs. I'm gonna nail his ass as well."

Looking around the room at his friends, his breath left in a whoosh as he said, "How the hell can I fix this with Eleanor if I can't talk to her?" His throat threatened to close as he said, "I can't imagine her anguish right now, having such a horrible article thrown in her face. And I can understand why she'd be pissed at me for not telling her everything, she opened up and I should have too, but a part of me also wonders how she could turn her back on me so easily, not even giving me a chance to explain... Jesus, how can I make this right?"

The front door of the apartment opened and Rosalie walked in, her eyes darting around the room, settling first on Zander's, offering a smile to him, before they shifted to Rafe. With a little chin lift, she moved from the group and into the bedroom, giving the men more privacy.

Standing, Rafe said, "Guys, thank you for dropping everything and coming here." As he moved toward the door, the others stood as well, offering back slaps along with their goodbyes. As he jogged to his truck, he thought of the one other person who would understand.

As he pulled up, Rafe saw her outside, near the rose trellises under the kitchen window, her floppy hat perched on her head and her garden gloves covering her hands. With clippers in her hand, she moved around the rose bushes, clipping some of the blooms and placing them in a basket. She lifted her head, watching him as he approached, her face kind with understanding, setting the basket and clippers on the ground.

As he reached her, she opened her arms wide, embracing him. He towered over her, but her arms were strong, giving off the same feeling of comfort as she had for so many years.

"Rafe, I'm so sorry, sweetheart," Miss Ethel said.

He stepped back, sighing audibly, his hands now on his hips. "Did Rosalie tell you?"

Her lips curved slightly, her head nodding. "But can you tell me what happened?" She bent to retrieve her clippers as he held her basket.

"We got close, Eleanor and me. We shared about our families...about our time in the military. We spent time together every day and she was even able to spend small amounts of time in the sun with me while I worked. At night, we would eat dinner and then read to each other."

His voice caught in his throat as he admitted, "I fell for her and I could have sworn she felt the same."

"And the article?"

Fighting the urge to curse, something he would never do in front of Miss Ethel, he grimaced, finding the words. "I know my agent was involved. Pissed that I was here and not in California. Pissed that my modeling contract was over and I hadn't renewed yet. Pissed that he was in the process of setting something up with some actress that was using him to get to me, and I was ignoring them both. I made a stupid mistake in telling him what I was doing this summer and I guess I must have said something that gave him the opportunity to do some digging to see where I was. I never realized he'd try to find me, much less use the information he found out as a publicity stunt."

"You hurt because she's hurt."

"Yeah," he bit out. "She once told me why she lived alone, shunning the outside world. Said it was too painful to be stared at, talked about. Without her safety net of a family, it was just all too hard for her to deal with, so she secluded herself. This has got to be killing her inside...the cruelty makes me sick."

Dropping his head, he stared at his feet for a moment, the heavy blanket of guilt weighing on his shoulders. She reached out and touched his arm.

"You fell for her but didn't tell her everything there was to know, did you? And that's what's really eating at you."

He lifted his eyes to hers, swallowing back the bile threatening to choke him. "No...I didn't. I just wanted to spend time with her getting to know the real me. Not the cold world I was living in California. I didn't want her to make assumptions about me like so many other people do. I wanted to be me...just Rafe."

"But that's part of you. Part of your past. You can't just pretend those years did not happen."

"It's part of who I was. *Was.* Past tense." His voice like gravel, he bit out the words before his face fell. "I wish she could trust me. After everything we've been through...she found out I was a model and judged me for it, just like everyone in California. I see the real her, but she doesn't see the real me."

"Oh, Rafe. She's hurt. That's all she can see right now. Give her time and she'll realize that."

"I hope so." With a self-deprecating laugh, he looked into Miss Ethel's eyes. "You know what's really ironic? I had already decided not to go back to California. I am done with modeling. I've already talked to Zander about what I wanted to do next with my life."

Cocking her head to the side, she peered up at him from under the brim of her hat. "What was that, sweetheart?"

"I want to start my own lawn care business. Like my dad. Spending time at Bellamy House gave me the push to finally do something that I want to do...love to do. Be my own boss, work outdoors, follow in my father's footsteps."

"And Eleanor?"

"I wanted her to be part of that...part of my life. But," his eyes held hers, "I've screwed up with her."

Placing the last clipped rose in the basket, she took it from his hands, turning to move toward the porch with him in tow. Moving to the steps, she lifted her warm gaze back to his. "Dear boy, do you remember what I used to always tell you? Whenever one of you would make a mistake, and you did because it is human nature to do so,

I would tell you that the true measure of a man was not in the mistakes he made, but in how he handled those mistakes." Reaching her hand up, she patted his cheek. "And you, sweet Rafe, are a good man."

"But I don't know how to make this better," he confessed.

Smiling, she turned to go into the house. At the top of the steps, she looked down in her basket of clipped roses, the scent wafting up, before glancing over her shoulder and holding his eyes. "You're a good man. You'll find a way."

26

Miss Ethel watched Rafe drive away before making her way into the house. Walking past the living room, she carried her basket to the kitchen, setting it on the counter. Leaving on her gloves to protect her fingers, she began to trim the thorns.

Looking over at the table, she said, "Funny, isn't it? Not many flowers have thorns, but the most famous flower of all is covered with them."

Eleanor sat, her eyes on Miss Ethel, knowing there must be wisdom she was trying to impart, but her muddled mind simply could not follow.

"I can't remember where I read it..." laughing, she added, "probably on a Facebook page, but I love the saying, 'A life filled with love must have some thorns, but a life empty of love will have no roses.' That's pretty, don't you think?"

"Yes, ma'am," she said, attempting to take a sip of herbal tea, praying for it to soothe her cried-out sore throat.

Miss Ethel lay the rose clipping down and walked to

the table, settling in a chair next to Eleanor. "Did you hear?" she asked, her head nodding toward the raised window overlooking the rose trellis.

Seeing her nod, Miss Ethel smiled. "My sweet girl, you're hurting... and rightfully so. The words were so cruel. But they were not his words."

"I know," she whispered. "But they were true, nonetheless. He is beautiful and I am...well, not." Sighing, she admitted, "It was easier, when I just thought he was a gifted gardener. I had no idea he had a completely different life, one that involved a world full of beautiful people."

"From what he has said, it was a life of very disingenuous people, and those are not beautiful people."

Lifting her shoulders in a slight shrug, she said, "I know. People should not be judged by their outward appearances, but it seems our society does."

"Including you? You heard what he said. You're judging him by his looks. You read an article and made assumptions about him based on his appearance, what he does for a living, what other people said about him. He has his own hurts, and people not seeing who he really is, is one of them. You think he doesn't know his own mind and would regret being with you? You're not taking into account who he *is*, instead of pressing a societal idea of who you think he should be."

At Miss Ethel's firm words, her eyes jumped to the older woman's, seeing kindness as well. "I hadn't thought about it like that."

"And now?"

Her gaze drifted out the window, spying the beautiful roses in full bloom. "I never meant to hurt him, and I wish I hadn't, but I honestly don't know. I told him everything, opened up so much, and he left out this huge part of his life. I just need some time. Time to think about what's next."

Reaching over to pat her hand, Miss Ethel smiled warmly. "And my dear, that's exactly what you shall have. For as long as you need."

"She was at Miss Ethel's? What the hell?" Rafe yelled.

Zander put his hands up in defense. "I didn't know. Rosalie just told me this morning. Said that Eleanor needed to get away and she trusted Miss Ethel to give her a safe haven and not tell you."

"I can't believe Miss Ethel didn't tell me," he argued, slumping in his chair. The group sat around a table at Grimm's before it opened.

"So, what are you going to do?" Jaxon asked.

"I'm going to keep working on the Bellamy House grounds." Seeing a few raised eyebrows as well as grins, he said, "She may have fired me but I'm not abandoning her. There's work to be done and I'm going to do it."

"And..." Jayden prompted.

"And I plan on a lot of groveling, explaining, begging... and just hoping that her feelings for me outweigh her hurt, because mine absolutely do."

"Sounds like a plan," Cael said, leaning his large body back in his chair. "You know, if you need help from any of us, you just gotta call."

Nodding, he shot a tight smile at his brothers, hoping his optimism was not misplaced.

"Thank you. I'll be in touch."

Eleanor disconnected while perched on the kitchen chair, her breath leaving her lungs in a whoosh. Sucking in her lips, she waited for the sense of panic, but only mild nerves landed in the pit of her stomach. *I can do this. I have to do this.*

Sally stood by the kitchen counter, her face unreadable. "Are you sure about this?"

Nodding slowly, she placed her hands on the table in front of her, pushing herself to a stand. Taking her coffee cup to the sink, she said, "Yes. It's time for a change, Sally. Time for me to move on with my life."

Sally stepped forward, lifting her hand to squeeze Eleanor's shoulder. "Well then, you have my support as well."

They embraced for a moment before a loud noise from outside jolted them apart. "What is that?" Eleanor stalked to the window near the front of the house and stared in shock. "Seriously?"

"What is it?" Sally asked, coming up beside her.

"Him!"

"Who?"

"Rafe. I thought you told him his services were no longer needed."

"I did. In fact, yesterday, before you came back from Miss Ethel's, I went to the cottage to clean it out. It was spic and span, he was definitely moved out."

"Well, since you are on your way out, would you mind telling him, again, to leave."

Sally did not say anything, causing Eleanor to look over her shoulder at her housekeeper bending to gather her bag. "Please? I know I'm not the only one hurt, but I need more time," she added.

"Of course, sweetie."

Satisfied, Eleanor dropped the drapery, refusing to stare at Rafe anymore. Kissing Sally's cheek, she turned to move into her father's study, ready to make another phone call.

Rafe shucked his shirt, the mid-summer sun beating down on his back. Using his booted foot on the shovel, he widened the hole. Once satisfied, he bent to pick up the small blue spruce, burying its ball of roots before filling in with more soil.

Standing back, he grinned at the small row of trees, all about five feet tall, ready to form another backdrop for a shade garden. The sound of someone clearing their throat had him whirling around. Seeing Sally, he dipped his head in greeting. "Ms. Sally."

She stood, her back straight, hands clasped in front of her. "Mr. Walker. I have been sent to inform you that your services are still no longer needed and Ms. Bellamy requests that you leave the property."

He grinned, leaning on the handle of the shovel, one booted foot crossed in front of the other. "Well, Ms. Sally, the way I see it, I'm not employed anymore, but she didn't say anything about me not doing a little volunteer work on the grounds. And I know for a fact that she needs help with her lawn, so I feel compelled to offer my services."

Her lips quirked and it appeared she was trying to hide a smile. "Mr. Walker, I think it can be surmised that your presence, in any capacity, is not wanted here."

"I appreciate your orders, but until Ms. Bellamy tells

me herself that she doesn't want me here, I think I'll just keep volunteering my time taking care of her lawn."

At that, Sally's lips curved into a full-blown smile and she offered a nod toward him. "Then I bid you goodbye." She turned and walked to her car without going back inside the house.

"Mr. Thomas, as always it's been a pleasure," Eleanor said, satisfied with her phone call to her attorney. "If you'll have Mr. Hayden call me directly, I'll talk to him myself."

"Are you sure, Ms. Bellamy?" he asked. "I want you to be very sure about this before you make a decision."

"I am. It's time for me to take charge and start dealing with people directly. Not," she hastened to add, "that I won't still need you. But, this is something I want to do myself."

"I understand," he agreed, before they finished their call.

Settling deeper into the cushions of the sofa, she leaned her head back, the idea of a nap taking over. Just then the rumble of the gas-powered hedge trimmers sounded, jarring her eyes open. Stomping to the window, she pulled the draperies back, no longer trying to be discrete. She jumped at the sight of Rafe, shirtless, his muscles on magnificent display, right outside her window. As his arms lifted the heavy trimmers, she was mesmerized by the play of muscles under the tattoos on his arms and abs. With her lips pinched together, she glared at him, only to be met with a white-toothed grin and nod. When it was obvious he was not going to stop to give her time to berate him, she dropped the curtain and stomped out of the room, moving to her father's study.

An hour later, she walked into the kitchen, ready to make a sandwich. *I wonder if Rafe is hungry—no, stop it. He can get his own food!* As she plopped her plate onto the counter, she realized it was now quiet outside. Biting her lip, she made her way back over to the window near the front door, but did not see him at all. Leaning to the side, she tried to see if his truck was still in the drive. Unable to tell, she threw open the front door and could finally see that he had left. A strange sense of loss filled her. Turning to head back inside, her eye caught something pink near the door, lying on a piece of paper.

A small rose. The stem neatly trimmed, the soft, pale petals beckoning her. Bending, she picked it up, holding it to her nose, breathing deeply. The delicate scent of the natural blossom swirled around her, filling her senses. Opening the folds of paper, she read,

"But he who dares not grasp the thorn should never crave the rose." — Anne Brontë

Unable to keep the corners of her lips from curving upward, she stepped back inside the house.

27

Rafe, determined to take care of the grounds of Bellamy House despite Eleanor's objections, was on the riding mower, moving back and forth over the lawn. A truck with Hayden Development Company emblazoned on the side pulled into the driveway. *Hayden Development? The man who was trying to strong-arm her into selling?*

Shutting off the mower before jumping down, he stalked toward the house in time to catch a short, stocky man standing at the front door. Before he could get closer, the front door opened and Eleanor smiled her welcome as she invited the man into her home. "Mr. Hayden. Thank you for coming. Please, let's go into the study." She eyed Rafe as he walked closer, but simply smiled just before closing the door in his face.

For thirty minutes he paced outside, fuming at the thought of Eleanor inside with the slick-talking developer. Fighting the urge to knock the door down and force his way inside, he continued pacing.

Suddenly, the front door opened again and Mr. Hayden walked out, turning back to shake Eleanor's hand.

"Nice to do business with you, Ms. Bellamy." He smiled at Rafe as he walked back to his truck.

Eleanor nodded toward Rafe as she turned and started to close the front door, finding it blocked with his large boot.

"What the hell are you doing, Eleanor? Hayden Development? Are you crazy?"

Looking up into his irate face, she felt the heat of anger rising. "Excuse me? It is not your place to question what I do as the owner of Bellamy House."

"You're going to sell your family home? Why would you do that? What are you running from?"

She reared back, his words a slap in the face. "Running from? I'm not running from anything."

"Then why are you selling?"

Poking her finger at her chest, she said, "I'm doing what I need to do to survive. You have no say in what I do."

"Even after all we became to each other?"

"What did we become, Rafe? As I remember it, I bared my soul to you and you never even told me what you did for a living." Before he had a chance to retort, she slammed the door in his face, throwing the lock.

On quivering legs, she walked into the formal living room, slumping down onto the sofa. Her gaze wandered to the family portrait over the mantle, the vision of her parents and brother. Captured in time, they peered down at her and her chest squeezed as it always did when she took the time to think of what she had lost. A tear slid down her cheek as she sucked in a shuddering breath. Thinking of Rafe, she angrily wiped it away, determined to chart her own course.

After a simple dinner alone, she walked out onto the

terrace, hoping the sight of the sunset would bring her peace. Stepping onto the stone patio, she viewed the ever-changing sky as the sun fell behind the trees. Leaning her head back, she closed her eyes, inhaled deeply, and let the cares of the day drift away. Sighing, she dropped her chin and moved toward the chaise lounge to watch the fireflies dancing across the lawn.

As she approached the chair, she noticed a single, peach rose on the seat, with another piece of folded paper. The stem was neatly trimmed and the blossom perfect in every way. Bending, she picked it up and allowing the fragrance to waft by, she opened the paper, reading,

"Then he kissed her. At his lips' touch she blossomed like a flower and the incarnation was complete." The Great Gatsby by F. Scott Fitzgerald

Unable to keep the smile off her face, she settled into the chair, the note on her lap and the rose resting over her heart.

For the next week, Rafe appeared every day in Eleanor's gardens. One day, mowing the expansive lawn. Another day, planting flowers in the many flower beds. Another day, continuing his work on the terrace trellis, now weaving jasmine plants amongst the wooden support pillars.

And at the end of each day, after he left, Eleanor stepped out onto the terrace to find another rose, neatly trimmed, lying there waiting for her. Red. Yellow. White.

Each day, she gathered the bloom close to her heart, the delicate scent so familiar. At the end of the week, she peered out of the family room door to see Rafe on a ladder, tying vines to the trellis. He was creating a beautiful haven for her, even better than it had been before the storm.

She headed to the kitchen to fix a sandwich, hesitating for only a moment before fixing a second, much larger, one. Plating it first, she carried it and a bottle of water to the family room, wavering in her decision before taking the plunge and opening the door. Avoiding his gaze, she moved to a small table and set the plate down.

Turning to head back inside, his voice halted her feet.

"Eleanor."

The one word caused an ache in her chest. Casting a glance at him over her shoulder, she forced out a thin-lipped smile. "Thought you might like lunch."

"Thank you," Rafe said, hurrying down from the ladder, his heart pounding at the sight of her. His hands clenched at his side, the desire to reach to her overwhelming. "Uh…will you join me? Sit with me?"

He watched her eyes dart from him to the table and back to him again, uncertainty moving through them.

Finally, she shook her head slowly, her gaze moving to his. "No…I don't think…no." With that, she hurried back inside, shutting the patio doors with a soft click.

Disappointed, he looked at the plate and water bottle, a smile beginning to curve his lips. *It's a start.*

Much to his delight, a new habit formed. She brought him lunch each day and he continued to leave a rose for her. Each day when she walked out with a plate, he asked her the same question. "Will you sit with me?"

After a week of turning him down, Eleanor stood in the kitchen, his sandwich ready. She stared at the plate and thought of her conversation with Sally that morning.

Sally had watched Rafe working in the yard and

turned to Eleanor saying, "Are you ever going to give him another chance?" At her silence, Sally continued. "That man out there? You judged him guilty—and I did too, I know, but Eleanor, I realized my mistake and I apologized. But you never gave him a chance to explain. Or apologize. Or even tell you what was going on in his life."

Planting her hand on her hip, she had countered, "I was hurt...duped into thinking he was something he wasn't—"

"And what would you have done if he told you the first day, 'Hey, I'm a famous model who's trying to get back to my roots this summer'? What would you have done?"

"I...I would have stayed away."

"Why?"

"Because...because...I don't know. Because someone like him would have never wanted to be around someone with my scars."

"And you would have judged him without getting to know him. Just what you hate people doing to you."

She had opened and closed her mouth several times, thoughts swirling through her mind. "You're right," she breathed out. "He gave me time to tell my story, but I never gave him the same chance."

Now, alone in her kitchen, she thought of what she should do to make this right. Miss Ethel had said something so similar to Sally. *"You're not taking into account who he is, instead of pressing a societal idea of who you think he should be."* If he had told her right away, she would have judged him and made assumptions without giving him a chance. Something he said others did to him all the time. *Something I did too after seeing that article.*

Steeling her resolve, she placed her sandwich, along with his, on a tray with two bottles of water and moved to the terrace. Stepping out, she was disappointed not to see him. With slumped shoulders, she set the tray down.

"Hey!" he called from above.

Jumping back, she jerked her head up, eyes wide as she peered at him in the trellis above her head.

"Sorry, I saw you had lunch and didn't want to scare you until you had a chance to set it down." Rafe deftly jumped down and wiped his hands on a rag from his pocket, his eyes alive at the sight of two plates on the tray. "Will you join me?" he asked, his heart in his throat.

Nodding, Eleanor offered a slight smile. "Yes...I will." His wide smile hit her in the chest, and she sucked in a quick breath at the response. Moving to one of the chairs, she sat hastily, taking the plate with the smaller sandwich in her hands.

He moved to the chair closest to her and did the same. After several minutes of eating in silence, she ventured, "The terrace looks lovely. You know you don't have—"

"Thank you," he interrupted. "I want it to be a haven for you." Rafe hoped she would decide not to sell her home if he could convince her it was still a safe place, inwardly cursing at the hidden photographer once more.

Nodding, not knowing what to say, she kept chewing.

Clearing his throat, he said, "I...I need to let you know how sorry I am...about everything."

Silence.

Continuing, he said, "I never meant to deceive you."

"I know that now," she said, her voice belying her nerves.

Scrubbing his hand over his face, Rafe set his empty plate on the table and leaned forward. Placing his forearms on his knees, his hands clasped together tightly, he studied his muddy boots for a moment. With a heavy sigh, he looked up, saying, "I never meant to hurt you. This summer...was supposed to be about me getting away from a life that I was no longer happy with. A chance to do something purposeful. Maybe a chance to walk in my father's shoes." He held her gaze as he added, "But falling for you was never part of the plan."

Swallowing deeply, she remained motionless, her face giving away nothing.

"For weeks, we had no contact. I thought I was working for an elderly, shut-in friend of Miss Ethel's. But that night...when I heard you sing, it drew me out. It made me feel...feel things I hadn't felt in a long time. The work had already given me a purpose but when I met you, you gave me freedom."

Her brow lowered. "Freedom?"

"The freedom to just be me. Not Rafe, the model. Rafe, the body. Rafe, the face. You gave me the freedom to just be Rafe, the friend, the groundskeeper."

"And lover?" she asked.

"Yes," he enthused, reaching out and taking her hands in his, elated when she did not pull them away. "You were falling for the real me. The man, not the reputation."

"The article—"

"Baby, if I could get my hands on the person who took that picture, they'd never take another picture the rest of their lives!"

She jerked at his vehemence, but felt his righteous anger. Finally, giving a slight shrug, she sighed. "I'm sorry for losing sight of who you are after reading the article. For not giving you time and understanding, like you gave me. For taking one look at that article and believing the worst." Sighing, she added, "Rafe, I'm also sorry that I can't stop seeing that picture and reading those words. As much as they hurt, they're true. You are beautiful. The world looks at that picture and sees me as a pity fu—"

"Don't you say it," he growled. "Don't you dare sully what we had."

"It's not me, Rafe. Don't you get it? I've been the subject of stares and whispers since I got back."

"The only thing that matters, Eleanor, is how you feel about yourself. You're standing in your own way by not seeing how beautiful you are. The beauty, inside and out, that I see. Everyone else can be damned."

"I hear you, but my ego took a beating," she admitted. "Actually, it's been pummeled for a while. I suppose it will take a while for that to heal."

"I'll do anything to help you see yourself as I see you, as you really are," he vowed, his hand sliding down her arm to grasp her fingers, remaining quietly watchful. "And to build your trust in me, too."

She thought for a moment and then said, "Can you tell me about your life, the one in California? If we're going to build something new, then I need to know all about Rafe Walker, not just the bits you choose to share."

28

Rafe leaned back in his chair, scrubbing his hand over his face. He hated exposing her to the world he used to exist in but it was too late for that. Mostly, he hated to face what she would think of him once she knew, but, he realized they had no chance of creating a new relationship if he was not honest. Sucking in a deep breath, he let it out slowly before he began.

"I've told you of growing up and joining the military, but I never told you much about my time in the Army. I was a mechanic, not because of any great love for trucks, just small engines, especially the ones like Miss Ethel let me use in the yard and garden. I used to take them apart and fix them when they broke." Shrugging, he said, "Figured I scored high enough on the mechanical part of the ASVAB, so that's the training I did. The work was physical, but we also had some downtime. By then, I was a big guy and we had weights we worked with. I bulked up even more and got in good shape."

Blowing out his breath, he continued. "One day, a group of us were shittin' around, working out without our shirts on, flexing our muscles, playing volleyball or something and a photographer came by to take some shots. At first it was just for an article on how soldiers spend their downtime, but this guy got excited and wanted to know if we would be interested in posing for a calendar. You know, hunky soldier kind of crap." He felt the burn of the blush on his face but he forged ahead. "We all said sure and the next thing I know, I was Mr. July. The damn thing went viral, some video of our photo shoot ended up on YouTube and Facebook. I figured that was it...fifteen minutes of fame. And we sure as hell only got paid about fifty bucks each and I know that calendar made tens of thousands of dollars for the guy who put it together."

He hesitated at her eyes, wide with surprise, as she shook her head, mumbling, "Mr. July?"

Blushing more, he nodded. "I only had about three more months left and I wasn't going to re-enlist. Zander was getting out and I wanted to head to Virginia. I had no clue what I was going to do, but I wanted to get back to my roots. I ended up getting an offer to do some modeling by an agent who saw the calendar. Figured, 'Why not?', and the next thing I know, I'm off to California. The modeling contracts came in and I kept doing it. Seemed like easy money and at first that was great. Then I got a big contract with a designer of men's swimwear and the next thing I know, my body is plastered all over magazines."

Eleanor watched his face carefully, noting the unease at his confessions. So far, there was nothing he had told her that gave her concern. Reaching over, she placed her hand on his leg. "It all makes sense, Rafe. I can see getting excited about the money and the freedom it gave you."

Rafe's heart clenched at her trust and, for an instant, he considered leaving the rest of it out, but dismissed that thought. Not only would an internet search show her more, but she deserved to know it all from him. *If she's going to take me back, she's got to know who all I used to be.*

"There's more, babe, but this is the part that's hard to admit." He watched with dismay as her hand left his leg and she sat back in her chair, visibly steeling herself.

"There was a certain lifestyle that went along with the modeling world. I had moved quickly into the national spotlight as far as modeling went and the invites poured in. Parties, being seen with actresses, red carpet escorting. I swear, I did not let it go to my head, but I sure as hell made some poor choices."

"Poor choices?"

Nodding, he dropped his chin to his chest as he rested his forearms on his thighs. Flashes of the parties bolted through his mind as he sifted through what to tell her. "Parties...lots of drinking...drugs, but I swear not by me. I never used drugs. But, alcohol was used to excess."

"And..."

Clearing his throat, he lifted his head as he admitted, "Women. A few famous, but mostly just groupies. They were looking to say they were with a model and for us, it was...just easy." His chest burned as he observed the understanding dawning in her eyes, followed by the wary coolness emanating from her.

"It was a lifestyle that I kept up for about a year and then I began to see how shallow it was. I hated it and withdrew into my own little existence. I lived alone in a small efficiency and only had two other good friends I would hang out with."

"And Cherelle Parkinson?"

Blowing out his breath, he shook his head. "My agent thought we looked perfect together and so we were photographed a lot, everywhere we went. A big mistake. We went on a few dates, but she was not my type. Fake, plastic, manipulative. I cut it off, but it took longer for her to get the message."

Her face paled, as she whispered, "Perfect...perfect together. I can see that." Shaking her head, she leaped up from the chair, backing away.

"No, Eleanor, please don't do this. She...none of them mean anything to me," he begged, jumping up as well, his hands fisting to his sides as he fought to reach out to her.

A tear slid down her cheek as she swallowed deeply. "All that was before me, Rafe, so I can't condemn your life-style, what you did, or who you did it with. But, don't you see? The world expects you to be with someone perfect. Someone...not like me."

"Not the world, baby. Just those who think they can continue to make money off me. But my friends, your friends, the people that care about us as real people...they don't have any expectations other than wanting us to be happy. And baby, you make me happy."

He stepped forward until she had to lean her head back to keep her gaze on his. Eleanor stared at his face for a long time, seeing nothing but sincerity in his eyes. Letting out a long, slow breath, she nodded before planting her forehead on his chest. Turning her face as he wrapped his arms around her, she felt his heartbeat against her cheek. "I know I've got a long way to go to gain my confidence," she admitted, her soft voice barely heard over the breeze.

"Baby, think of how far you've come since your injury. You survived. You were beaten down, again and again, but you survived. I'm here. I'm not going anywhere. That life is over for me and you are my future, if you'll have me."

Nodding, she started to pull back but he held her close. "There's one more thing I want to tell you."

Eleanor turned weary eyes to him, not sure if she could take much more.

"When I was a kid, early teens, the awkward stage hit me hard. I was lanky with big hands and big feet. There was this other kid, Dickie, and he made it his mission in life to torture me, calling me names. Shrek, ogre...beast." Her eyes wide, he cupped her cheek in his hand, "I can't say I know exactly what you're going through, not even close. But trust me when I say, the only people whose opinions matter are those you care about and those you love. But even more than that, is the opinion you have of yourself."

She stepped back, linking her hands with his. Looking down at her scarred hand, now nestled in his, she heard the conviction in his voice. With a little squeeze, she replied, "I guess I'll see you tomorrow." Turning to leave, she added, "I suppose if you are going to keep working here, you should move back into the cottage."

A smile spread across his face, watching her walk back into the house.

That night, she found another rose in the chair, this one accompanied with,

"I would rather look at you than all the portraits in the world..." Having a Coke With You by Frank O'Hara

---

Rafe hauled his duffle bag back into the cottage, the warm space greeting him as an old friend. He had no idea if this would lead to Eleanor back in his life as anything more than an employer, but he planned on earning her trust day by day.

Hearing a truck coming along the driveway, he stepped out onto the front stoop and looked up toward the manor. He watched as a Hayden Development truck pulled up and parked. *How the hell can she still be thinking of selling her family home?* The knowledge that she was so upset from a photographer with a long-range lens capturing her image that she was willing to give up something that meant so much to her, scored through him.

Stalking up the hill, toward the front door, he watched as Eleanor opened the door to Mr. Hayden, welcomed the man inside and closed the door before he could reach it. Standing in the middle of the lawn, his hands on his hips, he cursed loud and long before stomping to the tool garage. In the crowded space, he turned around, uncertain what to work on today. *Hell, if she's selling, why does it matter what I do?*

Dropping his chin to his chest, he slowed his breathing. *Trust. I have to trust that she knows what she's doing.* Loading the trailer with bags of mulch, he drove out to the flowerbeds, ready to start work.

Making sure to be on the terrace at lunchtime, Rafe smiled as Eleanor walked outside, another tray in her hand. Rushing to take it from her, he placed it on the small table, having pre-arranged the seats to be close together. "Here, let me get that for you."

Eleanor's lips twitched as she nodded, taking the seat indicated, realizing it put her scarred side closest to him... and that didn't bother her. "I made a pie earlier. I thought you might like a piece." If his enthusiastic smile was anything to go by, her idea was a good one.

Eating in companionable silence, Rafe appreciated the two sandwiches, chips, apple slices, and pie. Swallowing, he said, "You don't have to feed me, you know. I'd be satisfied to just sit with you."

"Rafe, we may not be what we were, but feeding you is not a hardship," she smiled.

He nodded, laying his fork down. "Can I ask you something?"

Tilting her head to the side in curiosity, she nodded.

"Can we ever get back to what we were?"

Eleanor sat for a moment, fiddling with her pie. Sucking in her lips, she said, "I don't think so, Rafe." She saw his face fall, but quickly added, "But that doesn't mean we can't build something new."

He eyed her warily, waiting for her to continue.

"When we became close before, you couldn't see me, so you had a chance to get to know me without the external scars...or internal scars, getting in the way. For me, I saw you as..." a crease knit her brow as she searched for the right words. "I...uh...don't know. Certainly not someone world famous."

"Would that have mattered? It was still me," he said, his eyes pleading.

A long pause filled the air between them as she considered his words, finding, to her chagrin that he was right. With another heavy sigh leaving her lips, she agreed. "You're right. It was my insecurities that made me reject you. At first, I was so thrown by the nasty headline that it was easy to cast that blame on you. But, that wasn't fair."

He leaned closer, careful, as though with a skittish

animal. "And now...can you just see me as you did? A man who wants someone, who's not impressed by all that fool's gold, and just see me."

She held his eyes, their soulful depths calling to her. His face, so handsome, and yet with a childlike quality of someone who wanted to be loved. Without thinking, she lifted her scarred hand and cupped his stubbled jaw. As soon as her fingers touched his skin, she sucked in a quick breath as the warmth moved through her, straight to her chest. Heart pounding, she said, "I can see the real you... but what happens when the glitter calls again and you're surrounded by people who don't want you to be with me? Who only see me as—"

"I'm not going back to that life."

She blinked slowly, her head jerking slightly.

"My modeling contract is over and I don't want that life anymore. It was empty. It was cold. I was wanted for a body, that was considered my only commodity."

A smile slipped across her lips and she said, "Well, it is a good body."

Leaning another inch closer, he said, "You're the only one I want to be impressed now. Yours is the only opinion about my body that I care about." His lips were barely a whisper apart from hers, but he hesitated, only wanting to take what she was willing to give.

Her breath halted in her lungs as she watched him move closer and then stop. She felt lightheaded, desire curling through her body. She met his lips, giving over to the pull. The kiss was soft, gentle. His lips molded to hers and his tongue slipped inside as she moaned. He moved one hand to her waist, his calloused fingers flexing against her hip.

He slowly leaned back an inch, her head following in

an attempt to stay connected. He smiled at her slight mewl of discontent when their lips were no longer touching. Seeing her eyes widen, he explained, "I just want us to get to know each other again. This isn't about sex, but about a deeper caring. I want you to trust me…trust that I'll always take care of you."

Forcing his legs to stand, which was no easy feat considering the hard-on he sported, Rafe took the now-empty tray and carried it to the door, ushering her inside. "It's getting hot, sweetheart. Stay in where it's cool." With one last kiss, he watched her go inside.

That evening, another rose was left for Eleanor to cherish along with another note.

"In vain I have struggled. It will not do. My feelings will not be repressed. You must allow me to tell you how ardently I admire and love you." Pride and Prejudice by Jane Austen

---

The sun had dipped below the horizon and Rafe sat in the small living area of the cottage reading, the room lit by a lamp next to the sofa. The room—and the activity—felt familiar and yet, lonely. He missed the evenings spent with Eleanor at his side as they read and chatted together. He looked back down at the book in his hand when a knock on the door startled him. Hopeful, his heart raced as he moved quickly to the door, throwing it open.

His heart did not slow down at the sight of her standing there, looking utterly adorable and ever-so uncertain.

"Hey," she greeted, her voice breathy.

"Hey," he greeted in return, his hand still on the doorknob, hope flaring in his chest.

"Um...can I come in?"

Jumping back, he felt the heat crawl over his face at his gaffe. "God, sorry. Yes, yes, come in. I was just thinking about you."

She walked by, the slight rose scent from her hair wafting by. "And here I am," she smiled.

"And here you are." Uncertainty now filled him as they stood awkwardly in the small room. "Did you need something?"

"No...not really. I just thought I'd make sure you have moved back in again. I was quite foolish to have asked you to leave."

Stepping closer, he replied, "You were hurt, upset... and rightfully so. Please sit with me." He took her hand and led her to the sofa, watching as she curled up on one end, facing him.

She looked down at the book on the coffee table and a smile brightened her face. "Charlotte's Web? I love that book!"

"Yeah, me too. It was one Zander read to us as kids. I always just thought of it as a children's book. I mean, it is, but..."

Nodding her understand, she asked, "Will you read to me? I've missed that."

Smiling, he picked it up again and began to read, relieved when she settled deep into the cushions, her eyes dancing. As the tale of Charlotte and Wilbur unfolded, he smiled.

"The barn was very large. It was very old. It smelled of hay and it smelled of manure. It smelled of the perspiration of tired horses and the wonderful sweet breath of patient cows.

It often had a sort of peaceful smell—as though nothing bad could happen ever again in the world."

He grinned, looking over at her. "You know, this is how I felt about Bellamy House when I first came here."

Pretending to be insulted, she placed her hand over her heart. "Are you saying you thought my home smelled like manure?"

"No, no," he laughed, happy to see her smile. "I just meant that it's as though nothing bad could ever happen here."

Settling back, Rafe's deep voice filled Eleanor as he continued to read.

"You have been my friend. That in itself is a tremendous thing...By helping you, perhaps I was trying to lift up my life a trifle. Heaven knows anyone's life can stand a little of that."

Rafe's eyes moved from the page to Eleanor's and observed her watching him closely. "I think I know what the author was trying to say. The help I gave you, here at Bellamy House, was really lifting up my own life."

"Is that why you kept coming back, even when I first told you to leave?"

Nodding, he said, "Yeah. I couldn't leave you alone. I didn't want you here by yourself. I couldn't stand the idea that I was still mired in the muck of my former life. Helping you, helped me."

Eleanor peered into his eyes, the light from the lamp illuminating their depths. "How can this work, Rafe?" she asked, her voice tortured.

"You and me? Oh, babe, we just become us...that's all we need to do."

Huffing, she said, "To quote Charlotte's Web, 'Most people believe anything they see in print.' You and I would always face that kind of cruel comparison. Your beauty to my beast."

He reached his hand to cup her face, his fingertips skimming the scars on her neck. "Oh, sweetheart, you can't let what others say interfere with what we have." He bent forward to place a soft kiss on her lips before pulling back, still seeing the doubt in her eyes. Picking up the book again, he began to flip pages until he found what he was looking for.

"Then you got up all your nerve, took a deep breath, and jumped. For a second you seemed to be falling to the barn floor far below, but then suddenly the rope would begin to catch you, and you would sail through the barn door going a mile a minute, with the wind whistling in your eyes and ears and hair. Then you would zoom upward into the sky, and look up at the clouds, and the rope would twist and you would twist and turn with the rope."

"Don't you see, Eleanor. I'll be your rope. You can take that leap of faith and I'll always catch you."

A single tear slid down her cheek as she sucked in her lips.

"And please, baby, please, don't sell your family home. I know everything seemed bleak but—"

Her sudden intake of breath halted his words. "Oh, Rafe, I would never sell Bellamy House."

His brow creased in confusion. "But, Hayden Development? The bastard's been here talking to you."

"He's not a bastard...honestly. I'm not going to sell Bellamy House to him. But I have been talking to him about something. I just wasn't sure I was ready."

"And you haven't been able to talk to me about whatever's going on?" he asked, the hurt obvious in his voice.

Reaching out to touch his face, she wiped her finger

over his frown. "There are some things I needed to do on my own. Figure out on my own. I needed to trust you again before I shared them."

"And do you?"

Nodding slowly, she whispered, "Yes. Even before you said you would catch me, I knew I had to learn to fly on my own again. Take chances." A small smile curved the corners of her lips and a light pink blush touched her cheeks. "But now...now that I know you'll catch me, I know I can do it."

"What are you planning on doing?" he asked, shifting his body so that he could see deep into her eyes.

She shifted her gaze away, staring at nothing, seeing the past. "When I was finally discharged from rehabilitation, I came back here, to my home. To the world, I might have hidden away here, but for me it was the only place I wanted to be. Even though being here meant I was faced with the loss of my family every day, I felt closer to them here than anywhere else I could have run to."

Watching him nod, she sucked in a deep breath before plunging into the next part of her idea. "I've toyed with an idea of how to help others for a long time, but could never seem to pin down any particular way. But slowly, being with you...helping you when you were injured, I knew I had to step back into the land of the living."

She gazed into his face, explaining, "I own acres of land that extend way beyond what you see here. Mr. Hayden is working up a proposal for my lawyer and me to look over. I want to take part of the land nearest the river and build a large rehabilitation center for veteran burn victims. For veterans who have completed their hospital and VA rehabilitation, but aren't quite ready to go back home, or don't have a home. It would have apartments and efficiencies, depending on what they need. Visiting nurses, physical and occupational therapists, employee trainers can come as well. It's ambitious and I'm nervous about putting myself out there—"

He grabbed her cheeks, pulling her in for a deep kiss, mumbling, "Oh, God…so fucking proud of you."

Eleanor reveled in his kiss, his lips bringing her cold ones to life. Pulling back, she held his gaze saying, "It's just in the initial planning stages."

Smiling, he said, "Babe, you jump and I'll be your rope. But just remember…you'll zoom upwards."

Her heart leaped with his words. Nodding, she threw herself into his arms.

29

Rafe's lips crashed into Eleanor's, the book falling to the floor as their bodies pressed together. She climbed over the cushions, crawling into his lap. With one hand on her ass he kept her in place, her core tucked against his cock, and the other hand wrapped around her back, pressing her breasts against his chest.

She clutched his hair before sliding her hands around his neck and down his back. Kissing until they needed to separate for air, her chest heaved as she drew in a shuddering breath. She shifted slightly, rubbing her breasts against his firm chest, need pooling in her core.

In a surprisingly fast movement, she grabbed the bottom of her shirt and whipped it over her head, her breasts bouncing right in front of him with the motion. Rafe's eyes devoured the mounds spilling over the top of her light blue bra.

"Are you trying to kill me?" he groaned, bending his head to capture a satin-covered nipple. Sucking, then nipping at the tender flesh, he smiled as a groan slipped from her lips.

Eleanor brought her hands up, unsnapping her bra, wanting nothing between them. She threw her head back, thrusting her breasts, like a gift, to him. Rafe shifted her higher on his lap, his cock aching to be free, but willed it to wait as he feasted on her breasts, sucking first one and then the other.

Eleanor's body quivered as she moved on his lap, his hard erection prodding her. He mumbled, his mouth still pressed against her skin and she leaned back slightly to see his face, raw with need. Taking charge, she pushed her palms against his chest, sliding backward off his lap. Standing, she slid her pants down, snagging her panties as they went.

Rafe's breath caught in his throat at the vision of Eleanor's naked beauty on full display. Grinning, he leaned forward to snag her back into his lap, but she skirted out of his grip.

Lifting her finger, waggling it in his face, she taunted, "Uh-uh. Not until you are as bare-ass naked as me."

Leering, he jumped to his feet, laughing as she backed away another foot. Loving the smile on her face, he decided to tease her a little more. "You want this, babe?" he asked, his fingers slowly moving to the bottom of his shirt.

"Hurry," she demanded.

"You want it faster, you come get it."

"Aughhh," she cried, running over to grab his t-shirt, trying to tug it over his head.

Whooping, he scooped her up into his arms and stalked into the bedroom. Laying her down he was filled with the memory of the first time they made love in this very room. Only, this time, it was with a much more at ease, playful Eleanor.

Unable to take the waiting, she bounced off the bed, her hands flying to the zipper on his jeans. He stood, feet planted wide, hands on his hips, grinning. "Come and get it, babe."

Shooting him a sexy smirk, she carefully lowered the zipper, her eyes devouring him as she pushed the denim and boxers down, freeing his erect cock. Thick and long, she took him in her hand, feeling powerful as his breath hissed through his teeth.

Dropping to her knees, she slipped her lips around the head, licking as she slowly took him into her warm mouth. Moving up and down his shaft, she bobbed her head, stopping occasionally as her tongue swirled around the head.

Rafe's hands grasped her head, his fingers tangling in her hair as her silky tresses flowed around her shoulders. "Jesus, baby," he groaned, the sensation overwhelming him as all thoughts centered on his dick. Finally, realizing he was just about to come, he jerked out, his cock bouncing as he lifted her from the rug. "Turn about's fair play," he said, laying her back on the bed before dropping to his knees.

Carefully placing her legs over his shoulders, he exposed her delicate flesh to his close perusal, the pink lips and engorged nub beckoning him. Hearing her gasp, he looked up as he licked her slick folds and grinned, seeing her head bounce back to the mattress.

Eleanor lay exposed, yet instead of self-conscious fear, all she felt was admired. And then, as his tongue took another swipe, all she felt was her sex quivering as sweet oblivion sent her spiraling.

Rafe felt her body shake as her orgasm rushed over her and he continued his ministration until she was still, her legs now laying to the side. Crawling over her body, he grinned, looking down at her hooded eyes, her body now limp. His hips settled between her thighs, nudging them apart as his cock nestled against her core.

Her languid eyes opened, a slow smile curving her lips. As her hands moved over his shoulders, fingers digging in, she welcomed him into her body. The fullness and pressure of his cock moving deep inside awakened her again, as electricity seemed to jolt from her breasts to her core.

Rafe, lost in the sensations of her tight inner walls milking him, suddenly was aware he was unsheathed. "Shit," he growled, starting to pull out.

"No," she protested, her fingers grasping at his back as her heels dug into his ass.

"Babe, I forgot a condom," he moaned, his body screaming to plunge back in as he forced himself to move away.

"I'm on the pill," she said, still trying to hold him in place. "I'm clean...there's been no one but you...not since I was injured several years ago."

"I promise I'm clean too," he vowed. "Honest to God, Eleanor, I didn't live a wild life in California. I wasn't a monk, but I never went without a condom. I was just tested not long before I came home to Virginia...I can show you—"

"I trust you," she interrupted, her eyes now wide, holding his gaze. Her lips curved and she repeated, "I trust you. We have nothing between us now. No secrets. Just you and me."

His heart leaped as his chest heaved with emotion. Bending, he kissed her lips, slow and sweet, as he gently plunged his aching cock back inside. Long strokes, in and out, flesh against flesh, her soft against his hard. Resting his weight on his forearms, he cradled her head in his hands, kissing her lips as their bodies joined.

Eyes open, they stared as the emotions swirled about them and their bodies hurdled toward climax. Chest heaving, her nipples grazed his chest as his hips ground against her clit.

"You close, baby?"

Panting was her only response, until she jerked her head back, biting her bottom lip as the waves of her orgasm crashed, the tremors shooting from her core through every nerve in her body.

"Jesus," he cried as he joined her, his cock pulsating inside her, filling her with his seed as he pressed his hips further into her soft body until every drop was drained. "Fuck, baby, fuck," he groaned, rolling to her side, his massive arms pulling her in tight. Reaching down, he grabbed the blanket at the bottom of the bed and jerked it over their sweat soaked bodies.

Tucking her head underneath his chin, he wrapped his arms around her much smaller body, feeling her tangle her legs with his. Perfect...she fit perfectly with him.

Her cheek pressed next to his pounding heartbeat, Eleanor listened as it slowed, a smile firmly in place.

Hours later, Rafe awoke and felt the warm body curled up in his arms, smiling as his hands trailed a path over her skin. He was learning the dips and curves, memorizing each one. He felt the rough patches of scarred skin, noticing she did not flinch when he moved his fingers over them.

"I can't really feel that," she said, lifting her head off his chest to peer down at him. "The scar tissue deadens the nerve endings."

He nodded, watching her carefully to see if she was upset, but she gifted him with a little smile. "It's okay, Rafe. I'm not going to fall apart. I just thought I'd let you know why some areas are sensitive and others aren't."

Moving his head, he kissed her, smiling as she laid her head back on his chest. Eleanor felt his chest rise and fall quickly as though he was about to say something and then change his mind. Waiting patiently, she knew he would speak when he was ready.

Finally, he said, "Eleanor?"

"Yeah, honey?"

"I'd really like you to meet my friends. Maybe somewhere safe, like at Miss Ethel's." He held his breath, waiting for her response.

Her hand splayed over his thick chest, her fingers tracing his tattoos. "I'd like that."

"Really?"

Laughing, she leaned up again. "I can't say it doesn't scare me, because I really want them to like me. But, if I'm going to join the world again, I guess I'd better start."

Rafe looked to the side, seeing Eleanor wipe her palms on her pants again. Reaching over, he took her hand. "It's gonna be fine."

She shot him a quick nod. "I know. It's just that this will be the most people I've been around for a while."

"Babe, if you're not ready, we can call 'em and let them have lunch without us. It's no big deal—"

"No, no," she rushed. "I need to do this. I want to do this."

They soon parked on the street in front of the familiar house, seeing a few trucks, SUVs, and a couple of motorcycles already in the area. He jogged around to her side, assisting her down. His gaze skimmed over her, noting the long-sleeved t-shirt she wore. The rounded neck allowed some scars to be seen, but most of the rest of her was covered.

Smiling, he tucked her arm underneath his as they made their way to the front door. Nerves hit him as he suddenly wished he had talked to the guys about this meeting. *What if they overwhelm her? Stare without thinking about it? What if—*

"Relax," she chided, looking up at him. "You're almost green with nerves."

Feeling foolish, he held her gaze, her smile warming him. Before he had a chance to respond, the front door opened and Miss Ethel stood there, her arms out in welcome.

Eleanor was immediately enfolded into the embrace before moving back to allow him the same welcome.

"Come on back," Miss Ethel instructed. "Rosalie decided a picnic outside would be a lovely idea. We're all just getting set up."

He started to protest, knowing it was not good for Eleanor to be exposed to the sun for long periods, but she halted him with her hand on his arm.

She whispered, "I'm covered and have sunscreen on my neck and hands. It's good."

As they followed Miss Ethel down the hall toward the

back of the house, he whispered in return, "If you start burning, you tell me." Giving a demanding look, he added, "Promise?"

She smiled, "Promise."

As they stepped into the kitchen, the room suddenly felt much smaller. Eleanor recognized Rosalie, but the women were dwarfed with large men. Next to Rosalie was a tatted man with piercing eyes that were staring at her, a wide smile on his lips. Before anyone had a chance to speak, Rosalie bounded over, enveloping her in a hug.

"I'm so glad you're here. It makes the balance against the testosterone so much better!"

She laughed as Rosalie introduced her to Zander, who took her hands in his and said, "Good to meet you." His eyes were warm and she relaxed, letting out a breath she had not realized she was holding.

Next up were two dark-haired men, almost identical, one with longer hair than the other, and she figured they must be the twins Rafe had told her about. Smiling, she offered her hand, pleased that their greeting was just as warm as Zander's.

Jaxon bent, kissing her scarred hand. Growling, Rafe pulled her back slightly. "You makin' moves on my woman?"

"I'd never pass up a chance to kiss a beautiful woman, yours or not," Jaxon joked, winking at Eleanor.

She laughed, turning to the others, being introduced to Cael, a man even taller than Rafe, and Asher, another handsome man. Zeke was last. Though he looked rough, he had a gentle touch.

"Well, that's all done," Miss Ethel announced. "Let's head outside."

The crowd each grabbed a platter from the kitchen

counter and moved through the door. As soon as Eleanor stepped onto the patio, she was pleased to see tables set up under a large oak tree, casting its shade over the entire area. She felt a squeeze on her shoulder and peered up at Rafe, seeing his smile.

30

Once settled, the group quickly dug into sandwiches of chicken salad, turkey and Swiss cheese, ham and provolone, and roast beef. Chips, nachos and salsa, potato salad, slaw, pickles, and a variety of condiments graced the table as well.

Eleanor regarded Miss Ethel's yard, filled with flower beds full of lilies and a rose garden in full bloom at the side of the house, and smiled, knowing Rafe grew up helping in the yard. Turning her attention back to the group, she watched the easy affection between the men and how they incorporated Rosalie into their circle. Biting her lip, she wondered if they would be able to do that with her as well.

Much to her pleasure, the conversation flowed all around her. Rosalie held her own with their gentle teasing, their admiration for her shining through.

"Eleanor, you used to be in the Army?" Cael asked, his friendly face focused on hers.

"Army Reserve. I was a nurse," she said, "but, uh...after

my injuries, I found it difficult to do the job. I have limited mobility in my right hand." Much to her surprise, she held her scarred hand up, showing the difficulty in wiggling her fingers. "I think I could do more, but well..."

Zander said, "I spent some time at the military hospital in Germany. I assume that's where they shipped you?"

Rafe startled, shooting Zander a glare, but Eleanor appeared to take it all in stride. She leaned around him and nodded toward Zander.

"Yes but, honestly, I don't remember it. The drugs I was on had me out of it for most of my stay, including the medivac back home and, even for a while, here."

"IED?" Zander asked. "That's what I went for. I've got some scrap metal pieces in my leg and arm that cause me pain sometimes."

This time, Rafe relaxed, realizing his friend was normalizing what she had been through, without trivializing it. Zander was offering her a way to share without feeling alone.

Smiling compassionately, "Yes. I was in a convoy. No matter my injuries, I was lucky, when most did not live." She glanced around the table, it hitting her that this was the first time since she had been home that she had been with a group of former military men who had their own tales to tell. And, for maybe the first time too, she realized she really had been the lucky one. *Not just a burn victim, but a survivor.*

The others nodded sympathetically, but she took a deep breath and plunged ahead. "I'm sure you know, I decided to just stay at home. My family..." She hesitated, uncertain what to say.

Rafe leaned over, whispering, "They know about your family, sweetheart. I told them, to make it easier on you."

Shooting him a grateful nod, she continued, "Withdrawing from the public eye became easier than facing the stares. I know that seems terribly cowardly to you."

The group immediately jumped in with protestations and she heard Rafe's the loudest. "You are not a coward, babe."

She held up her hand, saying, "That's kind of you all to say, but it did seem the safest thing to do at the time." Looking at Cael, she said, "I have taken on some nursing students as their online tutor. They send some assignments to me and I help them with some of the finer points they are struggling with." She lifted her shoulders, blushing. "It's not much, but for a long time, it felt like all I could handle."

Jayden shifted in his seat, drawing her attention. "You know, Eleanor, you're one of us. A veteran. We were all lucky...none of us were so severely injured. At least, not on the outside. Hell, I can't imagine what it was like for you."

"At first, I was so drugged that I don't really remember what anything was like. I was in the hospital in Germany for a long time, until I could be safely transported back to the United States. By then, I had been told of my family's deaths, but it all seemed like a bad dream. I didn't really process it until I was finally out of rehab and came back to Bellamy House."

"Like Rafe said, you are not a coward," Asher said, shaking his head in admiration.

Swallowing deeply, she glanced up at Rafe, gaining strength from him as he smiled at her. Looking at the others, she said, "Well, I'm trying. I'm learning that life goes on and hiding away is no longer who I want to be. Being here with you all? It helps. A lot, actually."

"You've made some decisions?" Miss Ethel asked, her gaze warm on her.

"I'm in the process of having a center built. Well, just at the beginning of the process." She fiddled with her napkin until Rafe placed his large hand over hers, stilling her fingers. She shot him a tentative smile, before continuing, "My grandfather's estate includes a large parcel of land that is about two miles from my home. I envision building a place for burned veterans who have no home to come to after their hospitalizations and rehabilitations are complete. Kind of a half-way house, as they figure out what to do next."

"Damn, girl," Jaxon exclaimed, his eyes wide, "when you decide to do something different, you really go for it, don't you?"

Blushing, she nodded. "I guess it does seem rather ambitious, but...well, I don't know if this will make any sense, but I've learned that living and moving through pain seems rather pointless unless we can help relieve someone else's burden."

"I couldn't have said it better, my dear," Miss Ethel said, reaching over to grasp her hand, giving it a squeeze.

A smile slipped over her face, returning the squeeze before leaning into Rafe's embrace.

"Have you decided to give up making a living off your ugly mug?" Jaxon asked, his smirk aimed at Rafe.

Throwing him a cocky grin, Rafe leaned back, rubbing his chin. "I think it's time I retired this face and did something a little more worthwhile."

The group laughed, then he sobered. "There's a favor I'd like to ask you all." Gaining their serious attention, he said, "I'm going to be flying to California in a couple of days to clean out the efficiency apartment I had. Don't have much there, but I did leave a few things. I'll only be gone about three days, but I'd like you all to keep an eye on Eleanor for me."

"I don't need babysitting," she protested, but was soon drowned out by the others immediately assuring their services. Smiling, she said, "Well, I shouldn't need anything, but it'll be nice to know I can call on you."

"I hate that I have a meeting with Mr. Hayden and my lawyer when you have to fly out," Eleanor pouted a couple of days later.

Standing at her front door, Rafe held her tight. Kissing her lips, he said, "I'd rather know you were tucked in safely here in your home than driving back from the airport. And, I'll be home before you know it. My plan is to stay there for three nights, get my possessions packed, go by the bank, talk to my landlord, and say goodbye to a couple of friends."

"Are you sure Marty won't try to talk you into staying?" she asked, accepting that a sliver of insecurity was showing.

"Doesn't matter what he tries to peddle, I'm not buying," he promised. "Anyway, I'll be back in time to mow the grass again."

Throwing her head back in laughter, she said, "Yes, yes, that's all I need you for...keep my grass perfect. Well, that and your body."

Rafe loved the joy on her face when she laughed and bent to kiss her once more. "Okay, I'm outta here. The sooner I go, the sooner I'll get back to your body, babe. Now, remember, you've got all the guys' cell numbers saved into your phone, so call if you need them."

"Rafe," she reminded, "I lived here in seclusion for a long time. I'm sure I can handle anything that comes up."

With one more kiss, he jogged down to his truck and, waving, pulled out of the driveway. Eleanor stood on the front stoop, looking at her expansive lawn and gardens, her gaze drifting to the woods where the small cottage could be seen. The sky was blue and the sun was rising over the trees. The scent of roses clung to the air and, as she moved inside, she decided the terrace would be a perfect place to get some work completed.

Waking up in his old efficiency apartment the next morning, Rafe stretched, the California sun shining in the window. He had packed his few belongings, glad that most of his modeling money had been saved so that now he could focus on building his own business. Looking around, the place appeared so bland compared to the stone cottage at the edge of the woods. Jumping out of bed, all he could think about was how much he missed Eleanor even though they skyped long into the night.

The day, filled with errands, moved faster than he originally planned and he hoped he might be able to fly back to Virginia a day earlier. Smiling at the possible surprise for her, he headed into the bar at the end of the day to have a goodbye drink with a few of the models he had become friends with.

The interior, modern and sleek, was nothing like Grimm's and he found it lacking compared to Zander's place. It was not full at this time and he easily saw the group waving toward him. He nodded and walked their way, shaking hands with everyone.

"So, you're really giving it all up?" John asked. He and Robert were the only two models Rafe had befriended, both having also served in the military, their experiences giving them a maturity not shared by the younger ones.

"Absolutely," he answered. "I'm going to start my own business, get to be back with my family, and I've found someone I want to spend forever with."

"Seriously?" Robert asked, his smile wide. "Damn man, good for you. So, who decided to take a chance on your sorry ass?" he joked.

Laughing, he said, "She was a former nurse with the Army Reserve." Seeing their wide eyes, he continued, "She was injured but is getting ready to build a veterans' burn center. A place where they can go after they finish the VA rehabilitation if they don't have a home to go to."

Whistling, John said, "Amazing. I'm really glad for you, man."

For the next hour, they enjoyed their drinks and catching up on each other's lives. Looking at his watch, he said, "I think I'll say goodbye—"

"Well, hello stranger," a familiar, but unwanted, voice sounded from behind. Turning his head, he observed Cherelle walking up.

"Fuck," he cursed, knowing Marty must have told her that he was in town.

She leaned over, from behind his chair, her breasts pressing against his shoulder, almost falling out of the low-cut dress she wore. Kissing his cheek, she murmured, "Missed you, babe."

Standing quickly, forcing her backward, he was

unconcerned when she rocked back on her heels, almost toppling over before righting herself. Ignoring her, he looked at his friends, reaching his hand out, "As I said, it's time for me to finish everything so I can get back to Virginia."

Robert and John, taking his cue, stood and shook his hand, well wishes coming from both of them. Turning, he pinned Cherelle with a glare, saying, "And that goodbye goes for you too."

"But Rafe," she whined, grabbing his arm, once more pressing herself tightly to his side. A tall woman, with her sky-high heels giving her added height, she easily planted a kiss on his cheek, cupping his head with her hand.

"Cherelle, if you think I won't cause a public scene, you don't know me at all. We were never anything more than convenient. And that's been over for a long time. You've obviously been talking to Marty to know I was in town, but then you also gotta know my modeling days are over. I can't help your career anymore." Disengaging her hands from him, he turned and walked out the door, leaving her standing in his wake.

Narrowing her eyes as a smirk crossed her face, Cherelle walked over to another woman sitting at the bar. Climbing onto the stool next to her, she asked, "You get it?"

"Oh, honey, from this angle, it looks perfect. Just like two lovers having a chat."

Throwing her head back in laughter, she took her phone and, within a moment, sent the video forward.

Her companion slid her a sideways glance, lifting her drink to her lips. "You know this isn't gonna get him to come back to you, right? I mean, the whole model pairing that Marty was setting up with you two isn't going to happen."

Popping the olive from her martini into her perfectly made-up mouth, chewing it thoughtfully, Cherelle nodded. "Yes," she grinned, "but revenge can be so sweet."

31

"I think we've got a good business plan," Eleanor said to Mr. Thomas and Mr. Hayden, as they stood to leave.

"I have to confess," Mr. Hayden said, "I had my eye on this place as an exclusive hotel at one time, thinking that it was abandoned. But, Mr. Thomas assured me a lovely, young woman lived here and he was right."

Smiling, she shook his hand and they walked through the foyer. "I could never leave my home, but I'm very excited to work with you on the building of the center."

Stepping outside, he looked over her lawn and said, "Whoever your groundskeeper is, he's got the gift. I need someone I can trust with some of my other properties."

"I happen to know that he'll soon be starting his own business. Can I have him give you a call when he's up and running?"

"Absolutely," he enthused, pumping her hand up and down before walking to his truck with a wave goodbye.

Mr. Thomas offered her a hug, smiling down at her. "My dear, your parents would be so proud of you."

"Thank you...that means a lot to me."

"I get the feeling that there is more going on than just the burn center. I just hope that you'll introduce me to your young man sometime."

Blushing, she agreed readily. "As soon as he's back in town, I'll have you over. And I hope it is the first of many gatherings here in Bellamy House again."

With a final goodbye, she waved him away, her heart light.

Rafe showed up at Marty's office, late that day, stepping up to his assistant, who looked as harried as usual. "Hey Donna, is Marty in? He's been blowing up my phone wanting to meet even though I've told him over and over my modeling career is finish."

"He didn't come in today, Rafe, which makes no sense because I know he's been dying to get hold of you and convince you to not quit modeling," she replied, her lips pinched together. "He took off from here and left me with a pile of meetings to cancel or reschedule, a shit-ton of models to placate, and didn't leave me his fucking itinerary."

Lifting his eyebrow, he asked, "Is that usual?"

"Which part?" she groused, lifting her hands to pull her hair back from her face before securing it in a knot on top of her head with a pencil. "Leaving the complaining models for me to deal with? Only when they're on the lower end of the spectrum and not a big name. Rescheduling meetings? Only when he has a more important meeting to take, which happens all the fucking time. But not giving me the itinerary? Nope, that's a new jerk move for him. I'd think he was off having a tryst with a sweetheart...if he had a heart."

Barking out a laugh, he said, "Honest to God, Donna, he doesn't pay you enough."

"Well, don't worry about what he pays me. Marty's losing clients every day after that dumbass stunt he pulled with you." Grinning, she said, "And I'm going with another agency. This is my last couple of days, just trying to put things right."

"Donna, you are one of only three people I'll actually miss from here. And Marty isn't one of them."

Now it was her turn to laugh, standing to offer him her hand. "Good luck with wherever life takes you."

"I'm staying in Virginia, starting a new business. And found the love of my life." With a dip of his chin, he walked out, sliding his sunglasses on his eyes. Smiling to himself, he realized that without having to meet with Marty, he was free to leave a day early. Pulling out his phone, he called the airlines.

By ten p.m. that night, he was sitting on a plane. Thrilled he had been able to get on an earlier flight from California to Virginia, he did not mind the premium he had to pay for changing his ticket or the last-minute fees. Before he had to power down his phone, he shot off a text.

Got finished early. On plane now. Will be in your arms before lunch tomorrow. Miss you!

Leaning his head back against the seat, he closed his eyes, his mind filled with the beautiful woman waiting for him at home.

Eleanor walked into the kitchen the next morning, a cup

of steaming coffee in her hand. The sun was peeking through the window at the front of the house that she'd moved through the rooms and opened the draperies. Her late-night text from Rafe had her smiling and she could not wait to see him and tell him of the latest plans for her project, and the fact that Mr. Hayden might hire him to do more landscaping when he got his business started.

Moving to the desk in the study, she opened the folder that they had been working on and perused the documents. The center would be comprised of a small apartment building, housing both efficiencies and one-bedroom units. A large therapy room, gym, and indoor pool would be on the first floor, along with offices and a large kitchen.

The windows would face the river below or the extensive lawn and gardens on the back. Only two miles from Bellamy House, it would be close enough for her to spend a lot of time there and yet far enough away to not feel like it was in her backyard.

Her mind rolled to the business Rafe wanted to start. He wanted to plan landscapes and she knew several of her parents' old friends would love to hire him. Ones that had not given up on her and continued to call, even when she tried to hide away.

Glancing down at her right hand, the scars still just as red and puckered as they rose up her arm, she realized they no longer held her captive. She smiled and had just looked back down at the papers when the doorbell rang.

Walking through the foyer, she opened the door, seeing a middle-aged man in a suit standing on the stoop. "Hello," she greeted. "May I help you?"

The red-eye flight had been long, but Rafe was pleased he had been able to sleep. Climbing into his car, he began the drive back home. *Home.* He liked the sound of that word. Not since he had left Miss Ethel's home at the age of eighteen had he felt like anywhere was home. *And all because of Eleanor.*

The drive, like his time working on the grounds of Bellamy House, gave him time to think. He realized he never saw her scars when he looked at her. Or when he made love to her. *Love. Home and love.* A huge grin split his face as he drove along, each mile bringing him closer to the place he never wanted to leave.

His phone indicated an incoming call and he hit the answer button as well as making sure it was on speaker. "Hello?"

"Rafe? This is Donna. I wanted to let you know that if you were back in Virginia today, you can have your meeting with Marty."

"What are you talking about?"

"I guess Marty must have been planning on meeting you and never told me. I got a look at his itinerary that he finally sent to me late last night. He had a meeting with a few models and agents in New York but then diverted his tickets to Virginia's Richmond airport before he planned on coming back here. I assume it's to meet up with you."

"Marty knew I was going to be in California," he explained. "I can't imagine what he'd be doing here in Virginia." An uneasy feeling slithered through him and, glancing at the time, he knew he could be home in another half hour.

"I don't know where he was planning on trying to meet you. The note on the side of his calendar says Bellamy House. Does that make sense?"

The uneasy feeling roared to life, his breath leaving his lungs in a rush. "Yeah, it does. Thanks Donna." Disconnecting, he pressed down on the accelerator, revving the engine, hoping to make it home in time.

Calling Zander, he barked, "Almost home, but I think Eleanor might need some help. My slimy, former agent, who doesn't like to take no for an answer, may be trying to get to her. Get over there as fast as you can."

"You got it," came the expected reply.

Sucking in a deep breath, he hoped he was wrong about where Marty might be heading, but was afraid his fears were right.

32

The man on the front stoop wavered slightly as he pulled himself up to his full height. Eleanor narrowed her eyes, catching a whiff of alcohol. Keeping one hand on the door, she cocked her head to the side, waiting for him to speak.

"I'm looking for Rafe Walker. He told me that he lives here."

"Yes, he does. But he is...out right now." Not wanting to offend a friend of Rafe's, she hesitated, fighting the unease the man created. "I can have him call you when he gets back, if you would like."

A slow smile spread across the man's face as he reached out his hand to shake. "Martin Robbins. I'm a friend from California. A good friend. I was nearby on business and decided to drop in."

She didn't take his hand, but she did assure him, "I see, Mr. Robbins. I'll make sure to let him know you were here."

Seemingly unperturbed that she had refused his handshake, he pulled back. "He's quite famous, you know.

Such a face…a physique. His life was very full in California. Being seen with the rich and famous." Chuckling, he amended, "Of course, they all wanted to be seen with him, since he had money and fame."

Uncertain what to say, she tried to smile politely, but could feel it was more of a grimace. Sliding her hands into her pockets, she nervously waited to see what he would say.

"I was hoping that perhaps he would move back, or at least move his girlfriend here with him. She misses him so. They could live in Virginia and work from here. He called to ask me to set something up for them."

"He did? When?"

Marty appeared to ponder before saying, "A week or so ago, I believe. Cherelle has been dying to be with him again." He wavered on his feet, his eyes narrowing on her. "Cherelle. Cherelle Parkinson. You do know who that is, don't you?"

Unsure what to say, she remained quiet, wondering why he was telling her this obviously false information. *Maybe Rafe hasn't told everyone in California his plans…or about me.* Shaking her head slightly, she realized it was ridiculous for him to have talked about her since their relationship was so new.

Taking a step backward, she nodded dumbly, about to tell him once more that she would have Rafe call him. Suddenly, his hand flew out, slamming against the door, and he leaned forward. Startled, she jumped, her small movement giving him the advantage to step inside her house.

"You cannot make him happy, you know. It would be so much better for you to let him go."

Eyes wide, her chest heaved with indignation. "You need to leave—"

"He was with her last night." Taking advantage of her stunned silence, he lifted his hand, his phone screen facing forward.

Eleanor wanted to step back but her eyes landed on the phone, Rafe standing in an upscale bar, a statuesque, drop-dead gorgeous blonde leaning against him, her hand cupping his face while she kissed his cheek. The time stamp on the video did show yesterday.

Her eyes flickered between the video on replay and the cold eyes of the man standing in her foyer. Swallowing deeply, she said, "You need to leave."

A smirk slowly curled his lips and he lowered the phone. "As you can see, my little beast, Rafe needs beauty. It's his career…it's his life."

Jolting, she stared at his expression, thinking how much like the Grinch he resembled with his lips curved in a smiling snarl. How ugly he was. How…*full of shit he is.*

"I asked you to leave and now I'm telling you to leave. Immediately. And I'll be sure to inform Rafe of your entire visit here. He'll be thrilled to tell you to go to hell, but I'll tell him that I've already said it to you."

His smirk slid from his face, replaced by pure anger. "Are you fucking kidding me? The little kitten has claws—"

She threw up her hand in his face, and said, "Please spare me any more of your diatribe." Laughing she added, "Do you really think your visit changes anything? That video you showed…his hands are at his side, not on her. Believe me when I say that when Rafe cares for a woman, his hands are not at his side."

Marty reared back, bloodshot eyes wide, and opened his mouth, but she got there first.

"And the ridiculous story that Rafe needs beauty for his career and his life? You're absolutely right…that's why he's a gifted horticulturist. He brings things to life that create beauty."

Gathering his wits, he snarled, "You stupid girl. How long do you think your scarred body will hold his interest when he sees all of you—"

"Good God!" she yelled, throwing her hands up from her sides. "What do you not get? He has seen me naked, and," leaning close, poking her finger at him, "he loves it." Standing straight, she took a calming breath and finished by saying, "So, you can leave, or I can call the police." Putting her hand back in her pocket, she pulled out her phone for him to see. "And, if you try more subterfuge, I've got this whole conversation on recording."

Growling, Marty whipped his hand out, his fingers closing around her throat. "You bitch! You're killing my career. Rafe's got clients dropping me left and right. I have got to get you out of the picture!"

The smell of alcohol on his breath hit her full in the face and she looked up in fright, noting, for the first time, his dilated eyes. A noise outside drew his attention and her Army training took over. Quickly using her hands to disengage, she broke his hold on her throat just before kicking him in the groin.

As he dropped to the floor, the front door flew open, slamming against the wall, her foyer filling with large men. Gasping, she watched as Zander single-handedly put Marty in a choke hold. Before she had a chance to answer the questions flying at her, Rafe raced through the door, his eyes wild until they landed on her.

His heart in his throat, he rushed to her, scooping her into his embrace. "Baby, are you okay?"

She leaned back, taking him in, from his rumpled shirt to his mussed hair. The day-old beard was attractive but the dark circles under his eyes gave away his fatigue. Before she could assure him that she was fine, his eyes dropped to her neck, where they narrowed.

"What the hell did he do to you?" His eyes shifted from her bruised neck to the man Zander held with ease. Transferring her to Cael's arms, he stalked over to Marty.

Rafe cocked his arm, Eleanor's cry for him to stop the only thing that could have halted him at that moment. Jaxon and Jayden moved to either side, Jayden calming him.

"Man, we've called the police. Let them deal with his ass."

He stood, his chest heaving with fury, and stared at the man now slumped against Zander. "What the hell were you thinking? If you had any career left, it's gone after this."

"You destroyed me after that article came out. Cherelle swore that kind of publicity would send you straight back to us but instead you dug your heels in to stay with *her*. And my client list began leaving me the next fucking day."

"I didn't destroy you," Rafe bit out, feeling Jaxon move slightly away and the gentle touch of Eleanor's arms encircling his waist. Wrapping his arm around her, pulling her in tightly, he added, "You did that to yourself. You and that stupid stunt Cherelle pulled last night."

"I saw it," Eleanor said softly, looking up at his hard face, a muscle twitching in his jaw.

He swung his gaze down to her, his eyes wide, but she shook her head. "I didn't believe it. I told him that when you're with someone, your hands aren't down at your side."

His breath flew from his lungs as he stared into her trusting eyes. Nodding slowly, he leaned down, kissing her forehead. "Thank you, baby."

"The police are here," Asher said, opening the front door, allowing them entry. "Oh, and I hope you don't mind, but I called the local press. Thought they'd like to get a story off this piece of shit being escorted out in cuffs."

Still hanging on to his anger, Rafe just nodded, allowing Eleanor to give her statement and letting them take pictures of her neck. He was so proud of her when she did not hide her scars, instead showing them the bruises on both sides.

Jayden, Cael, and Asher talked to the reporter outside until the police took Marty to their cruiser. Cael, stepping back inside, said, "Eleanor, we've talked to the reporter, but you don't have to."

"No, no," she said. "I want to."

A squeeze on her waist caused her to look into Rafe's eyes. "Babe, you don't need to—"

She placed her palm on his chest, over his heart, and smiled. "It's okay. It's time I stopped hiding and came out into the light. I need to let others know that scars don't define a person. But love can."

His heart stuttered at her words and he watched her invite the two reporters inside, leading them to the living room. Before following her, he moved to his friends, thanking each of them.

Clasping his hand, Zander shook his head. "No thanks needed between brothers." Looking over his shoulder, he said, "You go on in and make sure Eleanor is good. We'll see you after y'all get some rest."

Zeke grinned as he filed behind the others to leave. "You know, your girl is something else. She had him on the floor by the time we got here. Fucking brilliant to see him pissing himself."

Dropping his chin to his chest, he took a deep breath, thinking about the danger she could have been in...and then the surprise Marty must have felt at having his balls kicked by a former female soldier. Looking up as Zeke clapped him on the back, he closed the front door after his friends and turned to head into the living room.

A week later, after a late-night walk around the gardens ending on the terrace, climbing roses in bloom all along the trellis, Rafe halted and turned Eleanor in his arms, pulling her tight. She looked up and smiled, lighting his world.

Suddenly nervous, he stumbled, "Do you remember us...uh...reading *Jane Eyre*? A while back?"

"Of course," she replied. "I remember all the stories we read."

"Well, there was something I wanted to ask you." He peered into her eyes, her trust and love giving him courage. " 'I ask you to pass through life at my side—to be my second self, and best earthly companion.' "

Her eyes widened as she gasped, her fingers flexing on his arm. "For real?" she breathed.

Smiling, he said, "Of course. I want you at my side, to be my other half, for always."

Jumping into his arms, she cried, quoting in return, " 'Then, sir, I willmarry you.' "

Miss Ethel sat in her kitchen, sipping her cup of tea, the Sunday newspaper spread out on the table in front of her. She perused the colorful picture of Rafe surrounded by the beautiful roses in the Bellamy House rose garden, smiling down at Eleanor, tucked into his side, her smile as wide as his.

Her eyes moved to the article's headline and she read with interest.

The Rose Garden Beauties

Eleanor Bellamy celebrates with Rafe Walker over their plans to soon build Bellamy Center, an apartment and rehabilitation center for veterans suffering from burns. A former Army Reserve nurse, injured while serving in Afghanistan and enduring a long rehabilitation herself, Ms. Bellamy is excited to offer the center to other veterans who do not have a home to return to as they continue their convalescence after discharge.
Mr. Walker will soon be the owner of Walker Horticulture, providing the landscaping for the center as well as taking on a number of clients who desire the beauty of gardens surrounding them. He plans to use his landscaping skills to train interested burn victims and offering employment to those choosing to stay in the area. He stated that the cultivating of beauty is a positive rehabilitation in itself, and is eager to begin the service.

The two met under unusual circumstances and were recently the victim of a smear campaign calling the pair, Beauty and the Beast, a cruel joke by Mr. Walker's former modeling agent. One only has to spend a moment in Ms. Bellamy's presence to know that she is truly beautiful, both inside and out. And, one only has to spend a moment in the presence of both Ms. Bellamy and Mr. Walker, to see that they are truly in love. For readers who know of veteran burn victims that would benefit from the Bellamy Center, please contact either Ms. Bellamy or Mr. Walker at the address below.

Closing the newspaper, she leaned back, a smile on her lips as she sipped her tea, the scent of roses wafting through the open window.

33

SIX MONTHS LATER

The violins played softly as the small group gathered in the formal living room of Bellamy House. Rafe stood in front of the fireplace, nervously tugging on the tie's knot at his neck.

"You good?" Zander asked, standing next to him.

"Yeah," he whispered back.

"Hell, as much as you used to be in front of the camera, you think you'd be used to the attention."

"That was all pretend. This is real," he retorted. Eyeing Miss Ethel, sitting in one of the chairs facing him, her smile calmed him.

Rosalie walked toward them, smiling at Zander, giving Rafe a wink as she neared.

"She looks relaxed," Rafe commented, then turned his head to see Zander's complete attention on his wife. Just then the musicians began playing Pacabell's Cannon in D and his head jerked to the living room doors, his heart starting its staccato all over again. And then she appeared.

Eleanor, on the arm of Mr. Thomas, walked toward him. Her dress was ivory, the form-fitting bodice flowing out into a skirt of simple satin. Around her neck was the pearl necklace her mother had worn when she married Eleanor's father, and her grandmother before that. Her hair was pulled away from her face, draping down her back in waves, no longer worn to cover the scars on her neck. Her beauty took his breath away and for a moment he had to remind himself to breathe. Before he knew it, she was at his side, slipping her hand into his.

As they stood in front of their friends, they pledged their vows to each other. After slipping the ring on her finger, they kissed before staring into each other's eyes. Just before walking back down the aisle, Eleanor looked over the fireplace, her heart light as she viewed her family smiling back from their portrait, a rose resting in her mother's hand.

Five Years Later

Eleanor walked out of her office, past the fitness room, smiling at the few men and women inside working with the physical therapist. Making her way past the kitchen, she stopped to talk to the ones that were there with the occupational therapist, learning various techniques of holding utensils with their scarred hands.

The center had been built, passed the many qualifications needed to open, and now was fully functional, staying at capacity. People from across the country had visited, starting similar centers elsewhere.

Passing by the newest room, a child care center, she

stood at the door, watching as several of the veterans were in the process of being certified in child care. One child, in particular, captured her attention.

Rory...her and Rafe's son, now four years old. He had been raised around the various burn scars the veterans had, many disfiguring. And like most children, who absorb what is in their world, he saw no difference in their appearance. Waving at the workers, she continued through the building.

Going through the back door, she held her hand over her eyes to offer shade, while casting her gaze around. Finding what she was seeking, she smiled as she walked toward the large, dark-haired man standing in the middle of a group of clients. As she made her way closer, she could see him explaining the merits of a gas-powered hedge trimmer, while also making it clear that if needed, one that was lighter in weight could be just as good.

"Only you can determine what is the best machine for you. Use what feels natural."

Rafe instructed the group to try the various tools and as they moved away with enthusiasm, he watched Eleanor approach. His smile widened as he opened his arms, welcoming her into his embrace.

No words were spoken for several minutes as they stood, hearts beating as one.

That night Eleanor walked up the back stairs to the bedroom now decorated in blue and green. She heard the soft sound of voices and stopped at the doorway to peek in. Lifting her fingers to her lips, she stifled a chuckle, seeing her large husband's nightly routine of perching on the small bed with Rory curled up next to him as he read. Tonight's choosing was the Disney's *Beauty and the Beast* book. Rory had watched the movie numerous times and it was one of his favorites.

"Please don't leave me," Belle sobbed. "I love you."

"Daddy, if you were a beast, would Mommy love you?"

"Yes, she would love me no matter what."

"And if she were a beast, would you love her?"

"Of course, I would love your mother."

Rory thought for a moment before lifting his child's face to his father. "And if I were a beast?"

Eleanor stepped into the room, settling next to the bed, reaching over to hug both her son and her husband. "My dear, silly. Beast or Beauty, we would all love each other."

Don't miss the next Heroes at Heart
For all of Miss Ethel's boys:
Heroes at Heart (Military Romance)
Zander
Rafe
Cael
Jaxon
Jayden
Asher
Zeke
Cas

ALSO BY MARYANN JORDAN

Don't miss other Maryann Jordan books!

Lots more Baytown stories to enjoy and more to come!

Baytown Boys (small town, military romantic suspense)

Coming Home

Just One More Chance

Clues of the Heart

Finding Peace

Picking Up the Pieces

Sunset Flames

Waiting for Sunrise

Hear My Heart

Guarding Your Heart

Sweet Rose

Our Time

Count On Me

For all of Miss Ethel's boys:

Heroes at Heart (Military Romance)

Zander

Rafe

Cael

Jaxon

Jayden

Asher

Zeke

Cas

Lighthouse Security Investigations

Mace

Rank

Walker

Drew

Blake

Tate (August 2020)

Hope City (romantic suspense series co-developed

with Kris Michaels

Hope City Duet (Brock / Sean)

Carter

Brody by Kris Michaels

Kyle

Ryker by Kris Michaels

Saints Protection & Investigations

(an elite group, assigned to the cases no one else wants…or can solve)

Serial Love

Healing Love

Revealing Love

Seeing Love

Honor Love

Sacrifice Love

Protecting Love

Remember Love

Discover Love

Surviving Love

Celebrating Love

Follow the exciting spin-off series:

Alvarez Security (military romantic suspense)

Gabe

Tony

Vinny

Jobe

SEALs

Thin Ice (Sleeper SEAL)

SEAL Together (Silver SEAL)

Letters From Home (military romance)

Class of Love

Freedom of Love

Bond of Love

The Love's Series (detectives)

Love's Taming

Love's Tempting

Love's Trusting

The Fairfield Series (small town detectives)

Emma's Home

Laurie's Time

Carol's Image

Fireworks Over Fairfield

Please take the time to leave a review of this book. Feel free to contact me, especially if you enjoyed my book. I love to hear from readers!

Facebook

Email

Website

Made in United States
Troutdale, OR
07/26/2023